DEVILS UNTO DUST

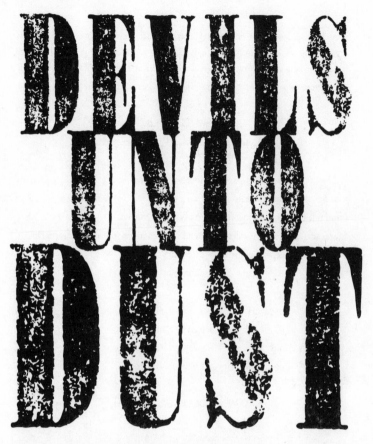

DEVILS UNTO DUST

EMMA BERQUIST

WITHDRAWN

GREENWILLOW BOOKS
An Imprint of HarperCollinsPublishers

This book is a work of fiction. References to real people, events, establishments, organizations, or locales are intended only to provide a sense of authenticity, and are used to advance the fictional narrative. All other characters, and all incidents and dialogue, are drawn from the author's imagination and are not to be construed as real.

Devils Unto Dust
Copyright © 2018 by Emma Berquist

All rights reserved. No part of this book may be used or reproduced in any manner whatsoever without written permission except in the case of brief quotations embodied in critical articles and reviews. Printed in the United States of America. For information address HarperCollins Children's Books, a division of HarperCollins Publishers, 195 Broadway, New York, NY 10007.
www.epicreads.com

The text of this book is set in 13-point Adobe Jenson.
Book design by Paul Zakris

Library of Congress Control Number: 2018935493

ISBN 978-0-06-264278-3 (hardback)

18 19 20 21 22 PC/LSCH 10 9 8 7 6 5 4 3 2 1
First Edition

GREENWILLOW BOOKS

For Mike
For all the reasons

PART ONE:

THE TOWN

Texas, 1877

———

The desert is white as a blind man's eye,

Comfortless as salt.

—Sylvia Plath

Life out here is hard, my mother used to say, so you have to be harder. Even she wasn't strong enough to fight off the sickness. By the end she was just a shell of herself, her skull showing through the skin on her face, talking nonsense when the delirium took her. Sometimes she didn't know who I was or what was happening. And then she remembered, and it was even worse.

She lasted longer than most do. It doesn't really matter, it didn't make a difference, but I like to think it means something. That she was fighting to stay with us. That her life wasn't wasted, digging into this patch of nowhere.

I love the desert, love the hidden beauty of it. When the light falls just so and the heat shimmers off the ground, the desert is as graceful and endless as the sky. I love the way the ground cracks open under my feet, the fissures spreading out like veins in a shattered mirror. The air so hot it burns your lungs, the dust collecting in the corners of your eyes, the sand whipping against your skin until it's raw; this is my home, and it is beautiful. If I could, I would turn my back on this town and start walking, leaving behind the unbearable weight. But I know better than that; the desert may have my heart, but this town will take my bones.

Glory, our town is called, for no other reason than irony. People here are bad at naming things, even my own parents. Daisies don't grow here, not in this hard-scrabble dirt. Not that anyone calls me Daisy, not since I was old enough to know better. The name does not suit me; it is bright and yellow and sweet, and I am none of those things. And Glory is dead as sun-bleached bone and twice as cursed. Maybe it was different when people first settled here, before the sickness started to spread; maybe it wasn't always a sandy hole of a town, but that's all I've ever known it to be. Those who could afford to got out quickly, leaving the rest of us to whatever fate we deserve. There's nothing standing between us and the desert shakes but some barbed wire and the men who hunt the sick. It's only a matter of time before this town crumbles into dust. When the sick finally outnumber the healthy, we'll all be as dead as my mother. Or worse.

Today I wake up the way I always do, gasping for breath. It's the panic that I shove down all through the day, but I can't hide from it at night. The dreams gnaw at me like dogs worrying old bones, the pressure on my chest tightening until I force myself awake, into the real and unending nightmare. It's still dark out, though dawn can't be far off. I wait for a minute, trying to swallow the fear away, breathing in the smell of the mattress: hay and old sweat. I can just make out the shapes of my youngest brother and sister a few feet from me, both curled up on their sides. They are identical in almost every way, down to the way they sleep; I hold my breath until I'm sure I did not wake them. Still, I am tense, tenser than usual; something else is wrong. I wait, and wait, and then I finally hear it: a scratching sound, faint but distinct. A new jolt of panic surges through me, and I am instantly wide awake, sitting up and straining to see through the dark. Shakes don't usually get through the fence, but it's been known to happen. When the guards are young or drunk they don't always walk the entire perimeter, and our house is about as far from the gate as you can get. My mind fills with images of blood splashed against the walls and I tell myself to calm down; even if one made it through the fence, there's no way a shake could get in the house, not when our door is locked tight and bolted. Still, to be safe, I make my way to the door, my bare feet knowing exactly where to step to avoid the creaking boards. Our house is nothing more than a large wooden box with the barest suggestion of walls. We have a stove and some furniture, but the bedsheets need airing and I can't keep the dust out.

My father built this house, laid the wood and did the chinking and daubing, and it is just like him: ragged and aging poorly. The sand and the heat are hard on everything. Pa did his best, I suppose, but he spent more time picking out flat stones for the foundation than he did building the roof, and it sags in places. I blindly feel along the wall until my hand closes around the butt of my revolver, hanging from a peg in its holster. One chamber in my six-shooter is always loaded; sometimes seconds can make all the difference. I put my ear to the door and listen. The soft scratching in the dirt and whisper of wood scraping could be a dog or a coyote, even a healthy one that was too quick for a shake to catch, but I am not willing to take any chances.

We strung up bits of broken glass all around the porch, and I strain to hear any tinkling. There's no wind tonight; the air lies warm and stagnant, trapping heavy smells and smoke close to the ground. I lie down on the wooden floor, revolver in hand, trying to peer through the crack between the door and the floor. But it is too dark and the space is too small. I bite the inside of my cheek, considering; it sounds too quiet for a shake, though I wouldn't bet my life on that. Whatever it is, it doesn't seem to be moving, which means I'll have to deal with it sooner or later. Might as well be now.

I get to my feet, my back protesting, and reach for the small barn lantern hanging by the doorjamb. I jiggle it and hear a faint splashing, so there's still some oil left. Surprising, since I haven't refilled it in weeks, but oil is more costly than candles and it's easy enough to go without. I light the lamp and turn the flame up, throwing the doorway into sharp relief. I fumble a bit to get the bolts open with my gun in one hand and the lantern hanging off the other. The last lock sticks and I have to force it back before easing the door open a sliver, bracing my body against it.

Light from my lamp illuminates a patch along the

wood and the prickly poppies that are dying by the steps. The scratching stops, and I wait a moment before opening the door farther. Lamplight floods the porch and the dirt beyond, and I take a step forward, scanning the ground with my gun pointed at what I hope is chest level. A flick of movement and my stomach drops as my finger tightens around the trigger.

But it's only a rabbit, a cottontail I think, though it's hard to say for sure with the tail and most of its backside missing. It's been a while since I've seen one; between shakes and hungry townsfolk, slow and soft creatures don't last long. I don't know if a coyote or a shake got to it, and the callous part of me is angry because I can't take the chance it's sick and it's a waste of perfectly good meat. It scratches at the dirt, inching itself forward, somehow still moving. I don't know how it got under the fence without back legs, let alone how it made it this far without bleeding to death. I lower my gun and walk over, setting the lantern down close. It blinks round wet eyes at me and I sigh. I take no joy in killing things, but it's kinder to put it down than to let it suffer. The noise of a gunshot will wake up the twins, so I put my hand on its back, feeling the soft flutter of its heart under thick fur.

"Sorry, boy," I tell it quietly. "It's no safer in here than it is out there."

I break its neck quickly and cleanly, flinching only a little when the bones snap. I use my fingers to dig a hole, the dry dirt crumbling quickly. When I'm done I dust off my hands and stand up, my breath hissing out slowly. I stamp down the grave with my foot and consider going back to bed, but it is close to dawn. I stare out into the night, the land made unfamiliar by the darkness, the shapeless ground receding and melding into the blackened sky. The view is no better by day; our acres are scant and unlovely. I pick up the lamp and watch the light quaver around me, feeling alone and insignificant in this small bright circle.

"Morning," a voice says, and I jump so hard I'm lucky my gun doesn't go off. I swear and turn to see the tall frame of my brother standing in the doorway.

"Or is it morning yet?" Micah asks. He sees my face, lit up by the light. "Sorry, Will, didn't mean to scare you."

"You didn't scare me," I say crossly, walking up the steps.

"Liar," he says. Micah never lets me get away with anything less than the bone's honest truth. He's a stickler, that one, but then Ma was the same way; she had no use for sugarcoating.

"What are you doing out here?" he asks when I get close, his brows knitted together over dark eyes.

"I didn't mean to wake you," I say, which doesn't answer his question.

Micah glances at the gun in my hand and frowns. He's a worrier; it comes from being inside his own head so much. He's smart, smarter than most in this place, and it hurts me to think of what he could be if things were different.

"I'm gonna make biscuits for breakfast," I say to distract him.

"What's the occasion?"

"I'm as sick of grits as you are, that's what."

The truth is I need a way to save this morning. I don't like waking up to blood and death, I get enough of that in my dreams. I don't want to remember this day as the day I killed a rabbit; instead, it will be the day I made biscuits.

I follow Micah inside and take one last look at the small mound of fresh dirt before I shut the door and bolt it fast. Poor, stupid thing. It should have known better. This is no place for the weak.

2.

I put the gun back in the rack and take a long drink of water from the bucket we keep in the kitchen. I'll have to boil more from the pump soon. It is a lengthy and tiresome process, but necessary. The shakes don't seem to like water, or fire, but it's still possible one of them could contaminate the pump. We can't take any chances, not when the sickness spreads so easily.

The floor is dirty. I can feel grit beneath my bare feet, and I really should try and sweep, but that can wait until after the biscuits. I can tell how much flour we have left simply by holding the flour sack, a skill we all learn early in Glory. A knot in my stomach is directly related to that sack, and it gets tighter and tighter as the sack becomes lighter. I will have to go to the Homestead and barter for more soon. We can't afford to buy it, not with the first of the month coming and our dues still to pay to the Judge. The prospect of talking to him leaves an unpleasant taste in my mouth. The Judge has little patience for women, and I have little patience for a man that cruel and greedy. He's technically the governor now, or at least he fancies himself as such, but everyone still calls him the Judge. I don't even know what his real name is, nor do I care. In Glory, his word is law, and if we cannot pay our dues, we lose the protection of the perimeter and are left to the mercy of the desert.

It wasn't always this way. Sure, Glory has always been a rougher kind of place, on account of us being the last town before the land gets too harsh to farm and too brutal to settle. Mostly folks just passed through on the way east to Best or north to Plainview. But when the Judge took over, he put the word out that he would grant clemency to anyone willing to turn shake hunter. Maybe he even meant for it to help, maybe he really thought he could kill all the infected and that would be the end of it. But the more men he sent out, the more the sickness spread. All it takes is a bite or scratch and it's only a matter of time before the fever and the ague and the tremors start. And now our town is crawling with former criminals, murderers and thieves, foul men who choke up our streets. There aren't enough jobs to go around, not with the number of hunters who swarmed to Glory. Mostly they drink and fight one another, waiting to go back out to the desert and shoot those left to a fate worse than death. What they can't take out on the shakes they visit on the rest of us, stealing and brawling and killing without consequence. I can't tell anymore which are worse, the shakes or the ones who took to hunting them. The hunters, I think, because when they kill they know exactly what they are doing.

I boil some water with a small scoop of coffee so I can think straight, then get to work on the bread. I mix flour and a pinch of our precious salt with the sourdough starter I've kept going for almost a year. I take out my anger at the unfairness of this life on my dough, beating it viciously. When my arms are tired I cover the bread with a worn and holey cloth and leave it on the table by the grimy window. The bread rises with the sun, the symmetry relaxing me. Sunrise is a glorious thing in the desert, the way the light breaks and spreads over the flatlands, a beacon of safety. The shakes are sluggish during the day, and easier to spot. They don't have their minds anymore, and I think the heat makes them tired, just as it does with the rest of us.

There are bits of flour on my hands and I realize that I am still wearing my nightgown as I wipe my fingers on the scratchy thing. I pull on a pair of worn trousers, the pant legs rolled up to fit and the waist held up by a snakeskin belt Pa made for my thirteenth birthday. That was back when he still had Ma to remind him of birthdays, and I've had to punch new holes in it twice. The pants were Micah's until he outgrew them; it annoys me that my little brother is already taller than me at fourteen, or at least it would if it didn't embarrass him so much. Micah is shy around strangers, though he talks back to me often enough.

I glance at where he sits at the table, tinkering with a penny knife with a loose catch. He's forever trying to figure out how to take things apart and put them back together. When he was eight he stole Pa's pocket watch, the one with his initials engraved, and pried all the gears out. He never figured out how to repair it, but Pa let him keep it and he still wears it, for show I guess. Since then Micah's gotten much better at the fixing part, which is helpful, seeing as how the twins destroy everything in their path.

"Can you watch the twins later?" I ask him. "I have to go to the Homestead. We need flour, and I need to pay our dues."

That gets his attention. "Aw, do I have to? Can't you just tie 'em to a post somewhere?"

"If you want to go, I'll stay here instead."

Micah makes a face at me. The Homestead's where the shake hunters convene and drink and fight and generally make a loud nuisance of themselves. It's where the Judge sits and collects his fees, where my father gambles away whatever money he makes. I'd be happy never to step foot in that place again, but Ma always said you need to pick your battles.

I give him a crooked smile. "It's only for a couple hours. If I have to suffer, you have to suffer."

By midmorning, the temperature is starting to climb. I tie back my hair, but pieces of it come loose and plaster to my face. I haven't cut my hair in more than a year, not since my mother died. She always cut it for me, and I can't quite bring myself to do it without her. It seems wrong, like a final admission that she's not coming back.

Once the dough has risen, I divide it into fat round biscuits to bake. Half I'll leave for my siblings to argue over and the rest I'll take to trade at the Homestead. I rummage around the tins on the shelf until I find the empty coffee can we hide our money in. I pull out the bills and I sit at the table and count it three times while Micah watches.

"Ninety-eight," I say, setting the bills down on the table. "Minus twenty for the fee . . ."

"Seventy-eight," Micah says, always quicker than me. "That won't last long."

"It will get us through next month." It amazes me that all we have in the world can be held in one hand.

I count out twenty dollars and put the rest of the money back in the can. I fold the bills and stuff them into a pocket sewn into my belt, where no one will see them. I don't trust the kind of people that frequent the Homestead. It's not much money all told, but there are hunters who would easily kill me for it.

"And after next month?" Micah asks quietly.

"I don't know. Maybe Elsie has work for me at the bar, or repairs need doing. Pa might send something."

Micah scoffs at me, and I hold up a hand to silence him.

"The twins are awake," I say quickly. I can hear tentative footsteps, and I don't want them to overhear.

Catherine has taken to hiding around corners and eavesdropping. She is too much like Micah; she understands too much for a seven-year-old. Calvin I do not worry about; he is more interested in lizards than conversation.

"You're up already," Cal says grumpily as he pulls out a chair. The twins like to jump on me to wake me up, and the crosser I get the more they laugh.

"You're going to hurt me one day, and then you'll be sorry."

"Prob'ly not," Cath says seriously, and I try to smile. The twins have our mother's coloring, sandy blond hair and light blue eyes. Micah and I take after our father, dark eyes and brown hair streaked light from days in the sun. We all have the same look about us, though, and it's easy to see we're related.

"I made biscuits, you ingrates. Clean your hands."

They ignore me as usual, knowing I won't press too hard. Breakfast is hardly a feast, but they eat the biscuits and some dried apricots with gusto. The twins try to see who can make Micah laugh first, which gets more difficult every day. They're happy; it's such a simple thing to please them. I watch the three of them, a smile frozen on my face. I love my brothers and sister, I do, but there is another part of me that wishes I could leave them all behind. It's selfish, but this isn't the life I wanted for myself. Some days it's all I can do to drag myself out of bed to face the washing and cooking and mending, the walls of this house slowly closing in on me, trapping me here forever.

It was different when Ma was alive. Ma knew how to stretch the pantry, she took in extra sewing on the side; she tried to teach me but I've never been much good with a needle. Things were tough, sure, but we got by. Pa—well, he was still Pa, but at least when he came home he had stories to tell, and he could always make Ma laugh. He would send money when he remembered, or when he won a big hand. Now, he never comes home unless it's to sleep off the drink and ask for cash that we don't have.

I keep waiting for something to change, but I don't know what that will be. All I know is that I can't keep on like this, I can't take care of all of them. Micah helps with the skinning, but between the two of us we only found three snakes yesterday, and two of those were rat snakes, not worth much. We have no money and there are four of us to feed. Hattie Jensen put a pillow over her baby's face eight months ago. The Judge put her outside the perimeter, but we all understood why she did it. If it's a choice between dying quick or starving, I know what I would choose. But I don't even have that luxury because I can't leave my family to die.

I wipe the plates down with a stiff rag and order the twins to clean their hands again. I can see the grime under Calvin's fingernails, and I vow to start enforcing some rules around here, though even Ma could barely control the twins. I don't think they're scared of anything, especially not me; that's what happens when you grow up in a place where danger is as commonplace as weeds. They've never known any other life, and maybe that makes it easier.

I'm debating whether or not to sweep; I'm fighting a losing battle with the dust, and some days it doesn't feel worth it. A knock at the door makes the decision for me.

"Micah," I call over my shoulder. Micah's friend, Sam, can be expected at least once a day.

"Hold on," I say, and I shove back the sticking lock on the door. I open it wide to find two hunters waiting on our front porch.

3.

The younger one's name is Yancey, I'm fairly certain. He's a sorry-looking fellow, sallow cheeks and thin hair that he hides under a wide hat. The other one, with the dark hair and the mean mouth, I don't know. I've seen him at the Homestead, playing cards with Pa, but I never had reason to get his name.

"What do you want?" I'm not rude as a rule, but I don't like surprises, especially on my doorstep.

"You Harrison Wilcox's daughter?" the stranger asks.

"Who wants to know?"

"Name's McAllister. We're looking for your father."

"He ain't here."

"That right?" And before I can stop him, Yancey

shoves his way past me into the house.

"Hey," I yell, grabbing at him and missing. "You can't just—"

"If you're hiding him, you better tell me now," McAllister interrupts.

Yancey knocks over a chair and my entire face goes hot. I start to call him all the dirty names I can think of, and the commotion brings Micah out of the back, the twins trailing after him.

"Willie?" he asks, confused.

"He ain't here," Yancey says to McAllister.

"I already told you that," I say, furious. "Now get the hell out of my house."

"One moment," McAllister says, and he very deliberately pulls out his gun. I go still, and he nods at me. "Now how 'bout we have us a talk."

I glance at Micah, but his eyes are on the gun. My own still hangs on the wall, useless with McAllister between it and me.

"I don't think so, missy," McAllister says, following my gaze. "After you," and he motions to the table with his gun.

Damn. I turn around, trying to remember where Micah left his rifle. McAllister takes a seat at the table where we just ate our breakfast, and my lip curls with resentment. Who the hell does he think he is, pointing a gun at me in my own kitchen?

"Sit," he tells me.

"Let them go," I order him, nodding at my family. Yancey stands to Micah's side, daring him to move. "You don't need them."

"I'm not going anywhere," Micah says.

"I'm staying if he's staying," Calvin says.

"If Cal stays—" Catherine starts.

"Enough," McAllister says, his voice clipped. "Sit."

I glare at Micah and pick up the overturned chair. Trust them to be difficult when I least need it. I sit and McAllister levels his gun at my chest. I cross my arms to show him I'm not impressed, not by him or his bootlicker. I'm scared, but more than that I'm angry. I know their kind, bullies and cowards, and I won't show him fear.

"Now then," he says, "like I said, we're looking for Harrison Wilcox."

"Why?"

"'Cause he has something that belongs to me, that's why."

I close my eyes for the briefest moment. "What'd he steal now?"

"Four hundred dollars. I won it fair off some boys last night. I maybe celebrated overly much, and when I woke up my money was missing, and your pa with it."

It figures. Only a fool would spout off about money at the Homestead; serves him right that Pa took it off him.

"I can't help you," I tell him. "I didn't even know he was back in town, I swear."

McAllister doesn't say anything for a moment, he just studies me. Then he nods at Yancey, who kneels down in front of Catherine.

"Hey there, darlin'," he says, smiling at her, and bile rises in the pit of my stomach.

"Leave her alone," Micah says.

"Did you see your daddy this morning?" Yancey asks.

Micah moves to jump in, but Cath doesn't need help; she rears back and kicks Yancey in the shin, hard.

"Son of a bitch," he yells, rubbing at his leg. "You little—"

My mouth fills with wild, panicked laughter that I swallow down.

"Look, he weren't here," I say quickly, before Yancey thinks to retaliate. "He hasn't been home in months. If Pa took your money, he wouldn't stick around. You can bet he's out in the desert right now. You want what's yours, you'll just have to go get it."

"I got a better idea," McAllister says with a nasty smile. "Seeing as how he's your pa, I think you should get it."

"What?"

"I'll give you a week to bring me my money."

I shake my head. "Look around you—you think I got money to spare?"

"That's your problem, not mine. You're gonna do it." He stands up. "'Cause if you don't—Yancey?"

I look over in time to see Yancey grab Micah around the throat, and my chest lurches.

"Stop it," I yell, jumping up from the table, but McAllister yanks me back down.

"Stop it, now," I say, trying to tug away.

"You're going to get me what I want, because if you don't, Yancey and I are gonna come back with some friends. And we're gonna do for you and your brother, and then I'm gonna put a price on your gutless father's head."

Micah's face is turning red; the twins are pulling at Yancey's arms and kicking, but he holds Micah tight.

"What's gonna happen to those little ones if you're

not around?" McAllister says with a smile. "One week." He stands up and motions to Yancey, who releases Micah. He falls to the floor and I rush over to him.

"We'll be at the Homestead," McAllister says. "Waiting."

Micah starts to cough, the veins on his neck bulging out in red strands. I grab him around the shoulders, and I'm just repeating, "It's all right, it's all right, everything is all right." Two small sets of hands hug my back and nothing is all right because I can't keep them safe, not even in our own house, not even if I have my arms around them.

"Y'all have a good day," Yancey says, tipping his hat at us. The door slams shut behind them and I press my forehead against Micah's shoulder and listen to him breathe while I try to remember how to do it myself. In and out, in and out, until my body takes over for me.

4.

My boots are old and worn, the leather soft and cracked in places. Before the animals started to get sick, my father used to tan all sorts of hides. Now these are the only shoes I have, and they've molded to my feet after years of wear. I check for scorpions by habit, but my mind is elsewhere.

"I told you I'm fine," Micah says, sipping on some water at the table. His voice is slightly scratchy, but he keeps waving me away when I hover. "He wasn't really trying to hurt me, he just wanted to scare us."

"Well, it worked," I tell him, tucking in my shirt, a faded blue blouse. "I'm good and scared."

"I still don't think you should go to the Judge."

"Micah, they said they'd come back—"

"We got guns, too, Will."

"Don't be stupid. There's more where they came from, and I don't trust them not to come at night and burn the house down around our ears. No one else is getting hurt if I can help it. I'll ask the Judge for a line of credit and we'll pay them off."

My slim jim holster goes on my belt, and my gun goes into my holster. My father schooled it into us that you don't carry a weapon unless you can use it. My revolver is long and heavy, and I'm a decent shot. Micah is better than me with the rifle, but my vision isn't as sharp as his.

"You think he'll lend you the money? He ain't exactly kindhearted."

"We can't just wait and hope Pa shows his face again. I know Milford and that widow borrowed from the Judge. It's worth a shot."

"How are we gonna pay it back? We barely have enough to get by as it is."

"We'll figure it out, Micah. We can't have this hanging over our heads."

I think about taking my knife, but it can be cumbersome on a long walk, so I decide against it. If I need to pull a blade on a shake, chances are I'm already dead.

Micah fists his hands on the table. "I could kill Pa."

"Hey," I tell him. "I'll get us through this. I'll find a way, I promise."

I shouldn't make promises I can't keep, but the biggest lies are the ones you tell yourself.

"I'm set," I say, standing up. "You sure you gonna be all right on your own?"

"Would you stop fussing at me and just go already?"

I smack him lightly on the back of the head and call for the twins.

"Take us with you," Cath says as I tuck my hair into a wide-brimmed hat; we're all tanned as dark as our skin will go, but it will keep the sun out of my eyes at least.

"Please, Willie?" Calvin asks, and a matching pair of wide, hopeful eyes try to guilt me. They look so much alike; Cath took a pair of shears to her hair when it got longer than Calvin's. They're easy to tell apart now, though, when Cal has his horrid yellow lizard draped over his shoulder. I keep threatening to skin it, but I haven't been able to catch it yet.

"You know better than that," I say, wiping crumbs off Cath's chin. "They won't let you in anyhows."

"Here," Micah says, handing me an empty sugar sack. He's wrapped up the extra biscuits in the ratty cloth to keep them fresh, along with three snakeskins and some of the warning chimes he makes, fractured pieces of colored glass tied with string.

"Thank you," I say, the glass clinking as I settle the bag around my shoulder. "I won't be gone more'n a few hours, I should think."

"Be careful," Micah says.

"Always am."

"Liar." He gives me a wan smile.

The door is heavy, and I yank it open with a scowl, squinting into the light.

"Behave," I say. "And fix this damn lock while I'm gone, will you?"

They watch me march down the porch and along the dusty path from our house to the fence. It's old and wooden and useless, a remnant from a time when these kind of fences mattered. At the gate I look back to see all three of them crowded in the doorway. This is my family, smaller than it should be, worn down and restless and resigned to losing. I don't want to give them more bad news.

"Love," I call.

"Love," they call back, even Micah, who sometimes feels he is too old to be shouting *love* to his sister. But this is Glory, and you always make time for good-byes.

5.

Hunters. It's always the hunters. It was a hunter's fault Ma got sick, the one who happened to be at the gate that day. That alone is enough to condemn them all. I don't remember his name, only that he was young and too drunk to remember to close the gate all the way. Ma was just dropping off some linens to Elsie, trying to get home before supper. She still made it home; she killed the shake that came for her and just kept going. Even bleeding and half-conscious she tried to get back to us. We shut the door behind her, locked it, and she never left the house again. I can't even hate the guard, because he's dead and gone beyond where hatred can touch him. But McAllister I can, and will, hate.

Anger fuels my march down the main road to the

center of town. It's less a road, really, and more of a wide expanse of packed dirt, worn down by feet taking the same trip hundreds of times. Horses aren't much good in Glory; they're expensive to keep and shakes tend to go for the animals first if you take them outside the perimeter. Some hunters are willing to risk it, but only the ones who can afford to gamble money for speed. At least it isn't awful far to the Homestead, maybe six miles, though it takes time to walk in the heat. I have wrathful energy to burn, and I set a sharp pace.

Our house is at the very edge of town, where the poor folks had to settle. We have a few acres Pa bought back when it seemed like a good idea, when it had only been a year since it had rained. Now all we have on our land is an empty chicken coop and an endless supply of dirt that's slowly making its way into the house.

Our land borders the Molinas' place, or at least it used to. They left three years ago, after their dog attacked their youngest son. It must have snuck out into the desert at night, and they never realized it was sick. Careless of them. You can't afford to overlook anything here.

The sun is high, turning the sky a blinding white. Heat shimmers on the road, and sweat is already beginning to trickle down my neck and between my shoulder blades. It's a good heat, clean and searing, burning away any moisture in the air. I lick my lips and swallow, wishing I had thought to bring a canteen. I left in too much of a hurry, I suppose, but I couldn't sit around and do nothing.

To my left the perimeter rises, wooden poles supporting row upon row of barbed wire. Tumbleweeds caught at the base rustle gently and the sun glints off the wire, turning each spike into a blinding spot in my vision that still flashes when I look away. Once Micah and I found a shake trapped in the wire along the road. We thought she was dead, but when we got close enough she opened her fever-bright eyes and began to scream and writhe, oblivious to the way the wire tore at her skin. I shot her through the heart, as much to stop her suffering as to keep us safe. The memory is like the spots of light; I blink and I still see it.

I was seven when the fence went up, and that was a good ten years ago. It wasn't long after the War Between the States, and I remember folks talking about how bad things were, how the war took the men and the crops and razed the cities to the ground. I remember Pa railing against the planters, saying it was a rich man's war and a poor man's fight; but then Pa is from the up-country of East Tennessee and never had any love for the rebels. He hid in the mountains for most of the war, a draft deserter. He wasn't particularly loyal to the Union; Pa's just always been good at avoiding a fight.

Then something changed, and people stopped talking, or if they did it was in hushed voices. I remember the fear in the air, and not knowing the reason. It hit Silver first, a mining town to the east. The docs thought it was hydrophobia, and that was bad enough; then they realized it was spreading too fast and people were taking sick too quick. So they said it must be something the miners dug up in the dirt, or caught from the red bats hunting at night, but even I knew they were just guessing by then. They started calling it the Silver sickness, and everyone shook their heads for the poor city folk. But didn't those people go putting on airs, thinking themselves better than the rest of us? Then the animals started dying, the cattle and the horses, and dogs stopped coming home at night. When it hit Hide Town and then Best, the fences went up and folks stopped calling it the Silver sickness. It didn't need a name anymore; Silver was gone, and the sickness was everywhere.

The fences kept the shakes out, but they couldn't keep folks in. And people still needed to go from town to town, especially when there's nothing out here to grow. Lots of folks died those early years, trying to get supplies through the desert. I reckon people even thought the Judge was a godsend, the way he came in and set up the stations. And at first his hunters seemed like a fine idea, to protect folks on the road. But the prices got higher, and the hunters got rougher, and the Judge started charging just to live in our own homes. By then it was too late. The Judge controls the hunters and the hunters control our movements, and I'm broke and half-starving with no way to get out.

I pass Old Bess's place and it snaps me out of a past that won't do me any good to linger over. Her front porch is cluttered with a rocking chair, clay pots, an ill-shaped bench, and an empty barrel with dirty cups on top. Bess has been ancient for as long as I can remember, and most nights she just sits in her rocking chair, drinking cup after cup of coffee and staring out at the desert. She's a strange old bird, but a tough one, and the only person the twins seem to listen to. My mother used to take us over to visit, and the inside of Bess's house is even worse than the outside, filled with all manner of odd knickknacks. Ma once tried to tidy up the place, but Old Bess just yelled at her and waved her cane around until she knocked the broom out of Ma's hands. I feel guilty as I walk by, and I lie to myself, promising to visit soon.

A volley of gunshots echoes up ahead, I reckon somewhere close to the gate. This early, that'll be the guards warning shakes away from the fence. I barely flinch at the sound of the blasts, that's how used to them I am—Glory's twisted version of a rooster's crow.

Doctor Kincaid lives with his son in the next house, which is in far better shape than the others. He could afford to live closer to town, but I think he likes the quiet. He's been the only doctor in town for some time now, and he delivered all my siblings and me. I don't know why he still lives in Glory, but I'm grateful he does. The door opens as I walk by and Samuel waves to me from the porch.

"Hi, Willie," he says with a small smile. The doctor's son looks just like him, round glasses, slightly hunched shoulders, and hair that refuses to lay flat.

"Hi, Sam. Your pa's out?" It's more of a statement than a question; Doc Kincaid is always needed somewhere.

Sam nods. I wonder if he gets lonely in that big house all by himself. His mother ran off years ago, lost to the safety and the comfort of the north, or maybe it was the west.

"I thought I might stop by today," Sam says hesitantly, and I try not to sigh at him. Sam comes over so often he's practically another brother, yet for some reason he still feels the need to ask permission. He's nearer in age to me, but he and Micah have always been close. Sam's a bit more outspoken, but they're both the shy, bookish sort, and particularly awkward around girls.

"Go on ahead," I tell him. "I'm sure Micah will be glad of the company. It's been a hard morning."

"Twins at it again?" Sam grins at me, looking so much younger than I feel. I open my mouth to explain, but if I start to talk about it, I'll only feel more helpless. Suddenly I'm tired, and I need to keep moving.

"They'll tell you about it. I have to go," I say quickly. "I'll see you later, Sam."

He says good-bye to my back as I walk away, and I raise a hand without turning. I focus on the road, watching my boots slowly coat with another layer of dust. The houses get closer together and then give way to shops the nearer I get to town. What used to be Jensen's Candy Store is now a hollowed-out square building with a faded sign. Along the side of the building is a row of small glass windows, most of them cracked or broken, with shards of glass clinging to the edges. Every once in a while, when the twins get too rowdy to be contained, Micah and I bring them out here to throw rocks at the windows. Their aim is decent; they'll be good with rifles, I think.

Only one wall of the church remains standing, with empty spaces where the glass used to be. The ground is scattered with split pieces of wood and fractured bricks, and the rest is just sand and brush. Every year more of the wall chips away, until at last we won't even have the sad reminder of what used to be. Ma told me when times get hard, people either turn to god or against him. People in Glory turned their backs on god years ago and haven't looked back since. We got no use for a god in these parts; we're already damned.

I breathe out sharply and kick up a cloud of dirt, mad at the world. I don't need to pay attention to where I'm going; I've taken this walk more times than I care to remember. My feet do the work for me, following the road as it forks and taking the path to the right. I thought the walk would settle me some, but the closer I get to town, the angrier I get. I keep picturing McAllister making this same trek back, only I'll bet he did it with a smug smile on his face. It won't do to get this worked up before I even step foot near the hunters, so I start to hum to distract myself, then sing in a low voice.

> *I walk beneath the desert sun*
> *I walk beneath the moon*
> *I'm looking for my one true love*
> *I hope I find her soon.*

> *I'll look until I die of thirst*
> *Until I fall from grace*
> *I'll look for my one true love*
> *Till I forget her face.*

It's an old song, and the tune is cheery if the words are not. At the very least it gets my mind off this morning, my feet crunching along the road to the beat. When my throat gets too dry, I switch back to humming and try to swallow some moisture back into my mouth.

I pass what remains of the school, empty since our teacher left and no one bothered to take her place, then a long-shuttered mercantile shop, and then I'm almost there. McNab's General Store is still open, though there's nobody in it but McNab himself. He's a stubborn one, there behind the counter, a look of grim determination on his face. Most folks get their food from the Homestead now, rather than the store; no one wants to spend real money, not when they can trade.

The path swings back to the left, and now the two rows of shops that make up Main Street come into view. In between the empty buildings are the shops that are still in service, the bootmaker's and the boardinghouse, the pharmacy and the firearms store. There's always a need for guns and medicine, especially out here. The storefronts are plain and sandblasted, the paint faded from signs and the windows dusty, but they have wide wooden banquettes to walk along and a welcome overhang to keep off the sun. I step onto the porch of the pharmacy, both to catch my breath and prepare myself, leaning against one of the beams that support the overhang.

My destination is at the end of Main Street, where a large, square, two-story building sits between the rows of shops. The Homestead started out as the courthouse, but now it serves as a trading post and a saloon, and the place where the shake hunters gather. The second story is a brothel, though it's not advertised as such.

I hate the Homestead; I hate the smell of the whiskey and the drunken laughs, I hate the men who populate it, but my need is stronger than my hate today. I square my shoulders and push away from the beam and run face-first into two hunters.

6.

I jump back, rubbing my chin where it glanced off something metal and cursing myself for being so addle-headed as to not see where I'm going.

"Sorry," I mutter, and try to force my way past them.

"Not so fast," the man on the right says, moving to block me. "Where you off to in such a hurry, little sister?"

He has deep-set eyes and a squashed nose. I don't know him, but the man next to him is called Vasquez, a regular at the Homestead.

"You know damn well where I'm going," I say crossly. "So let me get on with it."

"What you got in the bag?" Vasquez asks, nodding at my sack.

"Nothing worth troubling yourself about."

"We'll be the judge of that," the stranger says. "Hand it over."

I clutch the sack tighter and wonder if I can reach my gun before they get theirs, and if a bag of biscuits is worth killing over.

"Don't be stupid, girl," Vasquez says, his hand on his pistol. "Do what Grady says."

I clench my jaw hard, but relax my grip on the bag, glad I kept my money tucked away. The stranger, Grady I guess, closes in and lifts it from my shoulder while I glare at him; at least I can refuse to hand it over, a small and meaningless victory.

He opens the bag and digs his hand in, and to satisfy my anger I picture how he'll look when the shakes tear his arms off. Bloody, I reckon.

"What the hell is this?" he asks, holding up a fistful of chimes.

I don't answer, and he lets them fall to the ground, where they land with a jangle. He pulls out the snake-skins next, and the biscuits, and then rattles the empty bag.

"That it?" Vasquez asks, looking doubtful. He makes a long gargling sound and then spits a shiny glob into the dirt. It's not enough to steal; they have to be disgusting as well.

"I told you it weren't worth your time," I say.

Grady scowls at me. "You're hiding something."

Now my hand is on my gun, and I make sure they can both see it.

"That's enough," I say. "You've had your fun. Don't make this more trouble than it needs to be."

Vasquez sniffs, to prove he's not impressed. "Come on," he says to his friend. "She ain't got nothing."

Grady looks me up and down and sneers.

"Yeah," he agrees, shoving a biscuit into his mouth, which only partly muffles the name he calls me. He drops my bag on the ground and they walk away from me laughing. I squeeze my hands into fists and slowly count to ten to make sure I don't accidentally shoot them both in the back. Then I kneel down in the dirt and slowly repack my bag.

Hunters. I hate hunters.

I stand up and compose myself, sling my bag over my shoulder, and push open the door to the Homestead.

The noise hits me first, the roar of men's voices all speaking over one another and the tinny sound of a piano underneath. It's dark in here, and I take off my hat and wait for my eyes to adjust to the dimness after the bright afternoon sun. Tables are spread out across the room with mismatched chairs, more than half of them occupied. To the right stretches the bar, a long wooden counter that's lost most of its shine, stools and spittoons placed in front, a tall redheaded woman behind it. The floor under my boots is sticky with old liquor and tobacco spit as I make my way toward her. She's arguing with a sloppy-looking fellow who's swaying on his feet.

"Jus' one, Elsie, tha's all I'm asking fer," he says, his voice thick and slurred.

"Jessup, go sit down before you fall over. And don't even think of starting something tonight, or you can find another place to do your drinking." Elsie glares at him mean enough to send him stumbling away. "And that goes for Dollarhide, too," she calls after him, her hands planted on her hips. She turns and catches sight of me, worry flitting across her face. It's gone just as quickly and she gives me a wide grin.

"Well, here comes trouble."

"Hello, Miss Elsie," I say with a small smile, pulling myself onto a stool.

"What can I do you for, Willie?"

"I'm here on business."

"What do you got for me?" Elsie says, pouring me a glass of prickly pear juice. "Did you want something else, sweetheart? Coffee?"

"No, ma'am, that'll suit me fine." I put my sack on the bar and take a large gulp of the juice. It's not cold, but at least it helps clear the dust from my throat.

Elsie opens my sack, carefully taking out the biscuits and the chimes, which are only slightly dusty. They aren't worth much, but it's something, and I already owe Elsie more money than I could ever hope to pay back. She's kind that way; she was close with Ma and always looks out for us. She also knows more about the shake hunters than anyone in town, and I trust her judgment.

"Biscuits, those can go with supper tonight, and chimes. Micah make these?"

I nod and Elsie smiles. "I thought so. Clever boy, even if he never comes to see me. You want this back?" She holds out the worn cloth the bread was wrapped in.

"Yes, ma'am," I say, feeling my cheeks get hot at the obvious proof of how poor we are.

"And some skins, too. You do them yourself?"

"Micah killed them, but I skinned 'em."

"Well, you did good," Elsie says. "Now what are you needing, dear?"

"Flour, hominy, beans, coffee, dried fruit." I rattle off the list I made in my head. I'd love to get some meat, even salted, but beans are cheaper and they'll go farther. "Lamp oil, a spool of thread, and a brick of that yellow soap if you still have it."

"Anything else?"

I take another drink and meet Elsie's sharp gaze. "Some information, if you'll give it to me."

Elsie blinks, her face carefully blank. I don't say anything, just stare back and after a long moment she sighs. "Damn. I was hoping McAllister would let it go. He bother you?"

I give a quick jerk of my head that could be a nod.

"I'm sorry, Willie. I didn't think they'd be after you already."

"I didn't even know Pa was back."

"He came in a few days ago. I tried to get him to go home, I really did—"

"It ain't your fault, Elsie. He wouldn't have done us much good at home, anyhows. Did you see what happened?"

"Some of it. McAllister was sitting with Fullerton and them and he was winning big. Making a lot of noise about it, too, which didn't go unnoticed. Then this morning he's down here screaming that someone lifted his winnings."

"And that someone was Pa," I say bitterly.

"Looks that way. Harry took off sometime in the night, but everyone heard McAllister bragging. If it hadn't been your pa, someone else would've done it."

"Any idea where he might be headed?"

"That I don't know, but I can ask around. I'll get Ned to find out who was on the gate last night."

"Thanks, Elsie."

"Anything you need, Willie, you let me know. I'm sorry I didn't keep a closer eye on him for you."

I shrug. "Ma couldn't control him, neither. I don't know why she married him."

Elsie smiles crookedly. "She loved him, that's why. Sense and love don't always go together."

"Well I wish she'd had a little more of one and less of the other. McAllister wants four hundred dollars, and I ain't got anything close to that. So now I gotta go to the Judge with my tail between my legs, and that ain't a conversation I'm looking forward to."

Elsie doesn't argue with me, doesn't say it's a bad idea, doesn't ask any questions. She gives me no pitying glances, for which I am grateful. It is easier to be strong when those around you are, too, and determination is etched into every line on Elsie's face. She reminds me of my mother, a hard woman in a hard land, and I resolve to be the same.

"All right, then. Do what you need to do." Elsie looks over my head, scanning the sea of faces across the room. "The Judge is at the back. Be firm, be polite, and hold that tongue of yours."

"I'll do my best."

I push my empty glass across the bar and hop off my stool, squaring my shoulders for the unpleasantness to come.

I.

I weave through the tables toward the farthest corner of the floor. Even through the smoke and the dim lighting I make out the Judge, his balding head sitting atop the massive bulk of his body. Three hunters sit with him at his table, and they fall silent when I approach, stopping a few feet away.

"Miss Wilcox," the Judge says in his deep, cultured voice. He emphasizes the *Miss*, and already I am annoyed. But I try not to scowl, as it will only encourage him to bait me further.

"Your Honor."

"I assume you've come to pay your dues?" He gazes at me with disinterest, like I am of no more consequence than a horsefly, a look he has perfected.

"Yessir." I dig in my belt for the twenty dollars and hold it out. The Judge nods to the man on his right, who takes the money from me and hands it to the Judge. He doesn't even bother to count it; I reckon it's nothing to him. He's rich enough to leave Glory, to sit pretty in some place out west. He stays because he wants to, because here he doesn't have to bother pretending to be a decent man. None of them do.

I swallow hard. "I also—well, I wanted to ask you."

"What?"

I can't seem to get the words out right. "I was hop-ing—I heard it was possible—"

"Spit it out, girl."

"I would like to take out a line of credit with you, sir."

"Would you?" The Judge sits back in his chair, and he can't keep a smug smile off his face.

"I need—well, my father left me with a debt, and I intend to pay it off."

"And how much is this debt?"

"Four hundred dollars."

"That wouldn't be the money your father stole from Angus McAllister, would it?"

My cheeks flush and I duck my head. He knows damn well what the answer is, he just wants me to admit it; I won't give him the satisfaction.

"I see. Well, honorable as your intentions may be, I'm afraid I can't help you." He's enjoying this, and I count to five in my head before I answer.

"Please, Your Honor. I have three younger siblings."

"If you think appealing to my better nature will change my mind, you're wrong. I am not a charitable man."

"I'm not asking for charity," I spit at him. Then I take a deep breath, trying to regain control. It's almost physically painful to say, but I get it out. "Please, sir. I'm begging you." The words leave a sour taste in my mouth.

"Miss Wilcox, I do not lend money to people who cannot pay it back."

"I will," I tell him. "I give you my word."

The Judge raises his thick brows mockingly. "Oh? And how will you manage that? Are you looking for Pearl to find you a place? I suppose you're not hard on the eyes, if you would fill out some."

The men snicker amongst themselves, and there's a prickling at the back of my neck. My fingernails dig into my palms as I leash my building temper. I have to try. For Micah and the twins I have to try.

"If you won't lend me the money, then you could talk

to McAllister. Ask him to see reason."

"Your father stole money from the man; he has the right to demand satisfaction."

"Not from me," I say through clenched teeth.

"As I understand it, your father has made himself unavailable. Perhaps you should take it up with him instead of sniffing around at me."

"Please—"

"Miss Wilcox, I am not interested in your tears or your pretty pleas. Whatever trouble you've stepped in, it does not concern me."

I open my mouth and the Judge holds up a meaty hand.

"We're done here," he orders, and one of the men stands up and reaches for my arm to escort me away.

"Don't touch me," I snap at him, yanking my arm back.

"On second thought, perhaps Pearl wouldn't want you after all," the Judge says, and his men laugh again.

"I'll turn to whoring the day you get a woman for free." The words are out before I can stop them.

"Watch your mouth, girl." The hunter who took my money leans forward menacingly. The Judge raises a hand in warning, and the man falls back restlessly.

"You are young, and foolish. I will forgive you your impudence this once. Good day, Miss Wilcox." If anything, his smile has gotten smugger, but there is no mistaking the calculated hatred in his eyes.

I turn my back on him very deliberately and walk to the safety of the bar, welcoming the noise to drown out the thought in my head: that was my only chance, and I blew it all to pieces.

8.

That was woefully stupid. I sit at the bar stiffly, admonishing myself. Maybe if I hadn't lost my temper I could've convinced him. To make me feel doubly bad, my friend Clementine is coming toward me, and she's the very kind of girl I just slighted.

"I thought that was you, Willie," Clementine says with her dimpled smile, her hair curling just so to frame her wide face. Clem is everything I am not: small and soft, her skin all cream and sugar. She's lovely, even with her face all done up in white and pink and red. She hugs me gently and I smell flowers. I'm suddenly all too aware of the dirt under my fingernails and the fact that I can't remember the last time I brushed my hair.

"Hi, Clem. I didn't see you there."

"I was upstairs. It's been forever since I seen you, Willie."

What Clem doesn't say is why; she's been working for Pearl for almost two years, ever since her parents died on the road. Things haven't been easy between us since. Clem thinks I look down on her, for choosing this work, but it isn't that at all; it scares me to see her here and to know how easily I could fall into this life, too.

"How've you been, Clem? They treating you right here?"

"Pearl's been decent to me. She takes care of all us girls." Clementine glances back over her shoulder quickly, then leans in closer to me. "What about you, Will? I saw you talking to the Judge. Is everything all right?"

I can't lie, not with those big honest eyes staring at me. "No, it ain't." I put my head in my hands. "I'm hard pushed here, Clem, and I'm only making it worse."

"Here, now, stop that worrying. You're getting a fine wrinkle between those eyes." Clem gently touches my forehead with her thumb, smoothing out the line.

"Leave off," I say, swatting her hand away. "It's my wrinkle. I earned it, I'll keep it."

"So it's true, then?" Clem asks gently. "What they're saying about your pa?"

I sigh, long and loud. "Yeah, it's true."

"Is there anything I can do?"

"Not unless you know where to get four hundred dollars fast."

Clem crooks an eyebrow. "I do, but you won't like the answer."

I shake my head. "Clem, please . . ."

She slides gracefully onto the stool next to me. "Maybe you don't want to hear it, but it is a way to make money." She folds her hands neatly on top of the bar. "I know most folk look down on us line girls, but I don't go hungry and I always have work. Maybe it ain't what I wanted for myself, but one day I'll have enough money saved to buy my way out of this town."

I look up, surprised. Clem and I used to talk about getting out of Glory. It was just child's talk, though, running away to have adventures, before life became real and messy. I gave up on those dreams a long time ago.

"That's the whole point, ain't it?" Clem asks. "To get you and yours out? Isn't that what we always said?"

"I didn't think you remembered. Where will you go?"

"North. Edgewater, maybe. Anywhere that isn't here. I'll get as far from Glory as I can, and find myself a rich husband who will keep me in ribbons and lace, and I'll spend the rest of my years trying to forget the last two."

Clem sounds as bitter as I've ever heard her, and I feel a pang of regret that I never guessed what was hidden under those layers of makeup. I touch her shoulder lightly.

"Sorry, Clem. I know—I know it must be hard here."

The smile Clem gives me is brittle, but real. "Life's hard any way you take it, Willie. You know that."

And she's right; I do. All we have are bad options, and you pick the one you can live with. You keep moving forward, because what other choice is there? As far as I'm concerned, Pa made his choice, and now it's time to make mine. It comes down to this: I won't let anything hurt my family, not if I can help it.

"So what are you going to do?" Clem asks.

"Whatever it takes," I answer. "I'm going to track down my father and get back what he stole. And if it's gone, then I'm gonna drag his ass back to Glory and he can answer for what he's done."

"You can't go out there alone," Clem says, her eyes wide.

I survey the room full of rowdy, reeking men, men who would probably kill me for less than what I have in my pockets.

"No," I say, my stomach sinking. "No, I can't."

9.

My hands are sweating, but at least I made a decision. Maybe it's a bad one, maybe it's all kinds of foolish, but it's something, and I cling to it.

"Oh my," Clem says. "Here comes Ned to make sure I'm not corrupting you. Take care, Willie."

Ned Evans walks behind the bar, setting a drink in front of me. He nods a brief good-bye to Clementine as she eases herself off the stool and glides away with a rustle of silk and perfume.

"You look like you could use this," he says with a wink. He's Elsie's uncle and a kind one, even if he's partial to gambling.

"Thank you. I surely could," I say, and wrap my hand around the glass so hard I can see the white of my knuckles. The glass is cloudy and there's a chip in the rim; I wonder how old it is, how many lips drank from it, how many hands clasped it. I'd be willing to bet this glass is older than me, if I had money to bet. I take a sip, letting the amber liquor burn down my throat and settle in my empty stomach.

"Judge rattles everybody, sweetheart. Don't pay him no mind. Elsie says you're looking for your pa."

"I am." I take another small sip and grimace. "Any news?"

"Well, I spoke to Santos, he was on the gate. Said your pa ducked out just before sunrise with Washburne," he says, naming a hunter Pa likes to run with.

"Any idea where he was headed?"

"Santos says east."

"Best, then," I say, turning the glass around in my hand. He has a few contacts there who still bother to buy whatever sorry hides Pa's selling. Best is due east, maybe two days out; Pa's probably halfway there by now.

"That would be my guess. Can I get you anything else?"

I drain my glass and set it down hard. "A hunter to go with me to Best."

Ned blinks at me. "Aw, Willie, you don't want to get mixed up with a hunter."

"I don't want to. I have to."

"Is that the way of it, then?" Ned sighs. "All right. Elsie would know better than me who to trust. How much you looking to spend?"

"I guess as much as it takes. How much is a hunter?"

"A good one, not like Washburne? One fifty, maybe two hundred."

My heart sinks; it may as well be the four hundred. "I don't . . . I don't have that much," I whisper. Everywhere I turn is a dead end; I just can't win.

Ned leans forward, one hand rubbing the gray stubble on his chin. "You ever play cards, Willie?"

I give him my most withering look.

"Right, your pa. Well, you learn all sort of useful tricks playing cards."

"I'm sure." I'm not really listening. There's a burning pressure behind my eyes that I'm not sure has anything to do with the whiskey.

"Bluffing, for instance." Ned smiles at me. "Bluffing can be a very useful trick. Say, for example, you can't really spare the money to call a bet. If you got a good enough poker face, you bluff and you go all in. You play the game right, you may come out on top."

And suddenly I'm listening very hard to what Ned is trying to tell me. "What happens if—if your bluff gets called?"

Ned shrugs. "Well. In poker, you lose your money. But sometimes, could be you got nothin' left to lose."

I meet Ned's eyes and nod slowly, hoping I understand. The whiskey is making me feel fuddled, but in a pleasant, comforting way, like all the hard edges of life are blurred and softened. I can understand why men lose themselves to drink, if this is the way it makes them feel. For the first time in as long as I can remember, the hard knot of panic in my chest starts to loosen as the whiskey spreads its warmth. I feel bold, and almost happy. Ned gives me his bright smile and starts to whistle as Elsie comes up behind him with her hands on her hips.

"Uncle, what in tarnation is Willie drinking?"

"It's hardly more'n a drop, Elsie."

"Ned, I swear, sometimes . . ." Elsie shakes her head. "You're gonna get the child drunk, her with nothing on her bones and you with nothing in your head. Willie, you need to get some food in you."

"It's all right, Miss Elsie—"

"Hush, child. It's on the house, on account of Ned's poor judgment."

I should protest harder, but I can hardly turn down a free meal. I try not to look too much like a poor orphan when I smell the stew that Ned sets in front of me.

"There you go. Best SOB stew in town," Ned says proudly.

"Ned!" Elsie smacks him lightly on the arm, a look of long suffering on her face.

"Beggin' your pardon." Ned winks at me. "Son of a gun stew, that is."

It's been so long since I've had any meat other than snake, I have to force myself to take small bites and chew. Even though the meat is offal, and old offal at that, it's still the best meal I've had in days. I feel somewhat guilty, thinking of my family and the empty pantry at home.

"Now then," Ned says as I eat. "Elsie, our Willie here needs a hunter."

Elsie narrows her eyes at me. "You sure about that?"

I nod. "I am."

She purses her lips and breathes out hard. "All right then. Let me see who's here." Elsie looks over my head, scanning the sea of faces across the room. "You don't want

Jennings, that man can't hit the broad side of a barn."

"And not Grady," I tell her. "I'm not feeling kindly towards him today."

"I'd trust you with Lady Jane, but she's holed up with a bad leg. Ramos, maybe? How much you looking to spend?"

I swallow a mouthful of stew and shoot a quick glance at Ned. "One hundred," I lie, hoping my voice sounds steady.

"Hmm. That's too low for most of the practiced hunters, them that's been at this awhile. You got two choices. If you want to hire a professional, you'll have to settle for an old-timer or a drinker. Someone like Dollarhide or Sanchez."

Ned snorts. "Dollarhide is half in a whiskey barrel, and Sanchez can't see farther than I can spit."

"What's the other choice?" I ask. I've seen Dollarhide around the Homestead, and he's a wicked drunk. Word is he killed a horse trader up north before he came under the Judge's protection. I wouldn't trust him to watch his own front, let alone my back.

"You could hire one of the amateurs. They're inexperienced, mind you—"

"Green as deer grass, you mean," Ned interrupts.

"But affordable," Elsie finishes, ignoring the old man.

"And maybe it's better you hire one of the new boys. Most of these men would rob you soon as they get you outside the fence. They'd leave you stranded and steal everything, even your virtue. These youngsters may be all hat and no cattle, but at least they'll try to bring you home in one piece."

I think it over for a moment. I can shoot well enough and I don't tire easily. What I really need is someone I can trust. "All right, one of the new hunters it is. You got a name for me, Elsie?"

Elsie nods decisively. "What you want is the Garrett brothers."

"I can't afford two hunters." I can't even afford one, I remind myself.

"They work together and split the single fee. They'll be able to watch your back, and they're honest. Well, as honest as their kind can be. Benjamin and Curtis. They ain't been here long, but I've heard nothing but that they're decent folk."

"You think they'll hire on for the price?" I look at Ned as I ask, though it's Elsie who answers.

"I don't see why not. That's Curtis sitting by his lonesome next to the staircase. Why don't you ask him yourself?"

10.

"I'm looking for Curtis Garrett."

"I'm Garrett. What can I do you for?" His voice is cautious but polite, which is more than I can say for some of the men in Glory. He's tall, I can tell from the way his boots stick out from under the table; newer boots than mine, stiffer leather with shiny roach tips. He has an open, honest face, round and clean-shaven under sandy brown hair. I put his age closer to thirty than twenty, judging by the laugh lines around his mouth and the wrinkles at the corners of his eyes. He could be younger; the sun is unkind and takes its toll early here.

"Mr. Garrett, my name is Wilcox." I avoid telling people my first name if possible, and I see no reason to give it to this man, even if I'm inclined to take a shine to his friendly face. "I'm in need of a hunter to go east, most likely all the way to Best. I was told to speak to you." I hold out my hand to him, and he gives it a firm shake.

"Nice to meet you, Miss Wilcox," he says, like he actually means it. "It must be my lucky day; I've never had the pleasure of being recommended to so lovely a lady." He smiles at me, still holding my hand, and I can't help but smile back; his teasing is gentle and harmless. I wonder how long he's been a hunter, if those hands did something I'd rather not know about.

"You're a fair hand at flattery, Mr. Garrett, but how are you with a pistol?"

Garrett gives a surprised laugh and releases me, clapping. "Full of piss and vinegar, ain't you? I'm curious as to what you said to the Judge to make Vargas put his hackles up." He pushes out a chair with his boot for me, which I settle into.

"We had a—a misunderstanding." Garrett raises his eyebrows, but I refuse to say more. My mouth has gotten me into enough trouble for one day.

"I see. There's not many would want a misunderstanding with the Judge. Now tell me, Miss Wilcox, why I should go up Best way." He's still smiling politely, but his eyes are serious. To his credit, they stay on my face, which is a rarity for the hunters.

"You're new to Glory, Mr. Garrett, but it may be you know of my father. Harrison Wilcox?"

Garrett nods. "I've met Harry. Trapper, right? Not that there's much in the way of hide these days."

"Mostly we do snake and lizard skin." I pause, biting the inside of my cheek. "Well, the thing is, I'm in a tight spot of trouble, and I need to find my pa."

"I see. Any chance the name of that trouble is McAllister?"

I scowl. Does the whole town know my business? "What if it is?" I ask him. "It doesn't change what I need."

"Well, you certainly have a situation, I'll give you that. Now if I go looking for your father—"

"Mr. Garrett, you misunderstand me," I interrupt, straightening my back, glad the whiskey has made me bold. "I intend to look for him myself. What I need are extra guns and eyes." As if I would send hunters to track down my father alone—he'd come back a body, or not at all.

He makes a small coughing noise, which I take to be surprise.

"That does complicate matters, a bit," he says.

"I don't see how. Since I'll be funding this expedition, I make the terms. And the terms are, I go to Best. The only question is who I go with."

Garrett rubs his chin thoughtfully. "Fair enough. Can you use that?" he asks, pointing to my holster.

"I wouldn't carry it if I couldn't."

He nods approvingly. "All right, then, Miss Wilcox, here's the deal: my brother and I charge one hundred for Best and back. We take care of food and transport, but you provide your own weapons. Take no more than you can carry; we travel fast and light. If it's sunup we're on the move, and we bed down at the way stations on the Low Road. Those are few and far between, so if you can't keep up, we're in trouble. We don't want to be caught outdoors at night."

"I'll keep up. And as for the money, I can pay you fifty now, and the rest when we return." My stomach churns at the lie, and I hope he doesn't notice that I can't meet his eyes.

"I can agree to that." Garrett looks at me, considering. "When were you wanting to leave?"

"As soon as possible," I say. "I have to make a few arrangements, but I was hoping to leave by tomorrow."

Garrett gives a low whistle. "You don't give a fellow much notice. I need to run this by my brother, but I think I can safely say we have a deal, Miss Wilcox." He stands up and holds out his hand, and we shake on it. I'm slightly stunned at the swiftness with which this is happening; some part of me did not expect it to work.

"I am—grateful to you," I tell him haltingly. "And you can stop with the *misses*; everyone calls me Willie, or Will."

"Call me Curtis. We're going to be seeing a lot of one another, might as well get familiar. If you'll excuse me, I have to see Miss Elsie if we're going to leave tomorrow. We set out at dawn. Meet us at the gate and we'll take it from there. It was a pleasure to meet you, Willie."

"And you, Curtis."

He pauses for a moment and rests a hand on my shoulder. "Get some sleep while you can; lord knows there's little enough to be had on the road."

My stomach twists as he passes me by. I don't want to cheat this man, who smiles at me with kind eyes. But I have no choice, I tell myself, and cringe as one lie begets another.

11.

The heat hits me like a solid wall when I step out into the sunshine. I breathe in the scorching air and the heat sears my lungs, clearing out the smoke and noise from the bar. I don't know how folk can stand to live in there, crammed together with no space to think. I put my hat back on and tuck up my hair, adjusting my sack on my shoulder. It feels full to bursting, and I suspect Elsie threw in a few extra items.

I haven't taken more than a few steps when I hear the door to the bar swing open behind me.

"Girl!"

I turn, confused, and find myself staring into a wrinkled face, uneven stubble darkening the crevices. It takes me a minute to match the name to the face;

Dollarhide glares at me, his eyes small and folded into the corners.

"Can I help you?" I ask, feeling uneasy. Just how many hunters are going to accost me today? And it's only the afternoon.

"I heard you're lookin' fer a hunter," he says, his lips curling back to reveal tobacco-stained teeth.

"Yessir, I was. I'm afraid I already made a deal, or I'd be happy to consider you." Like hell, but I'm hoping the lie will appease him.

"It ain't about that." He moves close enough that I back up without thinking. "I hear your daddy took a lotta money, little girl. He pass any of that along your way?"

I let out a sharp laugh. "My pa takes money from me, not the other way around."

"Then where you get the money fer a hunter, I wonder?"

"None of your damn business," I say, prickling because he's not all wrong. "Just leave me alone."

"I got a better idea," he sneers.

I start to move back and he grabs my arm just below the shoulder, pulling me so close that I almost gag at the reek of alcohol on his breath.

"How much he give you? Hand it over and I won't hurt you none."

I try to yank away, but Dollarhide's fingers are like iron, and I grit my teeth as he starts to squeeze. I aim a punch at his face and my knuckles connect sharply with his cheekbone. Dollarhide howls in anger, but doesn't loosen his grip on my arm; he's too soaked to feel much pain and I'm not as good with my left hand.

"Let me go, Dollarhide," I order him, trying to keep calm.

"Give it up, girly."

"I don't have any money, you blame idiot," I yell, tugging at his fingers. He's drunk but strong, and I'll have bruises to show for this tomorrow.

He shakes me hard, and he's got hold of my gun arm, but I can reach with my left. At this range it hardly matters how good my aim is. I call myself all manner of fool and swear I will never leave the house without my knife again.

"I want what's mine," he says, slurring his words. I don't really want to shoot this man, but I do want him to let me go. My hand is on my gun when I hear a voice.

"Need help leaving, Dollarhide?"

He spins clumsily toward the door of the bar, where

a man stands lazily against the wall.

"This ain't your business, Garrett."

"I'm making it my business."

I use Dollarhide's momentary distraction to aim a well-placed kick at his knee, and there's a solid crunch as my boot connects. Dollarhide yelps and stumbles as he releases me, both his hands going to his injured leg.

"I got nothing that belongs to you, Dollarhide," I tell him evenly. "You keep your mucking hands off me or next time I won't be so polite."

Dollarhide looks from me to the man at the door, and swears. He struggles to his feet and stamps back to the bar. There's a moment of silence as the stranger and I regard one another.

"You must be the other Garrett brother," I say finally.

"That I am." His voice is low and slightly gravelly, but I suspect that may be an affectation. He's tall, like his brother, but slimmer. Darker, too, enough that I would bet some of their kin come from over the border. He's younger than Curtis, but it's hard to guess his age with half his face obscured by a beard. Only his eyes stand out, a shrewd amber peeking out from dark hair in bad need of a trim.

"Nice to meet you," I say, holding out my hand.

He doesn't shake my hand, instead folding his arms across his chest.

"I guess Curtis does the talking." I put down my hand when it's clear he's not going to shake it. "And the smiling."

"Miss Wilcox, it's my understanding that you wish my brother and I escort you to Best."

"Accompany, not escort." I don't like this hard case of a brother, and it's clear he doesn't cotton to me, either. "You got a problem with that?"

"Matter of fact, I do. We're hunters, not babysitters."

"Mr. Garrett, I don't need looking after. I would go on my lonesome if I knew the way."

He snorts disbelievingly. "You ain't serious."

"I usually am. I can take care of myself."

"Like with Dollarhide there?"

"I was handling that," I say crossly.

"Looked more like he was handling you."

The hot, familiar buzz of anger bubbles under my skin, and I'm starting to regret hiring Curtis if this man is attached. "I made an agreement with your brother; if the deal's off, then stop wasting my time and tell me so."

Garrett shakes his unkempt head. "Curtis is holding firm. But I ain't as tenderhearted as my brother."

"What the hell does that mean?"

"It means that the only payment we take is cash money." Garrett eyes me levelly, and I stiffen at the implied insult.

"That is all I am offering," I say, making my voice as cold and unflinching as I can.

"I hope so. 'Cause I'm not moved by pretty words or pretty eyes like Curtis. If you bilk us, I got no problem turning you over to the Judge. I think you know his brand of mercy."

A chill creeps up my neck despite the heat. Garrett's bright eyes bore into me, and it's like he knows; somehow he knows I'm lying. I should call this off now, while I still have the chance, just turn my back and go home. Something inside me balks then; I know what waits for me at home. My life stretches out endlessly before me, an unwavering path of snake meat, ill-fitting pants, and a crumbling house. Three pairs of eyes pleading at me, the constant fear that it will never be enough; nothing ever changing, until I'm too old and broken to care. There is nothing this man or even the Judge can do that scares me more than dying ancient and wasted in Glory, with only ghosts and regrets to keep me company.

"You'll get your money," I tell him.

"So long as we're straight."

"As the crow flies," I say quietly. "Good-bye, Mr. Garrett." I start walking away, not bothering to wait for his reply; just as well, because it never comes.

12.

It always feels twice as far going back home, and I may as well take my time because I got no rest coming once I get there. There's washing to bring in and dinner to start, and I begin a mental list of what to pack. Part of me can't believe I'm really doing this, and part of me thrills at the idea of leaving Glory. Micah will be mad, but then he's always mad at me for something. I adjust the bag on my shoulder, wishing my life could be simple. That's a long road to start going down, though; I could wish for a lot of things, and if wishes were pigs we'd all eat bacon.

My thoughts are interrupted when a commanding voice calls out to me.

"Daisy, is that you?"

I groan inwardly and squeeze my eyes shut for just a moment. "Hello, Miss Bess."

"Come here so I can see you."

"Miss Bess, this ain't the best time—"

"Hurry up, now, Daisy, I'm old and I got no time for dawdling."

I sigh softly, but I've learned from experience that it's useless to argue with the woman, she'll only pretend she can't hear you. I step around a wheelbarrow with no wheels and kick aside an empty can, weaving my way through the debris to the porch.

She waits for me impatiently, her hair stark white against her brown face, back straight as a board. Most old folks stoop, but then Bess ain't like most folks. I've never seen her smile, not in all my born days, and she has the kind of strength that only comes from being hard-pressed your whole life. She made her way here from Georgia, and even though most of her family kept going west, Bess stayed put. She still has the accent; her voice is round and deep, all burnt sugar and smoke.

"Now then," Bess says when I climb up the steps and knock over a birdhouse, "let me get a look at you, Daisy."

"Miss Bess, you know no one calls me—"

"You're too thin. You need to drink some cream; it'll fill your face out some."

"Yes, ma'am," I say, biting back another response. Drink some cream, indeed; as if it were that simple. As if my jaw doesn't clench at night with hunger, as if I'm not living on weak coffee and desperation.

"Sit with me, my dear," Bess says, easing herself into her rocking chair. She bangs her cane against an overturned bucket, which I reckon is for me.

"Only for a moment," I say. I clear the bucket of dirty mugs and perch on the edge, my knees almost to my chin.

"Would you look at that," Bess says, her eyes gazing at the flat land beyond the fence. Her dark brown hands curl over her cane, the fingers knobby and wrinkled. "It's gonna be a beautiful sunset, Daisy, mark my words."

"It always is, Miss Bess."

"Every day the same, but every one different."

I start to fidget. How long am I going to be stuck here? Maybe she'll fall asleep and I can just leave. I sneak a glance, but her eyes are wide open and glued to the desert. What she's looking at I can only guess;

maybe she sees the same beauty I see, the lines flat and unbroken, the dust drifting up hazily.

"Did I ever tell you about the painter I met in Llano?"

I blink, startled. "I don't think—"

"He did landscapes, now and then a portrait, but mostly pictures of the desert. And he told me the only way to get that sky right was to mix some of the dirt in with the paint. Now ain't that something?"

"I reckon so."

"Dirt," she says again, and shakes her head, like she still can't believe it.

"Miss Bess, I need to be heading home. The boys and Cath will be wanting dinner soon."

"All right, then, help me up," she says, and I give her my arm to cling to. "I have something for you, it's just inside."

Bess shoves at her front door and I hear something splintering behind it; it opens just enough for her to turn sideways and step inside.

"Miss Bess, if it's too much trouble—"

"No trouble at all," she calls from somewhere inside. "Give me a moment to find it."

I roll my eyes; she could be in there all day and still not find what she's looking for. There's a crash followed by the sound of something rolling and I push at the door.

"Are you all right?" I call.

"Fine, I'm fine." Bess slips back out onto the porch, her white hair slightly mussed but otherwise unmarked. "Here you are," and she hands me a small pouch of paper, twisted up at the ends. "Open it when you get home," she says, folding my hand over it.

"Thank you, Miss Bess," I say, and kiss her offered cheek.

"Of course, Daisy. Now off you go."

I drop the pouch in my bag and make my way down the steps. I turn when I get to the road and wave.

"Bring those little ones by to see me," Bess calls.

"I will," I call back. She's a good sort, Old Bess. Her, and Elsie and Ned, and Doc Kincaid. The Judge and the hunters, they take up so much space with their talk and their violence, it feels like there's nothing left for the rest of us. It's easy to forget there are still good people here. Sometimes I think this town may be worth saving, but mostly I think given half the chance I'd walk away and never look back.

13.

I'm tired to my very bones by the time our fence comes into view. I swing it shut loudly behind me, and in the space of a breath an answering shout comes from somewhere behind the house. The twins are like dogs that way, ears always tuned to the gate. They run out to meet me, and I'm not too tired to smile at them.

"Hey there, tumbleweeds," I say. "Where you rollin' to?"

"Willie, you were gone *forever*," Cal complains as I ruffle his hair. He has fingernail scratches across his forearm, from itching or fighting I can only guess.

"What did you get?" Cath asks, tugging at my arm. I use my thumb to wipe dirt off her cheek before she squirms out of reach.

"Wait and see. Why are y'all covered in dirt?"

"Micah made us go outside. And he called us names." The twins stare at me with matching expressions of noble suffering that I don't believe for a moment.

"Mm-hmm," I say. "Did he make you crawl underneath the house, too?" It's a favorite game of theirs, though I don't understand the appeal. At least they seem to have forgotten all about this morning; I envy them such short memories.

"Take this inside and tell Micah to meet me out back." I give my sack to Catherine, and the twins race to the house to sort through it.

I walk around back to our empty plot of land, trying to work out a kink in my neck. We have four snake traps set up back here, small boxes that Micah made out of wood and wire netting, and ten more outside the perimeter. I don't like to venture outside the fence much, not if I can help it. Only once a week do I risk it, and only with Micah to watch my back.

I'm not expecting to find anything; we need to move the traps again, find new snake holes. I grab the hoe, its blade dark with snake guts, and check the traps. The first three are empty, but when I tap my boot against the last one I hear movement.

"Lock's fixed," Micah says, appearing at my shoulder.

"I tightened the hinges, too. You got one?"

"Yeah." I nod and he moves into place, our routine familiar and well-oiled. I get a good grip on the hoe while Micah flips the trap open to reveal a rattler coiled tight as a fist. It hisses angrily but I strike before it does, severing the head cleanly. I pick up the body by the tail, disappointed; it's small, not even a foot. It's not worth skinning, but I can at least throw it in the pot for dinner.

"I need to replace the latch on this one," Micah says, kneeling down to examine the trap. "It's getting loose."

"Take this inside, will you?" I ask, holding the snake out.

Micah lifts his eyes to my face. "Did you get the money?"

I look away, too tired for what's bound to be an argument. "The Judge wouldn't give it to me."

He scoffs and stands up. "I told you he wouldn't. Closefisted bastard."

"Can we talk about this later?"

Micah shrugs and grabs the snake from me. I kick the trap closed with a bang and start pulling down the laundry. The shirts and underthings go over my shoulder and I head inside, knocking the dust off my boots. I walk through the front door slowly, dumping the clothes in a pile and taking off my hat and hanging up my gun. For months after our mother died, I couldn't stand to be in this house; every room, every piece of furniture was a painful reminder. Memory can be a terrible thing. It's still hard sometimes, to come in and expect to see her, but now I worry that I'll start forgetting, that the chairs will turn into ordinary chairs and not the ones she sat in. I shut the door and lock it carefully, leaning my head against the wood for a moment, ignoring the shouting in the kitchen and what looks like broken porcelain on the floor. I can feel a headache coming on, a slight pounding in my temples that promises to only get worse.

I sigh and brace myself for the kitchen, where the twins and Micah are yelling at each other, their voices overlapping so no one can understand what's being said. The whole scene is almost comical, as Micah towers over the twins, but their ferocity is equally matched. Sam sits at the table, watching the fight like an amused spectator trying not to laugh. He catches my eye and winks, suppressing a grin.

"—big ugly cactus brain—"

"—I'm telling Willie—"

"—if you bite me again—"

"Enough!" I yell, loud enough to be heard. "Were y'all raised in a barn? I know Ma taught you better than this." They fall silent, and Micah at least has the decency to look sheepish. "What, we don't get enough trouble from strangers, you gotta fight each other, too? Shame on you."

"Sorry, Will," Micah says.

I glare at the twins until they, too, mutter apologies.

"Too right, you're sorry. Now what happened to the plate?"

They all start to talk at the same time, and I close my eyes and sigh.

"Never mind," I say. "It don't matter. Just—just all of you, clear out and go wash up."

The boys and Cath file out of the kitchen dejectedly while I turn back toward the door to pick up the largest pieces of broken pottery. Of course it would be one of our good plates, the ones my parents got for their wedding, and not the usual dented tin ones. There's a tap on my shoulder, and I turn to see Sam holding the broom, sweeping the smaller pieces into a pile.

"Thank you."

"Sorry," Sam says with a guilty grin. "I shoulda been keeping a closer eye."

"You just would've seen it break closer."

"I guess y'all had a rough time this morning," Sam says. "It's enough to make anyone rowdy."

"Micah told you about it?" I dump the shards of porcelain out the window, where no doubt I'll step on them later.

"Yeah. That was a real low move of your pa, to skip town. It ain't your fault he stole that money, and y'all shouldn't have to pay for it."

Anger bubbles up in my throat, scratchy and sour. He may come over every day, it may be the truth, but Sam isn't kin; he hasn't earned the right to talk about Pa like that. I know he's a thief and a scoundrel, but he's still my pa. He still sang songs to us and made Ma laugh, and when he came home drunk and flush he would pick up the twins, one in each arm, and dance them around the kitchen.

"Sam, I appreciate your concern, but this is a family affair and I'm not having this talk with you. Now I need to start dinner, and I hate to be rude, but I can't feed any extra mouths."

Sam hands me the broom quietly and gets his hat from the rack.

"I didn't mean to offend. I'm sorry."

The door closes softly, and I wince. Now I feel mean; I wish Sam had slammed the door, so I could be self-righteous in my anger, but that's never been his way. I sit down heavily at the table, ashamed. Now I'm a bully as well as a liar; this has been a poor day for my character. Dinner doesn't wait for self-pity, though, and I have to set the beans to soaking.

I find the sugar sack abandoned on the table and start to unpack it, putting the hominy and flour in the pantry and the dried apricots in a bowl. I pour out a good portion of the beans into a pot and cover them with water so they'll soften before I cook them. I feel around the bottom of the sack and find Elsie has added a surprise: a small jar of sorghum molasses. I send out a silent thank you, hoping it makes its way to her. I save the twisted bit of paper for last, trying to guess what's inside; with Bess, you never know. I unwrap the paper carefully and almost cry at the handful of peppermint drops. They're sticky with age, but I can't help myself: I immediately pop one in my mouth and let the cool sugar melt on my tongue. The rest I pour into my favorite chipped coffee cup that I hide on the top shelf of the pantry.

There's still some meat left from the last snakes Micah and I killed, though it's maybe a day away from turning. I cut the strips into smaller cubes, stretching it as far as it will go. I'll throw it into the pot last, after the beans are all but done; snake is lean, and falls apart quickly. I turn to grab a rag to wipe my hands when a flash of brightness scurries across the wall and I jump back with a stifled screech.

"Calvin!" I yell, throwing my rag at the lizard now sunning in the window. "Get that yellow-bellied monster out of my kitchen or we're having lizard for supper."

Cal rushes in, crooning to his beloved pet. "Come here, Goldie," he says, gently prying the lizard from the glass and cradling it to his chest. I'll never understand his attachment to that scaly thing, but he loves it more than anything. Cal has always been like that with animals, and I guess you take what you can get when there's nothing soft and furry to hold. I doubt that lizard even wants to be here, but it hasn't found its way out of the house yet.

I drain the beans and start them cooking, adding a pinch of salt and some of the molasses for a touch of sweetness. This past year I've managed to become a half-decent cook. I would be better if I had more to work with, but like Calvin and Goldie, you do the best with what you're given.

14.

"So what now?" Micah asks, setting bowls out on the table. "Does Elsie have extra work for us? I can do repairs at the Homestead if she'll let me. We won't come up with four hundred selling skins."

I stir the beans, making sure they don't stick to the bottom.

"Will? What are we gonna do about the money?"

I fish a bean out of the pot with my spoon and blow on it. "I took care of it," I say, half under my breath.

"What? What does that mean?"

The bean is hot and doesn't put up any resistance as I chew. I take longer than I need to swallow, delaying my answer.

"Willie, what did you do?" Micah's voice is thick with distrust.

I steel myself and turn to face him. "I hired a hunter. I'm going after Pa."

"You hired a hunter." Micah stares at me dumbly. I take advantage of his momentary silence and shout for the twins.

"Catherine, Calvin, come sit down. Dinner's almost ready." Micah's still staring at me, so I keep going. "I'm leaving for Best first thing tomorrow."

"You're leaving for Best."

"Please stop repeating everything I say," I tell him crossly.

"A hunter? Will, he's likely to take you halfway and leave you for dead."

"What other choice do we got? We need four hundred dollars, and I don't know how else to get it."

"You really think you can find him?"

"He's only a day ahead—if I catch up, maybe I can get to him before he loses all of it."

"He could've spent it already, Will, you know how Pa is with money."

"I know. And if I have to, I'll drag him back to Glory. We're not taking the blame, not this time." My voice is steady, but inside I'm shrinking; I hope it doesn't come to that. I can feel Micah's eyes on me, feel the judgment coming off him. "I know he's our pa, but if it will keep us safe—"

"To hell with Pa," Micah interrupts. "He don't deserve any kindness from us. What about you? Do you know how many people die on the road? How many just disappear?"

"You got a better plan, I'm all ears." Micah looks down. "That's what I thought. Look, I'll have two hunters with me. That's as safe as I can make it."

"Two? How'd you wrangle that?"

"They're brothers, they work together."

"Willie," Micah says slowly, "how can we afford two hunters?"

Damn. I was hoping he wouldn't catch on. "We can't," I say, shrugging. "But they don't know that."

Micah makes a strangled sound in his throat. "They'll kill you when they find out."

"I'll cross that bridge when I come to it. And I ain't so easy to kill, you know." I smile, but Micah won't budge.

"I'm going with you," he says.

"Like hell you are."

"I'm serious, Willie. You want to go on the road with

two hunters who have reason to kill you? If something happens, what are the twins and me gonna do? Did you even think about that?"

I sigh. "Micah, please. Don't make this harder than it needs to be."

"Don't do that," Micah says, his face screwed up in frustration. "Don't act like this is only up to you."

"It is," I snap at him. "I'm the one responsible for everyone. You don't have to point out how risky this is, Micah, believe me, I know. But until something happens to me, I am in charge of this family, and I will decide how to take care of it. So you are staying here and watching the twins and that's final."

Micah glares at me and I glare back.

"Now sit down and eat your damn beans. Cath, Calvin!"

"We're right here," Cath says, skidding into me.

"Hands," I order, and it comes out harsher than I mean it. I take a deep breath and swallow my anger as the twins hold up their hands. Filthy; I doubt they used any soap at all.

"Those are the opposite of clean," I tell them. "Just sit down."

It's not a pleasant meal; Micah shoots daggers at me,

but when I look up he refuses to meet my eyes. I don't have much appetite, so I push my beans around in my bowl until the twins are almost finished.

"I gotta talk to you about something important," I tell them, setting down my spoon. "You remember what happened this morning."

"Of course we do," Cath says.

"It was only this morning," Calvin adds.

"Hush," I tell them, "and let me finish. You heard what that man said; we're in trouble unless we do what he wants. So I went to the Homestead today and I hired a hunter. I'm going to be leaving for a few days, but I'll be back soon."

I'm greeted with silence as the twins stare at me, stunned. Micah just looks bored, examining his beans closely.

"Micah will take care of everything while I'm gone. Make sure you mind him, now."

"Is this because we broke the plate?" Catherine looks like she's fighting back tears, and something inside me twists.

"No, Cath, it ain't about the plate," I say gently.

"We're sorry. We won't break things no more. Please don't leave."

"It was Micah's fault!" Calvin says, glaring at Micah accusingly.

"I'm not trying to punish you. I'm leaving to find Pa," I explain. "Don't you want me to find him?"

"No," Cath says, her face screwed up tight.

"You don't mean that," I tell her.

"Yes I do. He's never here anyhows."

"Micah, tell Willie she can't go," Calvin orders.

"Enough, both of you," I tell them. "This is not up for discussion. I'm leaving tomorrow, and that's the end of it."

"I hate you," Catherine says, and pushes her chair away from the table. She runs outside, slamming the door behind her. Calvin follows his twin loyally, his small shoulders hunched.

"They took it well," Micah says from across the table.

I sigh and cover my face with my hands. "You gonna start in again?"

He shrugs stiffly, poking at the last of his beans.

"Why should I? It won't make no difference. You're going whether I like it or not, so I won't waste my breath."

"Micah, it ain't like I planned this," I say angrily. "I don't *want* to leave."

"Liar."

"'Scuse me?"

"You do so want to leave." Always the bone-truth. "Tell me you're not happy it worked out like this. Tell me you're not itching to leave."

"Micah—" I don't know what to say that won't be a lie. "It's not forever."

"Sure it ain't."

"You think I'd do that? You think I'd leave you all behind?" And it cuts me, because I want to, I want to so badly that Micah can read it on my face.

"I think if I could I'd walk out of this life and never come back," Micah says quietly. And I wish he was still angry, because the anger I can handle, not this; not this calm resignation, like he's already seen all of the world and found nothing redeeming in it. He sighs mightily and shakes his head. "Just watch your back, big sister. I don't trust anyone else to do it proper."

"I will." I force a lopsided smile. "Finish up, little brother, and help me with these dishes."

15.

I can't sleep. I try counting my heartbeats, but every noise and stray piece of straw poking through my mattress conspires to keep me awake. This is the last night I'll have in my own bed for who knows how long, but there's no comfort to be found. My eyes are wide open and staring into the darkness, weaving shapes out of nothingness. I hug my knees to my chest, folding myself up into the smallest form possible. The twins are sleeping in Micah's bed tonight, a final act of punishment. I listen for their breathing; the silence is loud in my ears.

I wish Micah wasn't so smart, or I was less easy for him to read. I do want out of Glory. I want all of us out. There must be somewhere better out there, somewhere we can breathe and stretch and dream, somewhere we could have a future. Ma tried to get us out, years ago, when things started going cross-eyed. But hunters cost money, and by the time she'd saved enough the twins were here and no hunter in his right mind would take four children into the desert. So the money got spent and Ma got sick, and it's all I can do to keep us fed and inside the fence. We're good and stuck in Glory for as long I can see, and this may be the only chance I get to leave. Maybe it's selfish and greedy, but I'm going.

It's no use; I won't be sleeping tonight. I sit up and feel for the matches I keep on my nightstand. The stink of sulfur fills the air as I strike one and light the small stub of a candle by my bed. The flame flickers and holds, chasing back the shadows with one sharp, wavering point of brightness. I pick up the small pile of cloth on the floor and bring it to my lap, unfolding the corners of the rag to examine the items inside. A spool of thread and a needle, the penny knife Micah fixed, another set of matches, a spare shirt and drawers, wool socks, and a small mirror that my mother gave me. I don't expect I'll find much use for it, but I want something of hers to take with me. Funny how everything I own in life can fit into so small a bundle, seventeen years contained in my lap.

I tie the corners back together and peel my blanket off my bed, then roll the bundle in the threadbare quilt and secure it with two pieces of twine; it should not be too heavy, though five pounds can feel like fifty a ways down the road. I take off my scratchy nightgown and dip my hands in the washbasin, bracing myself for the cold water. In the soft light I can just make out a bruise spreading across the knuckles of my left hand and I flex it, testing the soreness. I splash some water on my face, and when the worst of the shivers have passed I get the washrag and go to work on the rest of me.

The almost-morning air dries my damp skin while I let my hair out of its braid. I run my fingers through the worst of the tangles before I tightly plait it again. I get dressed, pulling on my worn britches and boots and my second-cleanest shirt. It started life as a bright white, but I've washed it so many times it's turned gray. Still, it's soft and I've only had to mend it twice. My heart hammers in my chest as I button my shirt, and my fingers are nervy as I secure my belt. I take a deep breath, trying to relax. I'll never make it through the day at this rate.

I'm not hungry at all, but I know I'll regret it later if I don't eat. The leftover beans are cold and congealed, but I force myself to swallow a few bites. Some hominy goes into my trusty sugar sack, along with dried fruit and cornmeal. If I can find a way to boil water, I can make hoecakes. I fill a canteen with water, hoping the Garretts have more, or it's going to be a long and thirsty day.

I can smell dawn coming, a subtle shift in the air. It's time to go if I want to make it to the gate on time. I load my revolver, carefully slipping each round into the chamber. I holster the gun to my belt and fill up a small drawstring pouch with extra cartridges and fifty dollars, which I hang around my neck. This time I slide my long dirk knife into its sheath, reassured by the feel of a weapon on each hip. I get my hat and my duster coat, and put my blanket roll, canteen, and sugar sack by the door. I stare at my effects for a moment, certain that I'm forgetting something, but all that's left is the leaving.

I hesitate at Micah's bed, but I have to say good-bye, no matter how mad they are. A small body shifts in the darkness and sits up.

"Willie?"

"It's time," I whisper. "I'm sorry, Cath. Love."

I hold my breath until I hear her answer.

"Love," she says softly.

"Love," comes an identical voice.

"Will?"

"Yeah, Micah?"

"This time mean it."

My smile trembles in the darkness. "I'll be careful. Be good to each other. I'll be home soon."

16.

It's cool out with the sun still hiding. My legs feel jumpy, like I want to run, and I give them a firm stamp to get the nerves out. I can't be wasting my energy this early in the day. Picturing the look on Benjamin Garrett's face if I start to tire sobers me up plenty. I wish it were just his brother taking me to Best, but I suppose he wishes the same thing.

Sam's house is dark as I pass by. The doc is almost never home, he's too busy patching up the knife wounds and bullet holes the hunters like to hand out. I have a feeling Sam will be staying at our house for the next few days; he hates to be alone. I hope he and Micah don't ignore the twins for too long, or they're bound to set fire to the place. I'll make it up to them when I get back, I promise myself. I'll teach them how to sing "The Lonely Cowpoke," with all the dirty words. They'll like that, and it will annoy Micah to boot.

When I get to the fork in the road, I go left, instead of right to the Homestead. The gate is up ahead, a small break in the looming barbed wire. It's made of thick planks of wood as tall as a man and only opens from the inside. There're two guards on it at all times, bored hunters the Judge rotates through, and it's my luck that today one of them is Amos Porter. He's kin to Old Bess, a great nephew or second cousin or some such thing, and for all he's a hunter, he's never been anything but kind to me.

"Good morning to you, Miss Wilcox," Amos calls to me, his rifle cradled across his wide chest.

"Good morning, Mr. Porter."

"Where's your brother at? You goin' out snake hunting alone?"

"Not today," I tell him. "I'm headed to Best. My guides will be along shortly."

Amos whistles. "Well now. Ain't that something, first time on the Low Road. You know I see 'em all go out, don't always see 'em come back in."

"You'll see me, Amos."

"You know, I do believe that. What I want to know is, was that really you gave Dollarhide that shiner?"

"Whoever it was, I'm sure he had it coming," I say with a nonchalant shrug, but Amos isn't fooled.

"Ha! I knew it," he laughs, teeth flashing white against his darker skin. "He was out here at dawn, still tangle-legged. You watch out for that one, Willie, he'll be after you with a sharp stick. That your party?"

From the Homestead road I see the Garrett brothers walking, and just like that I feel woefully outgunned. It's one thing to know you're hiring hunters and another to see them decked out like the cavalry. Curtis has two long-nosed revolvers at his hips and a bandolier slung across his chest, the cartridges shining like so many rows of teeth. The hilt of a sabre juts up from his back, and his throat and forearms are covered with thick leather guards. Benjamin, too, is wearing the leather guards and a wide-brimmed hat tugged low over his forehead. He's carrying a revolver at his waist and a rifle on his back, the sun glinting off the polished metal. Best of all, in one hand he's got the lead of shaggy gray mule loaded with supplies.

"Where'd you find that piece of crow bait?" I call, walking to meet them.

"You hush," Curtis answers, patting the mule's nose. "Nana here is the finest pack animal that ever was. Show some respect to your elders."

The Garretts come to a halt and the mule eyes me with disinterest.

"Howdy, Nana," I say, and she gives me a slow blink. "I didn't think there were any soft animals left. Never thought I'd be so happy to see a mule."

"She's too tough even for the shakes to take. Load her up, then," Curtis says, and I hand him my bedroll and sack to add to Nana's packs.

Benjamin hasn't said anything, and I can't make out his expression under his hat. In the spirit of forgiveness, I vow to make a fresh start with him.

"Morning," I say politely, and get a grunt for my troubles.

"You'll have to excuse him," Curtis says. "Early mornings make my brother a touch grumpy."

"How can you tell the difference?" So much for a fresh start.

Benjamin pushes back his hat and glares at me with red-rimmed eyes.

"You got something for us, or you just here to visit?" he asks in his rough voice.

I tug open the purse around my neck and slap the stack of bills onto Benjamin's open palm. He counts it calmly, then folds up the money and puts in into his front pocket.

"Well?" I ask him, folding my arms across my chest.

"What do you want? We're square."

"An apology would be nice, but I guess that dog won't hunt."

"You got a big mouth for someone so small."

"All right, that's enough," Curtis interrupts. "Ben, you know better. I'm not going out there if you're gonna be tetchy the whole time. If you two can't be civil, you can be quiet."

I look down at my feet, embarrassed. I'm acting no better than him, and I feel like a reprimanded child.

"I can be civil," I say.

"Ben?"

Benjamin nods curtly.

"Shake on it, then," Curtis orders.

Benjamin holds out his hand, and I clasp it briefly. His hand is warm and callused, his handshake firmer than I would expect given his obvious disdain.

"That's settled, then. Porter, how's it looking?" Curtis asks.

"Mostly clear," Amos tells him. "Spotted a couple near the road, maybe a half mile down to the right. They're lying low enough our shots aren't scaring 'em off."

"We'll take care of them," Curtis says. "Ready?"

"When you are," he says, nodding. "Happy hunting."

"Open her up," Curtis says, and Amos whistles for his partner and they put their shoulders to the gate. It opens with a terrible reluctant screech that makes my insides crawl.

"Eyes out," Curtis says. Amos claps me on the back as we walk through the gate, and suddenly we're past the perimeter, breathing in the hot fumes of the open desert. I don't look behind, not even when the gate screams shut. It occurs to me that it's too late to back out now, and there's some small comfort in that. For better or worse, this is happening. The desert stretches out endlessly before me, and I could walk forever, as long as the road leads away from Glory.

PART TWO:
THE ROAD

In the desert
I saw a creature, naked, bestial,
Who, squatting upon the ground,
Held his heart in his hands,
And ate of it.
I said, "Is it good, friend?"
"It is bitter—bitter," he answered;

"But I like it
"Because it is bitter,
"And because it is my heart."
—Stephen Crane

17.

For the first few minutes we don't speak at all; the only sound is the soft tread of our boots on the dirt and the occasional snort from the mule. Two roads lead to and from Glory: the winding High Road that goes north, and the Low Road. This is the one we take, headed straight east, cutting a long razor across the land. The path isn't easy to see, just a slight depression in the ground from years of repeated use, but the brothers walk purposefully and I trust them to know the route. A change comes over Curtis, a stiffening of the spine and an alertness that overtakes his easy manner. I do not see such a difference in Benjamin, but my guess is he doesn't leave his vigilance in the desert. My opinion of him raises a hair; he must know, like I do, that a perimeter locks in danger just as much as it keeps it out.

I hum to myself for a bit, feeling lighter than I have in days. I dislike being caged, even if it's a big cage and even when I know it's for my own protection. My memories of Glory before the perimeter are hazy at best, but I remember a time when people weren't always afraid. When I didn't feel trapped, when I didn't worry about money or Pa coming home drunk. Ma used to sing, silly songs she would make up while she cooked or knit. She sang less and less often, and then she stopped altogether. The way I remember it, the day she went quiet was the day the fence went up, when the ugly wire started looming taller and taller. I feel like singing out here, like filling up the vast empty space with sound.

"Sign," Curtis calls, and I stop mid-hum. He points ahead to a small dirt mound to the right of the road. The dirt moves and separates into two figures and my stomach drops to somewhere above my ankles. I take a step back, as if that would help.

"Those'll be the ones Amos saw," Ben says, his voice remarkably even. He pulls his revolver from his belt and Curtis follows suit.

My palms are sweating, and I hastily wipe them on

my pants before I reach for my own gun. My hands are tight and it takes me two tries to cock it. I tell myself I shouldn't be afraid; I've seen shakes before, killed them before. Never like this, though, never without a perimeter in sight, never without somewhere to run to. Where can I run to out here, when there's no place to hide?

Curtis gives me a steadying look. "When we start shooting, they're gonna come for us," he says.

"I know," I say. My voice comes out only slightly high, but I hate that I give away any fear.

"Ready?" Ben asks.

"Ready," Curtis answers.

It happens so fast; Curtis fires a shot across their heads and the shakes leap away from whatever dead and rotten thing they were crouched over. They come for us, rail thin and snarling, teeth bared and blackened with dried blood. More shots go off, deafening and smoky. I take aim and shoot but it goes wide; they move so fast and erratically that it seems impossible to hit them. Then one shake goes down as a bullet finds a wet home in its neck. It scrapes at its throat as it falls, blood staining its hands. The other keeps running at us, and every instinct is telling me to turn my back and flee. Curtis takes aim and a shot hits the shake's thigh; it stumbles and falls over, and Ben darts forward to fire one shot directly into its head.

Everyone seems frozen in place: Ben, standing over the shake, Curtis at my side, my knuckles white where my hand grips my gun. Ben breaks the spell first, nudging the shake with his boot to make sure it's dead. I take a deep breath and then wish I hadn't, the smell of foul blood and gunpowder making my stomach churn. Curtis moves to check on the other shake; there's a gurgling sound that means it's still alive. I don't want to look, but I can't avoid it. It's hard to tell because it's so thin, but the long matted hair makes me think it's a woman. Her lips move wordlessly and blood bubbles up from her mouth. I turn my head away so I don't have to see what happens next, but I still flinch at the shot.

"All set?" Ben asks his brother.

"Yeah," Curtis answers. "We're done here."

I tell myself that I did the right thing, hiring hunters. That I never had to shoot moving targets like that before, that those shakes would've killed me. But I don't feel like singing anymore.

18.

The desert is still, no sign of movement, not even dust. But it's a calm stillness, ancient and unchanging. The desert was here before us, and it will be here long after, watchful and patient and unmoved.

The ground is hard and flat and endless. There is something comforting about the sameness of it all, the way the color has been leeched from the land until everything is a blurry brown. Even the whiplike ocotillo and the saw-toothed green sotol blend into the ground, the slight shadows they cast swallowed up by the dirt. The light is still low, but when it hits noon, the sky will lose all color as well, the blue bleached white by the blast of the sun.

I can see the first marker from a ways off; the red

stake in the ground is hard to miss. We reached it quicker than I expected; five miles in under two hours. This is the farthest I've ever been outside the fence, and I lightly tap the stake for luck. It's a reassuring sight, proof that we're still on the road and a sign of those that came before.

"If we keep to this pace, we should be at the first way station by around four," Curtis says, breaking the silence.

"Is that good?" I ask, not so much because I want to know as because I want to be distracted.

Curtis nods. "We're making good time. I think—"

"Sign," Benjamin suddenly interrupts, and my stomach lurches.

"Where?" Curtis asks immediately, snapping to attention.

Benjamin points due west, behind us, and I spin around to stare, my hand going to my gun. All I can see is a small swirl of dust rising up, but it looks ominous.

"What is it?" I ask.

"Movement. Could be nothing. Could be something," Benjamin says.

The dust floats up and dissipates into the air and everything is still again. The boys don't move for a long moment, then there's an unspoken word between them and they both shift away.

"Keep an eye on it," Curtis says to Ben. "There's a hotbox in a couple miles if it turns into something. Let's keep moving."

We start walking again and questions build up on my tongue. I keep looking over my shoulder until I almost run into Curtis, and then I keep my eyes on my feet.

"What's a hotbox?" I finally ask when my curiosity gets the better of me.

Ben snorts. "It's what it sounds like," he says. "It's a wooden box with a tin roof that gets hot as all hell."

"It's a blockhouse," Curtis says. "There's one every ten miles. It ain't much, really. It ain't tall enough for a man to stand up straight or long enough to lie flat, but in a tight spot it's something between you and a pack of shakes."

I suck in my breath through my teeth, trying to imagine being trapped in a box while shakes surround you. It sounds all kinds of awful.

"You ever had to use one?" I ask.

"Just once," Benjamin says. "Got caught out at night, outside Hide Town. Some tenderfoot thought killing a shake would be a good time, wanted to try it for himself."

"What happened?"

Curtis gives a small snort. "Late afternoon and the fellow tripped over his own feet and broke his ankle. He couldn't walk so we had to carry him to the nearest hotbox, and the last hour it was almost full dark. Longest night of my life."

Despite the heat, I shiver.

We fan out, Curtis in the lead. I walk a ways behind him, glancing to the left and right, watching for any flicker of movement. We head directly toward the sun; Curtis's shadow stretches long and thin, his distorted head moving under my feet. I slow my pace by a hair until my boots are clear of him. It seems impolite to trespass on someone else's shadow, like walking into a house without knocking. Benjamin follows last with Nana, turning every so often to look behind. We're too far apart to talk now, so I count my steps to keep my mind alert. I lose track twice, once at six hundred and thirty-six, and again at eight hundred and twelve. The road begins to curve north, and I wonder who first plotted out this course. A man, I wager, but what manner? And for what purpose? Was it before the sickness came, was it as easy as riding on his lonesome through the dust? No need to be watchful for anything but rattlers and hoof stones, no roof but the stars over his head at night. How simple life must have been, then, how exquisitely simple.

It was after most of the horses died that people started leaving, at least those who could manage. No one wanted anything to do with us anymore. The Union all but disowned anything south of Llano, which leaves us with the territories to the west and the border to the south. Then the railroads starting failing, and that was the end of any outside help. You can still see where they laid the track, just barely; the sand has erased most of the evidence. Even if they could get it up and running again, they wouldn't come here; why bother when we have nothing to offer? The cotton fields are too big to protect, and no one wants to die for a farm. It's not an official quarantine, but an effective one; if you want to go north you have to walk, and chances are you won't make it out alive. If the shakes don't kill you, the sun will. We're on our lonesome out here, trapped in this no-man's-land, hemmed in on all sides by dust and death.

Something rustles to my right and I jump slightly before I spot the lizard. I feel a pang, surprisingly sharp, thinking of Calvin. It is too soon to be homesick, but guilt pinches just as hard. I scold myself, reminding my traitorous conscience that I am doing this for a good reason. The lizard doesn't even look like Goldie; this one is brown and thin, blending into a creosote bush with branches so thin and wispy it looks like a cloud of smoke rising from the bowels of the earth.

The sun climbs in the sky and I angle my hat lower to keep the light out of my eyes. Sweat beads on my upper lip and I lick it away, tasting salt and the dust that has already begun to coat my face and clothes. By the end of this trip I'll be more dust than girl. The desert claims everything, in the end.

19.

When we reach the second marker, I catch sight of my first hotbox and Curtis calls a break. He halts by the post and it takes me a minute to catch up to him, and another for Benjamin to reach us.

"Let's take a breather," Curtis says, wiping his face with a red handkerchief.

Benjamin takes a swig out of his canteen and passes it to his brother. Curtis takes a generous drink and hands it to me. I hesitate for a moment, not wanting to dip into their water supply.

"Go on," Curtis says. "Nana has extra. You need to keep drinking or you'll pass out."

"At least I'd be lighter than that Hide Town feller," I say, and drink. "Thanks. Is there enough to last the day?"

"There's a well at the halfway point, if you don't mind the taste of iron," Benjamin says. I pass the canteen back to him and he takes another mouthful before replacing the lid.

"What's halfway?" I ask.

"About another hour."

I nod, calculating in my head. If all goes to plan, we'll cover around twenty-four miles today. Not a small feat. I'm not out of breath yet, but there's a fine sheen of sweat covering my face and the beginning of an ache in my right heel.

I study the hotbox while Ben rummages through one of the packs on Nana's back. It's an odd little structure; it looks like someone started building a house and stopped halfway through. There are no doors or windows, only a series of grooves on one wall and small loopholes that go all around the box, just big enough to fit a gun barrel. We'll pass another one before the day is over, and I hope we have no cause to use either.

"How do you get in it?" I ask. "There's no door."

"There's a hatch at the top. You gotta climb up the side," Ben says, emerging from Nana's bags with a small round loaf of dark bread. "Here."

"Is that Elsie's brown bread?" I ask. She makes it

especially for the road, and her recipe is a well-guarded secret. The crust is so hard it's impossible to break off a piece with only your hands, but the inside stays soft and light.

"What else?" Curtis answers, smiling. Benjamin cuts himself a chunk of bread and passes it to his brother. I open my rag bundle and sugar sack and get my penny knife and some dried apricots to go along with the bread.

"Why do you wear those?" I ask, chewing on the fruit. I point to the leather guards on the brothers' wrists.

"Shakes go for the arms and the neck first," Benjamin answers. "The most exposed areas. The leather helps deflect, some."

Curtis hands me the bread while I think this over. My neck suddenly feels very vulnerable with nothing around it but a bag of bullets. I open my penny knife and go to work on the bread, making a mess of it.

"Sign," Curtis says abruptly, and I startle, the knife slicing across my palm sharply. I ignore the stinging pain and look where he's gazing, back along the road.

"Wait for it," Curtis says. Everything is silent while we all stare intently at nothing, and then it happens: a bright flash of light as the sun glints off something. I blink rapidly, waiting for the spots in front of my eyes to clear.

"Something's following us," Benjamin says grimly.

"What is it?"

Benjamin doesn't answer me, but he reaches into one of Nana's packs and pulls out a small brass object. He fiddles with it for a moment, but it isn't until he holds it up to his eye that I realize it's a scope. He swears under his breath and shakes his head.

"How many?" Curtis asks.

"Angle's wrong. We're too low."

"Could just be hunters."

"Could be," Ben agrees. He pulls his revolver from his belt and aims almost straight up. Curtis backs up a step and motions for me to do the same. Confused, I obey, unsure what's happening until Ben fires directly into the air. Both brothers tilt their heads expectantly. I don't know what they're waiting for, but when nothing happens, Ben looks even grimmer as he puts his gun away.

"Break's over," Curtis says, and his tone doesn't invite questions. He packs the food back up while I examine my left hand. The cut isn't deep; my penny knife can't do any real damage. The bleeding has already slowed, so I lick my palm to clean it, grimacing at the salty, metallic taste. I tear a thin strip of cloth off my rag bundle and tie it around my hand tightly, cursing myself for being so jittery.

"What happened?" Benjamin asks, and I cringe. I was hoping it would go unnoticed.

"It's just a scratch." I can feel my face turning red and I tug my hat even lower. "Do we need to get in the hotbox?"

"Not unless it's a pack."

"Do you think it's a pack?"

"Won't know till we reach higher ground."

Curtis motions for us to move out, and this time he takes the mule. I can tell he's anxious or he'd be the one talking to me.

"But if you had to guess?"

"I don't guess," Benjamin says sharply.

"But if—"

"You always ask this many questions?" he interrupts.

"Are you always this unhelpful?" I counter.

"Listen, girl—"

"Quiet," Curtis says, turning around to face us. His mouth is in a thin, tight line, but his voice is calm. "Let's just get to the well. It's on a rise and we can take it from there. Ben, let up on the kid, can't you see she's afeared?"

"I'm not," I start to say, but my words lack conviction. To their credit, the brothers don't contradict me, and I glance sidelong at Benjamin as we start moving again. If he's afraid, he's doing a good job of hiding it.

"You think it's a pack." I make it a statement, not a question.

He struggles with annoyance; I can see him fighting back a rude reply. Self-control wins out, and his answer is civil. "No, I don't. We would hear or see a pack. It might be one shake, but I never seen one track a party for more than a mile. It could be a hunter, but he didn't sound off. I don't know what it is. And I don't like not knowing."

20.

The Garretts are tense. Curtis's gait is rigid, like a soldier headed to an uncertain fate in battle. Benjamin keeps glancing behind us, his head jerking around every few seconds, almost unwillingly, like a spasm he can't control. We're walking faster now, and I'm breathing harder and shallower.

"How much farther to the well?" I call to Curtis.

He slows his pace to let me catch up to him.

"There," he says, pointing ahead.

"That's a well?" I ask, doubtful, squinting at a mound to the right of the road. "It looks like a pile of dirt."

"Stone, actually. It used to be taller."

We quicken our pace even more, spurred by the sight of our target. The ground rises under my feet, or maybe

I only feel it because I know it is. I keep my eyes fixed on the well; as long as I can see it I feel safe. This is our destination, our goal, and it seems so simple to accomplish. My tired mind tells me that when we reach it, everything will be all right, and I give a huge, unearned sigh of relief when we finally come alongside it.

The well is bigger up close, but crude, little more than a ring of crumbling brown stone with a thick rope descending into darkness. I throw one arm over Nana and lean against her gratefully, giving my legs a rest.

Benjamin immediately pulls out his telescope again and he and Curtis stand shoulder to shoulder, gazing back at the way we came. They don't speak, and the silence stretches out long and apprehensive. I brace myself for a shout of warning, my muscles tense and ready. The minutes pass, five and then ten, until I don't think I can bear it any longer. My jaw hurts, and I make an effort to unclench it, yawning widely.

"There," Benjamin calls, and my stomach lurches. I push myself away from Nana and go to stand next to him.

"It's not a shake," he says, his shoulders sagging with relief. "Two people. Maybe they're new hunters."

My breath comes out in a rush that leaves me almost

giddy, and I suppress the inappropriate urge to laugh.

"Anyone we know?" Curtis asks.

Benjamin hands the scope to Curtis and rubs his eyes with his palms. "Never seen 'em before."

As my body starts to relax, I realize what bad shape it's in. Sweat is dripping into my eyes and pooling down my back, and I can feel at least two blisters on my heels. My palm stings where I cut it and I'm thirsty again. I take a step back and stumble, my legs like liquid.

"Whoa, there," Benjamin says, grabbing my arm to steady me. I wince involuntarily as he squeezes the bruises Dollarhide already put there.

"Sorry, princess," he says, dropping his hand immediately.

"No, it's not—it's just from yesterday." If you can't talk sense, don't talk, I tell myself and clamp my mouth shut.

Benjamin stares at me like I'm a roach he scraped off his boot.

"I'll get some water." I walk away as quickly as I can without running. I can't seem to go more than an hour without embarrassing myself, and I can't stand the idea that Benjamin Garrett may be right, that I need looking after. Not that it matters what he thinks of me, but still, it's infuriating. I'm not some addle-headed child who can't handle herself.

I go to the well and grab the rope that's tied to a stake in the ground and begin to haul it up, hearing the splash and dull clink of the bucket on the other end. It's not overly heavy, but I'm tired, and my arms are trembling slightly by the time I get the bucket free. I set it on the edge of the well and take off the bandage on my hand. I wet the rag and use it to clean the dried blood off my cut before dipping my hands into the water. As I raise them to splash my face, I notice the odd color of the water. It has a reddish-brown hue to it, almost like rust. I let the water spill out of my hands, and it hits the ground in a soft trickle, soaking instantly into the dirt. Curious, I lean my head over the well to peer inside, and the smell hits me: a smell like rotting flowers and decaying meat, rank and sickly sweet. I gag and stumble back, the smell following me like a wave.

"What now?" Benjamin moves to my side as I make retching sounds. I clamp my mouth shut, refusing to give up what little food I have in my stomach. Bile stings my throat, hot and sour. Curtis puts a solid and reassuring hand on my shoulder and I try to steady myself. In between dry heaves I point frantically to the well.

"Get her some water," Curtis says, but I grab Benjamin's arm as he starts to move away, shaking my head violently.

"N-no," I manage to say in between coughs. "The water. Smell—" I gag again as I remember.

Curtis immediately strides to the well and leans cautiously over. His face turns pale and tinges green and his jaw clenches as he swallows hard.

My breathing slows and I stand up, using Benjamin as a crutch. I'm too sick to be embarrassed this time.

"What in blazes is going on?" I croak, my throat raw.

"You ever smell a dead body? One that's been dead for a time?" Curtis asks, and I shake my head.

"Well, you have now."

"There's a body down there?" I shudder, feeling ill.

Curtis holds a handkerchief over his mouth and nose and leans forward, peering down into the well. "What's left of one."

Benjamin and I both move closer; I hold my breath and look down. The walls of the well turn from sandy white to brown as it sinks, the sun bright enough to illuminate the inside. The well is not as deep as I would have guessed; I can see where the bucket touches the water, bobbing gently where it fell.

The water is scummy and dark, like it's turned solid. Something bumps against the bucket, and at first I can't tell what I'm looking at; my mind can't reconcile the image of this bloated, gray object with anything remotely human. Then I see where the mouth used to be, and the features rearrange themselves into a terrifying mask of a face.

I back away quickly, taking deep breaths. I close my eyes and lift my face to the sun, as if the heat could sear away the image of the bloated face from my memory.

"Did you drink from the well?"

I open my eyes to find Benjamin too close for comfort.

"Did you drink the water?" he almost shouts in my face.

"No," I say angrily, putting some distance between us. "I didn't. I swear."

"Poor bastard," Curtis says, the handkerchief muffling his voice.

"Are you sure?" Benjamin is still insistent. "If you drank any of it, you could be infected."

"Yes, I'm sure. How do you even know that's a shake? I thought they were afraid of water."

"Did you see his mouth?" Curtis asks. "Couldn't

swallow, so he tore his tongue out. I've seen 'em do that, near the end."

"We got no idea how long that body's been in there," Ben says. "Whole damn well is contaminated, and who knows who drunk from it."

"But the smell," I say. I feel shaky all over.

"They don't start to smell like that for a few days, at least," Curtis says grimly. "We need to put the word out."

I look back at the well and my stomach lurches. Pa could have drunk that water, could have missed the stench until too late. I need to find him, before things go from bad to worse.

Benjamin nods, swearing under his breath. "We should get to the station, have the boys pass it along."

"We can't leave it like this," I say. "What about the men behind us?" The brothers turn to look at me, wearing matching faces of confusion. I let out a small sigh of exasperation. "The people behind us on the road? What if they try to drink from the well?"

"She's right," Benjamin says after a moment.

"You don't have to sound so surprised."

Curtis rubs his chin thoughtfully, then pulls out a knife that makes mine looks like a child's toy. It only takes him one quick slice to cut the rope holding the bucket, and he throws the frayed end down into the well.

"Aren't you awful clever," Ben says. "But they could still find a way."

Curtis shrugs. "I'm hungry anyway. Might as well wait for 'em."

We can save the ones coming after, but how many others came before? They may not even know what it is they carry. How many are walking around with death running roughshod through their veins?

21.

We have to ration our water now, but I use the first sip to rinse my mouth of dust and the sour taste in my throat. My stomach is still queasy and all I can manage to nibble on is a dry biscuit.

"You all right, young'un?" Curtis asks me around a mouthful of apple.

"My belly's unsettled, some."

"What's wrong, Willie, don't like the boneyard perfume?" Benjamin sneers at me, and I flick a crumb in his direction.

"Go boil your shirt, Garrett. And it's Miss Wilcox to you."

"I call you Willie," Curtis says.

"You I like."

"Ouch." Benjamin feigns a look of injured feelings. "Wait, now," he says, "your parents called you Willie Wilcox?"

I give him my most withering glare and refuse to answer.

"No? What's your name, then?"

I've had well enough of this line of questioning, so I brush my hands and march away before I lose my temper or my dignity. I curse my parents for giving me an insipid name, and then feel an immediate pang of guilt and grief. I hate that this still happens, that I have to constantly remind myself that my mother is gone. I'll threaten the twins that I'll tell Ma on them, and then remember that I can't, and it hurts every time.

I stand on the dusty road, breathing deeply to calm myself. My heart is beating slowly and reassuringly, every thump a reminder of how alive I am. A slight wind blows hot air, drying the sweat on the back of my neck and sending wisps of long brown hair into my face to tangle in my eyelashes. I push the strands away and gaze along the road. There are no footprints to show the way we came, no sign that we've been here. Is this the path my father took? Are his footprints here, too, invisible beneath the dirt?

It would be so easy to disappear this way, to wander off the path and leave no trace of yourself behind; to become nothing but a ghost, a name whispered in hushed tones.

Boots crunch close by, but I don't alter my gaze from the road.

"My name is nothing to nobody."

"Surely," Curtis says. He stands next to me, crossing his arms over his chest. "But I like Willie. It suits you."

"Thank you," I say, somewhat mollified. "I always thought so."

"I should apologize for Benjamin. I hope his rudeness don't offend you terribly. He never learned good manners."

I give a lopsided smile. "You forget, I've lived in Glory my whole life. If I put any stock in manners, I'd be offended every minute of every day."

"Just the same, he's been mighty offish, and I'm sorry. I think you rattle him, some."

I shake my head. "I don't rate to rattle anyone. That them?" I ask, cutting off whatever Curtis was about to say. I point down the road to two dark figures moving clearly against the sand.

"Ben, glass!" Curtis calls, and Benjamin tosses him

the scope. Curtis holds it to his eye and takes a moment to focus.

"That's them. Took 'em long enough. Look mighty young to be out on the road. Don't look like hunters, neither. What do you think?" Curtis hands the telescope back to Benjamin.

"Not hunters, I only see one rifle. They can't be more'n sixteen."

A horrible idea crosses my mind.

"No," I say, firmly. "No, no, no."

Benjamin lowers the glass. "You know something?"

Wordlessly I hold out my hand and he places the telescope in it. I hold it to my eye and swing it around until the tiny specks become clear. My heart sinks: walking the path, not a care in the world, are my little brother and Samuel Kincaid.

22.

"I'll kill him," I say flatly, lowering the scope. "I'll kill him dead."

"They belong to you?" Benjamin asks.

"Micah, my idiot little brother. And he dragged along Doc Kincaid's son as well." I swear, low and harsh. "What is he thinking, coming out here? I'll tan his hide for this."

"Now, calm down," Curtis says. "At least they made it here safe."

"They shouldn't be here at all!" I start to pace, fuming. "That's it, I'm going to meet them."

"Just wait," Curtis says, putting a hand on my shoulder. "They'll be here in a minute."

"They'll be dead in a minute," I growl. But underneath

the anger is pure fear. Micah is lucky to be alive. Sam's never been outside the fence; I don't think he even knows how to shoot a gun.

I can hear the boys laughing, and I grind my teeth. I'm sure they're having a rousing good time, unaware of the noise they're making and how it carries. They don't even notice us waiting for them until Curtis raises a hand.

"Howdy," he calls out to them, and Micah and Sam startle. "You boys lost?"

Micah looks up, and his eyes move from Curtis to me; he halts in place, frozen to the spot. Sam nudges him, and they move forward, reluctantly now.

"You're in a world of trouble, Micah Wilcox," I yell at him, unable to contain myself any longer.

Sam reaches us first, though he keeps his distance. Micah stands a little behind him, shielding himself.

"Hey, Sis," Micah says, and he has the temerity to smile at me.

"Don't you *hey, Sis* me, Micah. What the hell are you doing here? Where are the twins? I swear, if you left them alone—"

"I would never! They're with Old Bess; she promised to look after them."

"Old Bess?" I repeat, my voice going high. "We'll be lucky to ever find them again! You addle-headed, half-witted—"

"Listen, Willie," Sam says gently, and I round on him.

"And you," I say, jabbing my finger at him. "You're supposed to be smart. Turn around. Both of you, turn around and go home right now."

"No," Micah says, scowling.

"Micah, so help me, you will do as I say."

"I'm not goin' back. You can't make me." Micah crosses his arms stubbornly.

I ball my hands into fists to keep from smacking him across the face. "Watch me. You're lucky you stayed alive this long, I will not have you out here."

"I can't just sit at home, watching the twins fight and wondering if you're comin' back," Micah says, his cheeks going red. I feel a lurch of guilt; it must be costing him a lot to say all this in front of strangers.

"I can handle myself, you know I can," I say, calming down some. "And the Garretts are good at what they do."

Curtis holds a hand out. "Hi there," he says, like he hasn't heard us hollering at one another. "Curtis Garrett."

"Micah Wilcox," my brother says, shaking his hand.

"Samuel Kincaid," Sam adds.

Benjamin doesn't offer a hand, watching the exchange with narrowed eyes. At least I know now he's rude to everyone, not just me.

"No offense to you, Mr. Garrett," Micah says, "but I don't know you. And I don't trust anyone I don't know to look after my sister. And I especially don't trust two men alone with her."

This is the longest speech I've ever heard Micah give to anyone outside our family; I would be proud if I weren't so mortified.

"I don't blame you, son," Curtis says evenly. "I wouldn't want two strangers on the road with my sister, if we had one."

"Then you understand why I won't go back," Micah says.

"Micah, two extra people will slow us down and make us an easier target. Curtis, tell him he can't come," I say.

Curtis rubs the back of his neck and mutters something under his breath.

"Oh, for pity's sake!" I should've known Curtis would be no help. Benjamin had it right; his brother is too tenderhearted. "Sam, your father is going to be worried sick."

"By the time he realizes I'm gone we'll be halfway back," Sam says. "And I already tried to talk Micah out of it. He was set to go himself if I didn't come along."

In desperation I turn to Ben. "You," I say. "You can't want them along."

Benjamin clears his throat and does his glaring thing. "We don't take in strays, boys," he says. "And we ain't free."

Sam squares his shoulders and digs in his pocket. "I didn't reckon you were," he says, holding out a fistful of bills. "I got the money, for both of us."

I should've known a doctor's son would have money.

"This is ridiculous. Sam doesn't even know how to shoot."

"I do too!" Sam says, affronted.

"You know how to aim?" Benjamin asks skeptically.

"You have plenty of gun hands," Sam counters. "What you don't have is a doctor."

"You're a doctor?"

"Closest thing there is to one out here." Sam shrugs off the pack he's carrying and flips it open. "Bandages, alcohol, needles, laudanum. I can patch wounds and keep 'em clean. That's worth more than any gun."

Benjamin and Curtis exchange a glance. It reminds me of the twins, how they can read what the other is thinking without words. I'm losing this fight, is what that look means.

"Willie," Micah says quietly to me. "We can walk with you or behind you, but we're not going back."

"I hope you brought your own water," is all I say.

23.

We pass the third marker while I am not speaking to anyone. I don't think any of them notice my silence, or if they do they don't consider it punishment, but it's a small kind of satisfaction. I keep my head down, watching my feet and reciting the names of cacti; shin-dagger agave, prickly pear, devil cholla, twisted rib. Half are named for what they'll do to you, and I've been on the receiving end of their tender mercies before.

Micah and Sam are walking behind Curtis, occasionally asking questions. They're not laughing anymore, not after they got a chance to see the well. I reckon it was a game until then, but a dead body makes for a rude realization. I hoped it would make Micah rethink coming with, but if anything he looks more determined. He and Sam are different out here. I never would have thought Micah would prove to be so strong-willed or that Sam would be prideful. Am I different, too, I wonder? All I feel is angry, and scared. And that's nothing new to me.

The blisters on my right heel have broken, and now the skin is being rubbed raw inside my boot. I try not to wince as I walk, but it slows me down some. I fall farther behind the others, coming level to Benjamin and Nana. He looks my way but doesn't say anything, not that I expect him to. I watch the others up ahead, my brother easy to spot. He's almost as tall as Curtis, but so much thinner, like someone took a small child and stretched him.

"I woulda thought I could count on you to send them packing," I say to Benjamin.

"Maybe you can afford to turn money down," he answers.

"Not me." I shake my head and sigh. This is not how I wanted this day to go.

I keep my thoughts to myself after that, and by the time Ben and I catch up to the rest, my anger has cooled some. It's too hot and bright out here for me to be burning inside as well. The best I can manage is a tired scowl when Micah comes alongside me. He takes a breath like he's about to launch into a speech, so I lengthen my stride until I pass him. If he has something to say, he can talk to my back.

I haven't gone more than a few steps when something small strikes my leg. It's a cheap trick, throwing rocks; I thought we'd grown out of it. Another pebble glances off my back and I twitch. It's not that it hurts, but Micah knows how much it annoys me.

"Stop it," I tell him, breaking my vow of silence. It doesn't help that his aim has improved. Another rock hits my shoulder and falls to the ground with a ding.

"Cut it out, Micah."

The last one hits me right in the rear, and I round on him, hands on hips. "I said cut it out!"

Micah grins at me and drops a handful of rocks back onto the ground.

"Come on, Sis," he says, dusting off his hands. "Ain't you just the littlest bit happy to see me?"

"No."

"Liar."

That does it; I take a wild swat at his face, but Micah knows my temper too well and he's tall enough now that he can hold me off. We wrestle for a moment, and then he has an arm locked around my head and I have my shoulder shoved against his stomach.

"What. Is. Wrong. With. You?" I punctuate each word with my fist, hitting Micah wherever I can reach.

"You! You never listen to me," Micah says, and he pokes me in the side with his bony elbow.

"Ow, stop it."

"You stop it."

We struggle against one another until it's clear neither of us has the upper hand.

"Truce?" I ask, breathing hard. Our fights always end the same way; since Micah started getting taller, we're too evenly matched.

"Truce," Micah agrees, and we both let go.

I straighten up and find Curtis and Sam watching us with matching expressions of amusement. Ben, of course, looks just the same, maybe only slightly more disgusted.

"What?" I ask defiantly, trying to cover my embarrassment. My cheeks get hot; I'm too old to be scrapping in the dirt.

"Nothing," Sam says, but I can tell he's trying not to laugh.

"Then keep walking," I tell him.

I glance at Micah; his face is bright red and he looks like he wants to stick his head in the sand. I sigh, and the fight goes out of me.

"Why couldn't you just do like I asked, Micah?" I say quietly, not wanting the others to overhear us quarrel again. "I got enough to worry about without you here."

"You're not the only one who worries, Will. I got just as much at stake here. This is my family, too."

"I know that, Micah. But what happens to the twins if we both get hurt?"

"Fine, then you go back," Micah says, not bothering to keep his voice down. "You go home and babysit the twins and wait by the door, hoping I come back alive."

I open my mouth to protest, but I have nothing to say. I couldn't, of course. I couldn't stand not knowing what was happening to my brother. I couldn't stand any of my family getting hurt; it's why I'm out here to begin with.

Micah smiles. "That's what I thought."

"I woulda come back, Micah," I tell him quietly. "I would."

"Maybe," he says. "But how long you think it'll take McAllister to put a bounty on Pa? It's only a matter of time, and then there's nothing to stop these boys from killing you and Pa and taking the money for themselves. I won't leave, Will, so don't ask me again. We're in this mess together, like it or not."

I shake my head, beaten. "Fine," I say. "Suit yourself. But you took the twins to Old Bess, and you're the one who has to go get 'em back."

From the look on Micah's face, he didn't think that far ahead. I smile to myself, pleased with the punishment; Bess doesn't get much company, and if the last time I visited is any indication, getting the twins to leave her house will be just as hard as getting her to let Micah go.

"That's low, Will," Sam says, eavesdropping on our conversation. He laughs and I narrow my eyes at him.

"I don't know why you're laughing, Kincaid. I'm sure the boys at the station will be happy to hear we brought a doctor with us. How many coughs can you listen to? How many blisters you think need tending?"

That wipes the smile off his face. "You wouldn't."

"Watch me."

"Willie, please—they'll make me lance things." Sam looks so horrified I almost relent.

"You shoulda thought of that before you left."

I leave the boys to commiserate with one another and

make my way over to Curtis, feeling fairly revenged.

"You're a mighty cruel one," he says, suppressing a smile.

"It's their own damn fault for crossing me. And you were no help."

Curtis raises his eyebrows at me. "You think my brother would stay put if I told him I was hunting alone?"

I glance over at Ben. "I don't know. Have you tried?"

Curtis chuckles. "I haven't been able to tell Ben what to do since he learned how to walk. He's that stubborn."

"I hadn't noticed," I say dryly.

"Sign," Ben calls out, putting all thoughts of mule-headed little brothers out of mind.

Curtis snaps to attention. "Where?"

"South," Ben answers, pulling out his scope.

I look to our right and squint against the sun: human-shaped figures moving against the dirt, darker than the desert, their shadows stretching long and low.

"What is it?" Curtis asks, and for a wild moment I allow myself to hope it's another rogue brother, or hunters, anything but—

"Shakes," Ben says, and my neck prickles.

"How many?" Curtis asks.

"Six."

"You sure?"

"Here." Ben hands the glass to his brother. I wish he would stop talking in single words; it sets my heart beating faster.

Curtis presses the scope to his eye and makes a grunting sound I take to mean he agrees with Ben.

"There's a bleeder," he says, and I suck in my breath. Bleeders, the injured shakes, are the worst; their wounds never heal properly, so they don't even have to bite you to get you sick. All they have to do is get close enough to bleed on you.

"What do you think? Half mile?" Curtis asks.

"Not even," Ben says, his voice maddeningly calm.

I glance at Micah, and I don't need a mirror to know we're wearing the same face: creased brow, tight eyes, lips set straight across like a knife slash. I would bet we're thinking the same thing, too: How fast can a shake cover less than half a mile?

Ben tugs his rifle off his back. The movement startles me, and I flinch and then curse at myself for flinching. At least this time my hands don't tremble when I reach for my own gun.

"You ain't gonna need that just yet," Curtis says.

"What?"

"There's a reason I let *my* little brother come along," he says with a faint smile. He nods at Ben while I stand there blinking, feeling like I'm missing a large part of what's happening.

"Stand clear," Ben says.

I'm not close, but I still back up a few steps, putting even more distance between us. Ben raises the gun to his shoulder and takes careful aim, his breath coming out in a slow hiss. He stands stiller than I thought a human being could, his eyes unblinking and his chest quiet. He doesn't shoot, and I glance back at the desert, wondering what he's waiting for. The shakes are getting closer, their movements uncoordinated but purposeful. I look away before I can make out their features; I don't want to remember their faces.

The shot takes me by surprise, the blast echoing across the flat plain. A heartbeat later one of the shakes collapses. Then the howling starts, high-pitched and wild; the sound an animal makes when it's in pain.

"You got it in the arm," Curtis says, the glass glued to his eye.

"Make it stop," I say, shutting my eyes. "Garrett, put it out of its misery."

"I'm trying," Ben says, his voice a low growl.

I ball my hands into fists, the shrieking grinding into my bones. Another shot rings out, sharp and cold, and the screaming abruptly cuts off and I can breathe again. I relax my hands and open my eyes, afraid of what I'll see but unable to look away. The shakes aren't moving forward anymore; they fold in on themselves, converging into a mass of wet mouths and dirty teeth. I know it's only my imagination, but I swear I can see a streak of red.

"It's down," Curtis says, lowering the telescope. "Nice shot. That should keep them busy for a while."

I look away, feeling ill. I tell myself it's like buzzards eating a rotting possum, but it's not. It's not like that at all.

Ben casually tucks his rifle onto his back, like shooting a shake at far range happens every day. I suppose, maybe for him, it does. But screams echo in my head, and I risk a glance at Micah. His eyes are slightly wide, and Sam's eyebrows are so high they almost touch his hair. I reckon I could say I told them so, but I don't much feel like it just now.

24.

We're all walking slower and I'm not the only one limping when we cross the fourth marker and the next box. My eyes feel hot and heavy and my tongue is like sandpaper. I try to swallow, but I can't get a lick of moisture in my mouth. My backside is one large ache, and I thank the stars for Nana. If I had to carry my pack this whole way, I'd be crawling by now. The only thing taking my mind off my poor feet is my hand, which is itching and throbbing something awful. The cut is deeper than I first thought, and the skin around it is red and puffy. It hurts to scratch it, but the tickle is driving me mad and I keep forgetting. Finally I tie another scrap of cloth around my hand; it may not help the itch, but it will keep me from scratching at it.

The back of my neck is starting to burn and I tilt my hat back for some shade. I find myself wishing the sun would go down, before I realize how stupid that would be. Still, between the heat and the dust I feel less like a girl and more like a tough piece of jerky.

A gun blast shatters the air and I jump so bad I think I leave the ground. All my pains and itches are forgotten in an instant as I look around for the source of the shot.

"Did that come from ahead?" Micah asks.

"Most likely," Curtis says, squinting along the road. "Everyone stay calm. Single shot is usually a sound-off from another hunter."

Ben already has his scope out, and he nods at Curtis. "It's that feller with the glass eye. Warrens, I think?"

Curtis tugs his gun out and points it straight up into the air. He gives us a moment to back up and then fires. He waves his gun around to clear the smoke before he puts it back on his belt.

"All right, keep sharp," Curtis says, and we keep walking.

It takes a few minutes for the other hunter to come into focus. I recognize him from the Homestead; he's a shorter fellow with brown skin and a graying beard.

"It's Aarons," I say. "Not Warrens."

"You know him?" Ben asks, one brow cocked.

"Not to speak to him, but I've heard his name. Didn't know he had a glass eye, though. Which one is it?"

"Hell if I can figure it out," Curtis says. "Aarons," he calls when the hunter comes alongside us. He holds out a hand, and Aarons clasps it.

"Garrett," he says, scowling hello. "And other Garrett. You boys out long?"

"Since this morning. Clear ahead?"

"All clear. Clear behind?"

"All clear. You on a job?"

"Clean-up patrol," Aarons says, sniffing with annoyance. "Caught a pack last night at the fence. Think we got most, but could be some stragglers made it away."

Curtis nods. "Make sure you keep outta the well; we found one in there."

"That's some bad medicine. I'll pass it along." Aarons scratches his beard and gets a good look at the rest of us. He starts to frown, and I realize how we must appear; two underfed boys and a girl with ill-fitting pants. We couldn't be more out of place.

"Well, we won't slow you down," Curtis says, clapping the man on the shoulder. "Take care, Aarons. We should be getting on to the station."

"Right. You'll be seeing it soon enough. Mind the cookout," he says, laughing harshly.

I don't understand what he means, and from their frowns, Ben and Curtis don't find it funny.

"Good hunting," Aarons says.

"Good hunting."

Aarons gives us one last look-over and goes on his way. He's right about the way station; the land is so level we can see it long before we get there. It's almost cruel, like teasing a dog with a bone just out of reach. With every step we take, the station seems to move farther away, so we're always the same distance from it. Maybe my mind is playing tricks on me, like dying men who see a lake in the middle of the desert. A stumble jolts me out of my reverie, but I manage to catch myself before I fall. I don't even feel where my toe hit the rock, my feet are that numb.

When I look up, I see a large black rock; beyond that a barbed-wire fence rises and behind that sits the station, near enough now for me to smell the smoke. Except the smoke has a strange scent to it, like charred meat mixed with burning hair and something foul.

"Where is that coming from?" Sam asks, frowning.

"You might not wanna look," Ben says, but it's too

late. What I took for a rock starts to sharpen into a tangle of blackened limbs and burnt clothes.

"They try for the walls at night," Curtis says quietly. "Some nights are worse than others."

Micah swears under his breath, his eyes wide. We burn our dead, but I've never seen a pile of bodies this big, thrown together like so much waste.

"I reckon this was a worse night," Sam says, and he sounds so calm about it. Maybe seeing people's insides numbs you to such gruesomeness, but I hope I never get to that point.

"Cookout," I say, pulling my shirt up to my face so I won't have to smell burning bodies.

"Yeah," Ben says, unsmiling. "Real funny."

25.

"At the gate!" Curtis calls, his voice weary but solid. Inside the fence, what I thought was an outhouse turns out to be a small guardhouse, and a slight man emerges with a pistol in his hand. He peers at us from across the fence with small dark eyes.

"How many?" he asks.

"Five altogether."

"Any of you touched? Afflicted, like?"

"Nary a one. Even got ourselves a doctor."

The slim man lets out a low whistle. "That so?"

"Well, I'm not really—" Sam says, but Curtis claps him on the shoulder before he can finish.

"Not really up to seeing anyone right now," he finishes for Sam. "Being on the road and all, but maybe get some food in him and he'll change his mind."

After that, the man can't let us in fast enough. The gate doesn't swing open, like in Glory; this one gets pulled up with ropes. We file in slowly, like cattle being led to feed, stumbling and gazing with wide eyes. A large wooden structure stands behind the guardhouse and there's a water tower to the right.

"Reyes," the man says, holding out a knobby hand.

"Garrett," Benjamin answers, and they shake.

"I seen you 'round here afore. Y'all be wanting tents and food?"

Ben nods and takes out a small leather coin bag from his pocket. "Meals and five beds, if you have 'em."

My stomach growls while they dicker over the price, reminding me it's been some time since I've had a full meal. Reyes doesn't look like he has enough imagination to haggle, but they come to an agreement. They shake on it and Reyes turns his attention to the rest of us.

"These boys know the ropes?" he asks, squinting at me and Micah and Sam.

"They're fresh on the road," Curtis tells him.

Reyes sniffs and spits into the dirt. I make a disgusted face until Micah elbows me.

"Right. Well, this is Backbone Station. Ain't much

to it; that there's the mess hall," Reyes says, pointing to the flat structure closest to us. This place was built to be a temporary stop, and it shows; the hall is only a roof and two walls, with long tables set up inside.

"Two meals a day, anything else is on you. Tents is there," and he points beyond the hall to a scattering of white shelters. "Any cot that's free is yours for the night. We ain't got many here right now, but it'll fill up some in the next few hours. Keep your valuables on you, less you want 'em gone. Water tower and hitching posts you can see, outhouse is behind the tents. Now listen close," he says, and his eyes get even smaller. "You bring any trouble here, you go outside the gate. You start any trouble here, you go outside the gate. Got it?"

"Got it," Micah and Sam say, one a beat behind the other. Reyes turns to his head to me.

"Got it," I say quickly, and his eyebrows shoot up when he hears my voice.

"You're a girl," he says accusingly.

"I know," I say.

"We don't get many women out here. This ain't a boardinghouse, we ain't got a separate place for you to sleep."

"I don't expect one, but I'm hoping you can help me,

Mr. Reyes. I'm looking for my—our—father," I say, glancing at Micah. "Harrison Wilcox. He would've passed through here yesterday maybe."

Reyes scratches the back of his neck. "I wouldn't know. Lewis was on the gate then, if'n you want to talk to him."

"Where can I find him?"

"He'll be around the mess hall later, pale feller with orange hair and ostrich boots."

"Thank you."

Reyes waves his hand, dismissing my thanks. "Welcome to Backbone," he says.

"Ben, get them watered and settled," Curtis says. "Reyes, I got some news I need to pass along."

Benjamin nods curtly and ushers us away, but not before I see Reyes's face go grim. Out here, there's only one kind of news, and it ain't the kind you want to hear.

26.

We go to the water pump first, and though it's warm and smells of minerals, it is the sweetest thing I have ever tasted. I swallow away the dust in my mouth and drink until I can feel the water sloshing around in my belly.

"Slow down, Will," Sam says, tugging on my shoulder. "You'll make yourself sick."

"I don't care," I say, but I stop and let Micah have a turn. Even my feet feel better now that I'm not thirsty.

We unload Nana and set her up at a post with water and feed. There's one horse hitched to another post, a mangy-looking dun with ribs poking out. The horse eyes Nana with disdain, and I give the mule a reassuring pat on the nose.

"You're better than any bony horse," I tell her, and glare at the dun. "Mind yourself, sir."

I pick up my small bundle and turn to find Benjamin frowning at the horse.

"What?" I ask him.

"Nothing," he says, shaking his head.

"You know him?"

"Don't think so. Come on, your boys are picking out cots."

"They're not *my* boys, Garrett. Don't go putting them on me."

A large pole stands in the center of the station with a red flag with black letters reading *Backbone*. As we pass it, I notice someone's added words in white paint to the pole: *The dead sleep free.*

The tents look larger and not so white up close. The canvas is ripped in places, and dirt stains the cloth where it touches the ground. They're solid enough, though, held up with wooden beams and tied with thick rope. Some of the tents look to be lived in, with guns and crates stacked in front. We walk by one with the flaps tied open and inside a flint-eyed hunter smokes a pipe, sitting on a camp chair with his legs propped up on a barrel. The sweet-smelling smoke drifts into my face and burrows in my hair.

"Over here," Micah calls, and he waves from a tent. "How's this one?"

Micah ducks back in and I follow him, pushing the canvas aside. Inside, the air is stale and smells like sweat and piss and whiskey. I wrinkle my nose, but at least it's cooler and keeps the sun off. There are six cots, two against each side of the square tent excepting where it opens. Two barn lanterns hang on the beams, but it's early yet for them to be lit. There's a small table with a washbasin and little else, but I reckon it will do fine for one night.

Sam and Micah have claimed the beds at the back, so I toss my pack on the cot to the right, nearest the opening and the freshest air.

"Is this all right?" I ask Benjamin when he comes in. "You and Curtis over there?" I point to the cots across from mine.

"Works for me. I'd rather be closer to the exit anyways," he answers. "Just in case things take a turn."

"We're surrounded by hunters," Sam says dryly. "How much safer could we get?"

I snort softly, and even Ben's lips twitch at that.

Ben throws his pack on a cot, leaving the other for

Curtis. The beds are old, straw-stuffed mattresses without a coverlid. I can see the imprint of where previous bodies have slept and yellowed sweat stains where their heads have lain. But I could sleep on a gravel road; I'm that tired.

"Go on and rest awhile," Ben tells us. Micah is already half asleep, sprawled out on the cot with his head propped on one arm.

I take off my coat and scrunch it into a pad for my head, then unroll my blanket and spread it out beneath me. It's too hot to get under it, but once the sun drops, so will the temperature. My gun and knife come off and get shoved under my makeshift pillow where they won't poke at me. I pull my boots off and let them drop to the ground, rubbing my sore feet. Every bone in my body creaks and settles when I lay down. The roof of the tent is vaulted, coming down low where I'm lying; I could reach out and touch it, leave my finger streaks in the dusty cloth. I turn on my side and study the beam close to my head, next to the entrance. There are names scratched in the wood, some deep and some barely visible. *Davis*, I read. *Rodriguez*. *Eames*. One that could be *Hicks*, or maybe *Ricks*. Why do they carve their names, when only strangers will read them? A name is only a meaningless word with nothing to attach it to. Maybe it is enough just to be remembered, if only for your name; here is proof of life, faceless and voiceless but unmistakable. Immortality of a strange sort: a eulogy in wood. I lift my hand to trace the names when sleep takes me.

27.

Someone is calling my name, and I struggle to swim out of the depths of sleep.

"Will, wake up."

It's my brother's voice, and for a blissful second I'm at home. Ma made breakfast and Pa is already up and working on the roof. The twins will be in any moment now, jumping on me and getting underfoot. I open my eyes a crack, expecting to see Micah leaning over me. But the light is wrong and the ceiling is too close and then reality comes crashing down around me.

"Will, come *on*, I'm hungry," Micah says.

I sit up slowly, my back protesting. My eyes feel leaden and my mouth tastes bitter. I rub my face and swallow and peer at my brother, long shadows on his face.

"What time is it?"

"Almost six. Sun's going down and they rang the bell for supper."

"Where is everybody?"

"Already went to the mess hall, where we should be."

"Nice of them to wait," I say crossly, rubbing sleep from my eyes.

"You wouldn't wake up, I told 'em to go ahead. Not their fault you sleep like the dead."

I give Micah a shove and ease my way to my feet.

"Shut it. I'm still mad at you." I pick up one of my boots from the floor and pull it on, hissing as it scrapes my heel. "Where the hell is my other boot?"

Micah grumbles, but he helps me find it and waits while I check it for scorpions and put it on.

"Can we go now?"

"Quit your bellyaching, I'm coming."

I stand up and follow Micah to the mess hall, feeling unsteady on my feet. My head is pounding something awful; I need water, food, and more sleep, in that order.

The setting sun changes the desert, orange light spilling out across the horizon, stopping only where the sky bruises blue. Through the open walls of the hall, light and noise pour out, the yellow glow of kerosene lamps, the metallic scrape of knives on plates. Heavy wooden tables stretch from one end of the room to the other, benches tucked in beneath. There are maybe fifteen men in all, huddled together in their own companies. Curtis waves Micah and me over to where he and Ben are sitting.

"Where's Sam?" I ask, but my eyes are on the steaming bowls in front of the brothers.

"Getting grub," Curtis says, and points behind him. "Go and help yourself."

We don't need to be told twice. Micah beats me to the table in the corner, where a man with brown skin and a tidy moustache stirs the most enormous pot I've ever seen.

"Evening, young'uns," he says cheerfully. "Grab a plate."

Micah picks up a tarnished tin plate and hands one to me, and the man ladles out the stew.

"Eat up, now. There's plenty more where that came from."

I could love this man, I think. I give him my best smile, teeth and all.

"Thank you, sir," I tell him.

"My pleasure, little lady."

Salt pork and potatoes, thickened with flour; no one speaks while we eat. There's a bowl of cornbread, only a little stale, and a pitcher of water set on the table for us. I don't remember the last time I ate this much or this well. Micah catches my eye and we grin at each other over our plates. I'm so full I could almost forgive him. I inhale my first serving, but I take my time with my second, chewing each bite slowly and deliberately. I study the other men in the hall, keeping an eye out for Lewis, listening to snatches of conversation, nonsense mostly. There's a rumor going around that the president might send the army to keep us locked inside our houses till the sickness dies out, and the hunters have been railing against Grant for days. I roll my eyes; the North has enough trouble, what with the strikes and the fires. Do the hunters really think anyone cares what happens down here? As long as the shakes stay confined to these few barren outskirts, the rest of the country is more than happy to ignore us. They've already stopped building railroads, now they'll wait for us all to die out and then come in and raze the ground and salt it for good measure. We're a speck on the map, a blight on the land, and no one's coming to save us.

Most of these boys look like hard cases and hard

drinkers. There aren't many old-timers, either; most of these boys are truly boys. Hunting isn't the safest profession; I reckon all these fellows know their odds. I count four other hunters I know from sight at the Homestead, though I disremember most of their names.

"Y'all aren't drinking," I say, turning my attention back to our table.

"What's that now?" Curtis asks.

"Most of these fellers are slewed already. I never knew a hunter didn't drink."

"We don't drink on a job," Ben says.

"Why not?" Sam asks.

"Bad idea," Curtis says. "You get loose, you get sloppy."

"Most don't care if they get sloppy," Sam says. "Long as they get some money up front."

"Where'd you hear that?" I ask Sam. I know it's true, but I didn't think Sam had anything to do with hunters.

"Willie, I've been helping my pa stitch since I could hold a needle. I hear plenty of stories. Remember Pickett? He killed his own client halfway to Barstowe. Didn't feel like taking him back."

"What happened to him?" Micah asks.

"Died in a bar fight, nasty knife wound."

I shake my head. "Ma said time was, Glory was a nice enough town. People didn't try to rob you in the street, folks didn't gamble away their savings. We even had lawmen, of a sort. Damn the Judge and his hunters. What did he expect, when he let killers loose in our town?"

"I don't suppose he cares," Micah says. "No offense," he adds belatedly.

"We ain't all like that," Ben says. "Some of us are just trying to get by. Judge might be our boss, but we don't deal with him any more than we have to. I don't know Pickett, but I reckon he got his."

"And we won't kill y'all," Curtis adds with half a smile. "That's just bad for business."

Micah regards Curtis thoughtfully, chewing on a dry piece of cornbread.

"You know, for hunters, you boys ain't so bad," he says.

Sam and I start to laugh, but Curtis nods his head solemnly.

"Here's how," he toasts, and raises his glass of water in salute.

28.

A clang comes from the left, and we look over to see a pale, slender man standing up and banging his cup against a table.

"'Scuse me," he calls, and it takes a moment for silence to come over the hall.

"Thank you," he says. "Sorry ter interrupt your supper, but we got some news for y'all heading west. The well on mile eighty-eight's been spoiled."

There's a low murmur as the news is repeated.

"We got some folks heading out tomorrow to seal her up, but in the meantime take whatever water you can carry and spread the word. Tha's all."

As the voices get loud again, I stand up and make my way over to the man, Micah on my tail. I'm betting this is Lewis; he has a shock of reddish blond hair and a spattering of freckles across his nose and cheeks.

"Are you Lewis?" I ask.

"I'm him," he says, turning to meet me. We're the same height, and he meets my eyes directly. "What can I do you for y'all?"

"Reyes says you were on the gate yesterday. I'm hoping you remember seeing my father, Harrison Wilcox?"

Lewis frowns, his brow wrinkling. "What's he look like?"

"Like me," Micah says, scowling, "but with a few more pounds and a lot more years."

"He mighta been with a man called Washburne," I add.

Lewis squints at Micah, considering. "I seen a man looked like him, but he didn't give the name Wilcox."

That's the first smart thing Pa's done. "That's him."

"Comes 'round a lot, don't he?"

"Yeah," I say. "He passed through often enough. Did you see him leave?"

"Can't say for sure. Maybe I did." Lewis rubs his hand through his bright hair.

"Please, sir. It's important. I need to know where he headed."

"Well, I suppose I saw him goin' east. Least that's how I remember it."

I nod in agreement, but the news somehow leaves me feeling more tired than before. At least I know we're going the right way. "Thank you, Mr. Lewis."

We walk back to our table quickly, my head heavy. Curtis sees me and raises his eyebrows.

"Well?"

"He was here," Micah says.

"I'm not sure when he left, but I reckon it was early," I say. "And he was going east."

"So what now? You think he'll stay in Best once he gets there?"

Curtis and Ben just wait, their faces carefully blank. Micah and Sam look at me, expectantly. The pressure starts to gnaw at me again, the familiar weight of responsibility settling onto my shoulders. This is what I tried to escape, came all the way out here to duck, and still it follows me. I don't want them to look at me like this, like I'm the one with answers when all I feel is lost. But it has to be this way; there's no one else I can look to, and they all look to me.

"I think so," I say, filling my voice with confidence I

don't feel. "At least for a few days. I've never known him to go any farther."

Micah frowns at me, but Sam claps him on the shoulder. "See? We'll find him, nothing to worry about. Willie always knows what to do."

His words pain me, but I force a smile. "'Course I do." I sit back down and pick up my fork before realizing that for once I'm actually full. There's even food left on my plate, a rare luxury.

Benjamin takes out a pack of cards with frayed edges, and starts to shuffle for a game of faro. I watch for a bit, not in the mood to play. I'm not a fan of card games, even if the boys aren't betting real money; it's just a way to pass the time. Curtis calls banker and deals, then burns off the first card. He's placing the banker's card when a loud horselaugh catches my attention from across the room. My eyes find Dollarhide immediately; his back is to me but there's no mistaking that dingy hair.

"What the hell is he doing here?" I ask, my fists tightening on instinct.

The Garretts crane their heads around to see who I'm glaring at.

"He who?" Micah nudges me, not following my gaze.

"Dollarhide," Ben answers for me. "I thought that was his horse."

"How in blazes did Dollarhide get a horse?" Micah asks.

"Stole one, I reckon," Curtis says. "You stay away from him, all of you."

"I intend to," I tell him, crossing my arms.

"Why?" Sam asks. "I mean, I know he's a bad sort and all, but lots of hunters are. Again, no offense."

"He's in deep to the Judge," Curtis says. "Gambling debts up to his eyes, and he's getting desperate."

"He was making noise a while back about Delgado fleecing him out of a job. Wouldn't shut up till some fellers made him. That was before he came after you." Ben nods at me.

"What?" Micah's eyes widen. "You didn't tell me that, Will. When? What happened?"

"Nothing," I tell him. "Dollarhide thought Pa gave me some of the money and tried to take it off me."

"Of course," Micah says, his lip curling up. "Leave it to Pa to pile on more troubles."

"That ain't fair," I tell him, but my heart isn't in it. I gave up on Pa a long time ago.

"It won't be long afore he follows your pa's example,"

Curtis interrupts, putting an end to our squabble. "The Judge ain't a patient man, and I hear Dollarhide owes two months in tithes."

"What tithes?" Sam asks. "I thought hunters didn't have to pay dues."

"No, but ten percent of everything we make goes to the Judge. Some goes to keep the patrols busy and these stations stocked, and the rest goes in his pockets."

Micah gives a low whistle, and I scowl. How much money does one man need? The rest of us barely scrape by, and the Judge still has his hand out.

"Is that why y'all are so affordable?" I ask.

Curtis shrugs. "Well, that and we're still green. But I don't like giving that man any more than I have to."

I nod in agreement, and glance at Dollarhide. Maybe he feels my eyes on him, because he looks right at me. I duck my head down, staring at my half-full plate. When I risk another look, he's making his way out of the mess hall.

"If he's smart, he'll get out of Glory," Ben says, watching Dollarhide leave. "Somewhere the Judge can't send hunters to collect."

"If he were smart, he wouldn't owe in the first place. Judge has long arms," Curtis says. "There's not many places he can't reach. His boys are everywhere from Savage to Rath City, and those boys are loyal. I know McAllister's after your pa, but I'd rather have a posse on my tail than owe one red cent to the Judge. All right, make your bets."

The boys use colored rocks instead of chips. A few fellows wander over to watch the game, introducing themselves as hunters from Plainview. They seem plenty nice, and one of them gives me a sidelong glance, but Ben and Curtis aren't enough to change my opinion of hunters entirely.

I watch the boys play without paying attention, my full belly making me sleepy and warm. Micah looks happy, laughing at Curtis's jokes and talking easily with Sam. At home he's so withdrawn, always sealing himself away. Is it my fault he's like that? Or maybe Micah feels it, too, the heaviness that lives in our house, the air thick with regret.

Breaking glass and shouts erupt from the corner, and I leap to my feet a second after the Garretts, pushing Micah behind me. Everyone is drawing guns but I can't see what's happening.

"Get back," someone yells. "Get away from him."

A space clears as everyone backs away from a man

lying on his side on the floor. At first I think he's been shot, but then I see him moving, convulsing in rapid and jerky spasms. His body contorts and as he rolls onto his back I see his face, twitching and distorted with pain.

"Oh no," Micah says softly, his eyes wide.

Sam takes a hesitant step forward, but Curtis puts a restraining hand on his shoulder.

"There's nothing you can do for him, Doc," he says. "Best not get too close."

It's the first rule we have drilled into us: Any sign of sickness and it's already too late. Sympathy will only get you killed. Lewis and Reyes run past us, shoving their way through the crowd. They stop well clear of the man, watching him jump like hot oil in a pan.

"Who came with him?" Lewis asks, his voice hard.

Two other hunters come forward, looking guilty and afraid.

"He only said he had a headache," one of them mumbles. "He weren't acting right, but we thought he was drunk."

"Tha's no excuse," Reyes says, glaring. "You know the rules."

The hunter nods rapidly and cocks his gun.

"Not here, you idiot," Lewis yells at him. "Take him outside the gate."

The hunters hesitate, not wanting to touch their friend.

"Do it now," Lewis says, "and we'll let you leave here alive. You might even make it to morning, if you're lucky."

They reach down and grab the man by his arms and start to drag him. He's making wet choking sounds, his eyes rolling in his head. He doesn't fight them; I don't think he's even in there anymore. The rest of the hunters move back, making a wide path out of the mess hall, and everyone is silent until they pass through.

"Anyone else tries to bring the sickness here, you get a night outside with your bullets for company," Lewis says loudly. "That understood?"

A murmur of assent ripples through the hunters.

"Then good evening."

"Well." Curtis sits down heavily, running a hand over his face. "Where were we?"

The boys settle back into place and the game resumes, somewhat subdued.

"He musta known he was sick," Micah says after a moment.

"It comes on fast," Sam says. "He mighta thought he had more time."

"He was wrong, then," Ben says.

My eyes start to blur as I look at the cards and I rub a hand over my face.

"Listen, boys, I'm dragged out. I'm going to lay down before I fall down."

Benjamin makes to stand up, but I motion him back.

"Finish the game. I think I can manage to walk a few steps on my own. Y'all come when you're ready."

"'Night, Willie," they call after me and I wave to them half-heartedly.

I know it's coming, but I still flinch when I hear the single gunshot.

29.

I trudge back along the path, the evening sky a dingy blue-gray, like a dog that rolled in dirt. There's a slice of moon tonight, pale in comparison to the swarm of the stars. A lantern hangs from the entrance of someone's tent, lighting the way in the dusk. I see the outline of a man standing stooped, a cloud of smoke around his head. I'm halfway to my tent before I make out his features, and then he moves up to meet me.

"Well, lookie here. I never expected ter see you out this way." His voice is harsh, tobacco smoke and rusty nails.

I groan to myself; I should've known he would be waiting after he saw me.

"Damn it, Dollarhide, I'm too tired for this."

Dollarhide drops his rolled cigarette and crushes it with his boot heel. The lantern illuminates his wrinkled face, and I can see a dark bruise across his cheek.

"That right? Had a long day, sweetheart?" I can smell whiskey on his breath, but he's steady on his feet this time. This could get ugly quickly; he's unarmed, but so am I, and I'm no match for him sober. I look behind me for help, but the hall is too far away for anyone to see us in the encroaching dark.

"Lookin' fer your boy to save you?"

"What do you want, Dollarhide? I don't have any money."

"And I say yer a liar," he says, pointing to my chest. "Give it to me now and you can go on your way."

I stare at him, confused, until I realize he's pointing at the drawstring pouch around my neck. I start to laugh, and his face hardens.

"Take it," I say, pulling the string over my head and tossing him the bag. "It's all yours."

Dollarhide catches the pouch in one hand, tearing at the strings to open it. He shakes out the contents into a waiting palm, holding them under the lamplight.

"What is this?" he says angrily, throwing the cartridges into the dirt. "Where you hidin' it?"

"I told you I got nothing."

"Do I look stupid to you?"

I hesitate a moment too long, and Dollarhide's face twists in anger. I have time to think *damn*, and then his fist connects with my nose. The pain comes a second after the impact, like fire racing along hot wires in my face. My eyes immediately tear up, and I blink rapidly to try and clear my vision.

"Dollarhide, you son of a bitch," I say thickly. Warm wetness runs down my lips, and my hand comes back red when I wipe it away. "That tears it." If he broke my nose, I'll break his neck; my patience is worn that thin.

"Give it to me," he says, his voice too close.

My sight is blurry and I'm too slow to move entirely out of the way as he comes at me again. The blow glances off my side instead of hitting my stomach, but my legs are tired and my right knee buckles. I end up on one knee in the dirt, with Dollarhide's fingers pulling at my pockets, searching for something I don't have. The sleeve of my shirt rips, and I've had enough of this. I shove Dollarhide's legs, using my weight to topple him. Surprised, his back hits the ground with a loud smack, and while he lies stunned I jump on his chest, digging in my knees. I aim carefully, then punch him directly on his bruised cheek, and this time I get to use my good arm.

Dollarhide yelps and I hit him again, and again, until the blood dripping down from my nose mixes with his. I think I have him beat, but then there's a roar from behind me and I jump up to see a man running toward me. I only barely recognize him as one of Dollarhide's men, the boys he drinks and gambles with. I set my feet and make a fist, but before he reaches me someone grabs him from behind, knocking him to the ground.

"Just a few steps on your own, huh?" Ben asks, and I have to grin at him. A moment later Micah and two other men are running toward us with a yell, and now it's a proper brawl.

Dollarhide scrambles to his feet, and I turn to face him. He pants, his hands braced on his knees.

"Are we done here?" I ask him.

As an answer, he rushes at me, trying to mow me over. He catches me around the waist and I punch at his back, digging my boot heels into the dirt.

A gunshot rings out, deafening and sharp.

"Have y'all lost your damn minds?" Curtis yells.

Dollarhide drops me and I leave off hitting him. Ben freezes in motion, his arm tight around someone's neck, and Micah picks himself up off the ground.

"Ben, let him go," Curtis orders. "Everyone, go about your business. And nobody says nothing about this, got it? Unless you want us all put outside."

Dollarhide straightens up, looking at me with pure hate.

"Come on, Dollarhide," one of the men calls to him. "It ain't worth it."

He starts to back away, but I can't keep my mouth from running.

"You come at me again and I'll kill you," I call after him.

"You just try—" Dollarhide yells back, but his friends shut him up and pull him back.

"You keep the hell away from us," Curtis says, his voice steely. "And we won't have a problem. Understood?"

Dollarhide's friends nod, and he goes quietly after that; his face is a bloody mess and he's holding his side awkwardly. Sure, maybe I don't look so nice, either, but he's got eighty pounds on me and I gave as good as I got. Not a bad fight after all.

"Willie," Curtis says insistently, and I realize he's been calling my name.

"What?"

"You all right?"

The pain will start to set in now that the fight is over, but I'm still riding high, jittery and scared. "I'll live."

I survey the damage to the others; Ben has a busted lip and what's bound to be an impressive black eye, but Micah looks unscathed.

"You all right, Micah?" I ask him.

"Fine," he says, looking almost disappointed.

"What the hell were you thinking, Ben?" Curtis asks, his mouth tight like he's holding in his teeth.

"Dollarhide started it."

"I don't care who started it; if the guards had caught you they'd throw us all out."

"We're supposed to be protecting her, aren't we?" Ben points at me angrily. "Should I just let him keep pounding on her?"

"He wasn't pounding on me," I protest.

"Everyone, just—quiet." Curtis sighs and rubs his eyes. When he lowers his hands, he looks more composed. "Willie, I'm sorry. That shouldn't have happened."

"Ain't your fault Dollarhide's a thieving scoundrel. I told him I didn't have nothing."

"Let's get inside," Sam says, trying to steer me into

our tent. "Will's face don't look so good."

"Aw, come on, I'm right here," I say, but I let Sam guide me back to our tent. We pass a few small groups on the way, and I guess from the stares we look pretty banged up. My nose is still dripping, and when I lick my lips I get a mouthful of blood.

In the tent, I sit down heavily on my cot while Sam lights the lantern and hands it to Micah.

"Hold this," he says, and Micah shines the light on my face. Sam bends down slightly, staring at my eyes. I squint at the brightness, but Sam shakes his head.

"Keep your eyes open," he says. His voice sounds different: calm, reassuring. He sounds just like his father when he's with patients. "Do you know where you are?"

"What? We're in the tent."

"Do you know your name?"

"Aw, Sam—" I start to object.

"Just answer the question."

I glare at him, but Sam stares back evenly. I don't know when he grew a backbone, but it must've been sometime in the last two days.

"Do what he tells you," Micah says, and it's the insistence in his voice that gets to me.

"Daisy Wilcox," I say, as quietly as I can mutter it.

I jut out my chin, daring anyone to laugh, but the boys stay silent.

"What day is it?"

"Why are you asking me these questions?"

"I'm trying to see if you bruised your brain."

"I didn't hit my head, Sam, so back off."

Instead, he gets even closer and places his fingers on either side of my nose.

"Ow," I say, and slap his hand away. "That hurts."

"Stop being a baby," he tells me, and I'm so surprised that he would scold me that I let him touch my nose again.

"It's not broken," he says, standing back up.

"Are you sure?"

"'Course I am." He pats me on the shoulder awkwardly, and just like that, he switches back into the Sam I know.

"Thanks, Sam."

"What about you?" he asks Micah.

"I reckon just a bruise where I fell," Micah says, scowling. "I only got in one good punch before I got knocked over."

"You sure? I better go check on Dollarhide and the others."

"What?" I'm sure I misheard him.

"Why?" Ben asks.

"Sam," Micah says angrily. "Don't be an idiot."

"I'm a doctor," Sam says, like that explains anything at all. "Or, almost one. I don't get to pick who I help."

"He's the one who started it," Micah tells him while Sam gets his bag from his own bed. "He attacked *my sister.*"

"I know. But Willie's gonna be fine, and I think he's got a cracked rib."

"Good," Micah says, harshly. "I hope it hurts."

"Pinch your nose and lean forward until the bleeding stops," Sam tells me, and then he's off.

Curtis sighs while I hold my nose and tilt my head down.

"I better go after him," he says. "Dollarhide won't take kindly to being poked at."

"Serves him right," Micah says. "Maybe when he gets a black eye for his troubles, the good doctor will come to his senses."

The anger is coming off of Micah in waves. I'm touched, that he would care so much.

"Thanks," I say to him quietly, and I hold out my free hand to him. "For coming to help. It was good of you."

Micah shakes his head unhappily. "Why you always gotta go looking for trouble, Willie?"

"I don't go looking for it. Trouble just finds me, is all." I give Micah a reassuring smile. "Go with Curtis. Tell Sam you're sorry for hassling him."

"I'm not sorry," Micah says.

"Yes you are. Go on now."

I'm shook up from the fight some, my ears still ringing, and I welcome the silence when they leave. I slowly release my nose and wait for a moment, but I think it's done bleeding.

"Here," Ben says, startling me; I forgot he was here. He holds out a yellowed handkerchief folded into a fat square, eyeing my ripped shirt with a frown. I'm upset about it, too; I only brought the one extra.

"You're not gonna start fussing at me, are you?" I ask him.

"Not me," he says. "Take it."

"Thanks." I shake the cloth out and wipe my face with it, scrubbing my wet cheeks. Ben makes a strangled noise and I stop to look at him. "What?"

"Nothing, just—you're gettin blood all over," he says, his expression pained.

"Oh."

"Give it here," he says, and takes the cloth from me and dips a clean corner in one of the water pitchers. Before I can object, he turns my chin up and wipes my face, not gently but thoroughly. He's careful of my nose, though I can't help wincing when his hand bumps it.

"Sorry," he says quickly. "Does it hurt?"

"Naw. My baby brother hits harder 'n him. How 'bout yours?"

"Barely feel it. He shouldn't have hit you. Ain't right."

"I thought you weren't gonna fuss," I remind him.

Ben shrugs. I study his face as he cleans mine, trying to see what's beneath the beard. The eye that's not bruised and closed is bright and sharp, the light amber of thick honey. Up close I can tell he's young, younger than I thought; probably not much older than me. The beard, the scowl; I get it now, it's all to make him seem older, more confident. It's only artifice, a way to hide that he's shy and uncertain, just like the rest of us.

"There," Ben says, sitting back. "It's gonna look like hell tomorrow, but you're clean."

"Thanks, Ben."

"You're welcome . . ." He pauses.

"Willie," I say firmly.

"Not Daisy?"

I throw the bloody handkerchief at him. "No, not rotten Daisy. I'm gonna skin Sam."

"It don't suit you anyhows," Ben says.

"You think so?"

"I never knew a Daisy as could take a punch."

It hurts my bruised face, but I smile. "Is that all it takes to get on your good side? You shoulda told me that from the beginning."

Ben ducks his head down. "I reckon I owe you an apology."

Now that he's finally offering, I find I don't want it. "Not necessary. And I'd hate to put you out, especially since I would feel the need to reciprocate."

"I'm not—I'm not so good at talking to people."

"Me neither. Ma always said my mouth runs when it should shut and bites when it should smile. Let's just call it quits and start over." I hold my hand out. "Hi. I'm Daisy Wilcox, but you better call me Willie if you value your life."

Ben smiles, the first real smile I've seen. It's crooked and shy, and it makes him look younger, and almost sweet. I can see why he doesn't do it very often.

"Benjamin Garrett, pleased to meet you." He shakes my hand firmly. "Now sit still till Doc Junior comes back."

30.

Despite the throbbing of my face, I can barely keep my eyes open, and Micah has to shake me awake when he and Curtis get back.

"Sam's still patching up . . . that man," Micah says, refusing to call Dollarhide by name. "He said he'll be back right quick and he'll give you something for the pain."

"If I lie down again I'm not getting back up," I tell him, yawning wide. "I'll wait for him outside."

The night air wakes me up some and I tilt my head back and stare at the thumbnail of the moon. It's full dark now, the sky a black so soft it looks touchable. I never get to see the night like this, the stars spread wide and untamed. Nights are for locked doors and shuttered windows, hushed voices and bad dreams. I forgot how vivid the darkness could be, how it can wrap around you like old sheets. I breathe it in like I could keep it.

"Damn Dollarhide," Curtis says from inside the tent, his voice barely above a whisper. I stay still, listening closely. "What was he thinking, starting something at a station?"

"I shoulda guessed he'd try something, after the last time." Ben exhales loudly, and I picture his frown. "He needs to be put down."

"I don't disagree. I'm sorry we let you down, Micah," Curtis says solemnly. "We're used to looking for danger outside the fence, not inside."

"It ain't your fault," Micah says, echoing my words. "Willie's got a knack for trouble. Always has." He laughs, but there's an edge of bitterness to it.

"It was good of you, to come after her. Y'all seem close."

"It's just us now. The twins are young, and Pa's always gone. It's better that way; he ain't much help when he's home. I guess he's not much help when he's away, either."

"And your ma?" Curtis asks.

There's a long pause and something in my chest twinges.

"Sickness took her," Micah says slowly. "Last year. We hid it as best we could, kept her inside and away from anyone but us. Maybe it was wrong, but . . . we couldn't let her die like that, alone and outside the fence."

My shoulders hunch up and I press my feet farther down into the dirt. I don't want to hear this, and I certainly don't want the Garretts to hear it.

"Pa came home for a while, but he left before the end. Wasn't strong enough, I guess."

My throat gets hot. It should have been him. It was his responsibility, his wife. No one wants to become a shake, so the merciful thing to do is have someone end it for you, end it before you hurt the people you love. Ma put on a brave face, she fought as long as she could before she asked for help. It was Pa's burden, and he couldn't even give her that bit of peace.

"Ma didn't want to lose herself, didn't want us to see her . . . like that. Like she wasn't our ma anymore." Micah keeps talking, and I wish I could shut out the sound of his voice. "But Pa said he couldn't. I think I hate him, just for that. He left her, left her when she needed him most. She tried so hard to fight it, but she was so sick—"

"I think that's enough, Micah," I say loudly, cutting him off before he says something he can't unsay. My voice is harsh in my ears, and I swing back into the tent abruptly. "Or did you want to air more of our dirty laundry?"

Micah won't meet my eyes, but at least Ben has the courtesy to look embarrassed.

"I'm sorry," Curtis tells me. "It's none of our business."

"We lost our mother almost thirteen years ago." Ben's voice makes me jump. I turn to him, and he nods solemnly. "Out east, in Ennis, where we're from. Smallpox. I don't remember it well. They wouldn't let me too close, on account of me being so young. Mostly I just remember how the whole house smelled of illness. Even after she was gone, it took ages for the smell to finally leave my clothes."

"What did it smell like?" It's an inappropriate question, but I want to know if it's the same smell I remember. Or does each disease have its own particular scent, the way some people smell like cut tobacco or old soap?

"Sweet, mostly. Like melted butter, but with something rotten underneath."

I can almost smell it, and I shake my head to clear it out. The pox is almost as bad as the sickness, but at least some folks come through it with only scars to show. Every now and then it roars through a town to remind us there's more than one way to die. Last time Best had a pox outbreak, Ma took Micah and me straight to Doc Kincaid for vaccination. He pricked us on the arm with the cowpox inoculation and afterward we both got lesions for near a week, but Ma said we had enough to worry about besides the pox. I reckon I should get the twins in sometime, but I'll probably have to hold them down.

I should say something else to Ben, thank him, maybe, but that would sound strange. Maybe it's enough to say I'm sorry, but Sam returns and saves me the trouble of figuring it out.

"I can take a look at that eye," he says to Ben.

"I don't think so, Doc."

Sam doesn't even try to argue, and I glare at him while he opens his pack, digging around until he finds a vial. Maybe it's the beard; I would grow one if I could, and the unfairness stings.

"Here, drink this," Sam says, and gives me a spoonful of clear liquid. I obey without arguing and swallow it. Bitterness coats my tongue, so sharp it burns. He hands me a canteen of water and I down it in one gulp, washing away the acrid taste.

"Sakes alive, that's awful. What kind of snake oil are you giving me, Sam?"

"It's just laudanum; it'll help dull the pain."

"How's our friend?"

"Worse off than you. I'm pretty sure you cracked his cheekbone, but there's nothing to be done about it."

"That's a shame," I say, examining the knuckles of my hand. "I hope it doesn't give him much pain."

"It surely will," Sam says.

"Pity." I shake my head sorrowfully. "Thanks for patching me up, Doc. I owe you."

"On the house," Sam says, smiling. "I figure I'll get plenty of business from you in the future."

I smack him on the shoulder, like he's one of the twins, but he catches my left hand.

"What's that?" Sam turns over my hand, looking at the cut on my palm.

"Proof that I'm clumsy," I tell him, snatching my hand away.

"You need to dress that, Willie, it looks infected." Sam frowns at me until I nod my compliance. "Good. And next time don't let it go so long."

"What do you mean?"

"That looks like you let it fester a couple days. If you'd come to me sooner, I coulda fixed you up." Sam gives me half a smile. "Now get some rest and stop trying to make my job harder."

I lay down flat on my back, staring at the blank white walls until my eyes feel numb to the world. Curtis and Ben are talking softly to one another, though I can't make out the words. Micah and Sam start up a game of mumblety-peg, which Sam will win like always. Micah's a better shot, but you should never go against a doctor with a knife. They tried to teach the twins how to play; I found all four out back throwing knives at the side of our house. I put such an end to that, Sam didn't come over for nearly a week. Seems silly now.

I turn over onto my side and slowly open my hand. The pink line of the cut rakes across my palm, definitive and resolute. From one corner of the wound pus weeps out, yellow and evil. Angry red streaks creep along my hand and move up my wrist. The skin is puffy and smooth, all the lines in my skin erased by the pressure underneath. My fingers start to tremble. It's been hours since I cut it, not days; infection shouldn't move this fast. Couldn't move this fast, not unless—no. I turn the truth over in my head until it loses all semblance of sense. It doesn't matter; I know what it means. I put an open wound in diseased water. It makes no difference if I bandage it or bleed it; no one survives once the sickness takes root. I have only days until the infection reaches my brain and I forget everything that makes me me. I'm going to lose myself, and Micah and the twins will lose the last parent they have left.

The pain in my nose is nothing compared to this. I feel like I'm drowning, like I cannot breathe. I know what happens next, I remember too well the madness and the pain and the stink of blood. This is not how I wanted to go, it was not supposed to be this way. Nothing in my life was supposed to be this way.

I'm not ready to die.

The laudanum is dragging me under, and I fight it. I have so few hours left, I don't want to spend them sleeping. But the drug is too strong, and I am too weak. Sleep takes me roughly, and I have only one thought as I surrender: I've damned us all.

PART THREE:
THE STORM

A woman in the shape of a monster

a monster in the shape of a woman

—*Adrienne Rich*

31.

I'm swimming, which is strange, because I don't know how to swim. I've never even seen anything bigger than a creek, but here I am, weightless in water black and thick as oil. I swim deeper, farther into the darkness, each movement becoming harder as the water turns denser. It's not water I'm swimming through, but blood; the blood of the already dead, congealing and hardening, so red it looks black. I open my mouth to scream and the blood pours in, coating my tongue and throat with its hot metal taste.

I wake up panicked, gasping for breath. This part is familiar, and I tell myself to calm down, that I'm safe in my house in my own bed. But that's not true; this isn't my bed and my face feels wrong and something terrible hovers at the edge of my consciousness. The night before comes rushing back, and the knowledge is no less painful with time to dampen the impact. I curl up, hugging my knees to my chest, making my body as small as it will go. I used to rock myself to sleep like this, when I was a child and so afraid of the world outside my door. If I could make myself small enough, I would disappear; if I could hide I would be safe. But I can't hide from what's inside me, and I can't run from myself.

"Will, you up?" Micah's voice pierces through my thoughts. I want to answer, but my mouth is not responding to my mind. I'm so tired; even drugged, the intermittent gunshots were loud enough to wake me up throughout the night.

"Let her sleep," I hear Curtis say.

I can feel the sun streaming bright through the tent, but I keep my eyes shut and listen to the bustle around me; the clearing of throats, the splashing of water, and the clink of guns being polished and loaded. Everyone is moving, busy, so aggressively alive. It's not fair.

Stop it, I tell myself. I am not some self-pitying fool, given to bouts of misery and mawkish tears. My mother did not weep when she got sick, or if she did she didn't let us see. Maybe I'm wrong; maybe it's not the sickness, only some fast-moving infection from whatever lingered on my knife. Whatever it is, I will not spend my last days curled up with my grief. I will be strong, and I will be silent. I can't tell anyone, not yet. If I tell them, they'll kill me. Or the Garretts will make us turn back, and I can't let that happen. I need to find Pa, because my family needs him now more than ever. So I'll wait, until I know for sure, until the very last moment. I'll hold on as long as I'm able, and then do what needs to be done. I won't let myself become a monster, I won't hurt the people I love. I will bring Pa back and it will be the last thing I do.

"I'm awake," I say, my voice raw. I sit up clumsily, my limbs heavy from the drugs, my back sore from the cot. My head begins to pound as soon as I raise it, but my eyes are clear and the pain in my nose is bearable.

Curtis whistles when he sees me. "That is one colorful face, little lady."

"Thanks," I say.

"What about mine?" Ben asks. His eye is a smarting shade of purple tinged with pink.

"It looks better on Willie," Curtis says.

I rummage through my sack until I find my mirror, glad to have use for it. I press the catch and flip it open to examine my face. It's not as bad as I thought; my nose is swollen but not misshapen. I angle the mirror up and see what Curtis meant: the skin beneath my eyes is bruised blue and green. I grimace and snap the mirror shut.

"Not the worst I've had, but bad enough," I tell Curtis.

"What was the worst?"

"That honor goes to one Micah Wilcox," I say, pointing at my brother.

"I had to do something to stop you kicking me," he says, grinning. A stab of regret clenches my stomach, and Micah's smile falters.

"What's wrong?"

"Nothing," I say, forcing a laugh that echoes harsh and hollow in my ears. "Just trying to remember why I was kicking you."

Micah frowns, but I hold a smile on my face like a false note hanging in the air long after it's done sounding. Finally he shrugs. "I think I put a scorpion in your bed, but it could've been a snake."

"Scorpion," Sam says. "I helped you catch it."

"Then I owed you those kicks," I tell him. I put on my gun and knife and gather all my belongings together with my duster and blanket. When no one's looking, I change my ripped shirt out for the spare one and hope it lasts longer than its predecessor. Before I get up, I strip off a length of fabric from my rag bundle and tie it around my hand, then tug my sleeve down as far as it will go. I can't let anyone see the infection, whatever it is, spreading up my arm.

When the boys have their coats and bags together, I tug on my boots and we leave the tent. It's early morning yet; the moon is still visible in the sky, a ghostly horseshoe mocking the sun. My legs are stiff and my muscles protest moving again so soon. We stop by the hitching post on the way to the mess, empty now except for Nana. She looks mighty put upon as we load her up, like a tired mother trapped with unruly children.

The mess hall is quieter than it was last night; there's no relaxed chatter or drunken laughter. Breakfast is a somber affair when no one knows what the rest of the day will bring. And I suspect the drinking last night didn't improve anyone's mood this morning.

Our group, too, is quiet while we eat. Breakfast is a plate of eggs over mashed beans, with real boiled coffee to go along. I've been drinking watered-down belly wash so long, I forgot how good it tastes. It's strong and sweet, and after my second cup I feel wide awake and looser. The coffee fills me with an optimism I know is false, but I can't help feeling hopeful; even my headache is better.

"Listen up, folks," Curtis says as we finish eating. "The second day is always the hardest. You're tired from yesterday and we got even longer to go. But this is where we're gonna start to see some action, so I need y'all alert and focused. Understood?"

We nod solemnly across the table; I understand the stakes out here now more than anyone. I knew when I left Glory that I was risking my life. Would I have chosen differently, if I had known what would happen? Even now I can't say for sure. I did what I thought I had to do, and I have to live, or die, with the consequences.

We fill up on water and leave the station with little fanfare; the gate closes behind us and it's like we never left the open desert. As we head forward, I take a quick inventory of my injuries: bruised face, stiff legs, cut hand, and a poison spreading slowly through my body. I've never started a day off in worse shape. But I'm still here. I'm still here, and I'm still walking. And for now, that's enough.

32.

We see a body the second mile in. Ben, from the lead, whistles two notes, high and then low. I shield my eyes from the glinting sun and look where he points, to a mound of rags off the road. We make our way over slowly, subdued by the presence of death so early in the day. It seems out of place, in the brightness of morning.

"Stand back," Curtis says as we gather slowly around the tangle of limbs and scraps of clothing. He unholsters his gun and he and Ben level their weapons at the unmoving body. I put my hand on my revolver, but I don't draw it. I see a tangle of brown matted hair, knotted and patchy in places. From the length, I guess it's a woman, but she's facedown on the ground.

Micah moves toward the body and we all jump. Ben grabs him by the shoulder and yanks him back.

"Are you cracked?"

Micah shrugs off Ben's hand. "She's not moving, she's dead."

"Just cause she ain't moving don't mean she's dead," Curtis tells him.

"Well, we can't know for sure until we turn her," Micah points out.

I use their momentary distraction to inch closer to the body. By the time they see what I'm doing, I've seized the body by the shoulder and rolled her over. Ben snatches me around the waist and lifts me away as the rest of the boys hightail it backward. We're more than a horse length out of reach when everyone realizes the body hasn't shifted. Curtis slowly lowers his gun and Micah stops fumbling for the rifle on his back.

"I think you can put me down now," I say to Ben, who still has one arm around me and the other full with his gun. He sets me down, none too gently.

"What the hell are you thinking? You got a death wish?" He's genuinely mad, and I wish I could tell him the truth. There's nothing that can hurt me now. In a way, I finally feel free; I have nothing to fear, because the worst has already happened.

"She's dead," Sam interrupts, kneeling by the body.

"You sure?" Curtis asks.

"Why do y'all keep asking me that? I may not be the best doctor, but I can tell when someone's not breathing," Sam says crossly.

He's right; now that she's on her back, we can all see that her chest is still and lifeless. It's hard to tell how old she was; her body is so thin, almost mummified, the bones jutting out plainly. Her skin is like paper, dried out from the fever that burned up her insides. No breath issues from her cracked lips, and her eyes stare out, blind and milky.

"I don't see any gunshots," I say, moving my eyes away from her face.

"Maybe other shakes killed her?" Micah suggests.

"Naw," Ben answers. "They don't attack one another like they do us. They'll eat their dead, but they don't kill their own. Don't know why."

"Something about the way they smell, maybe," Curtis says.

"Then what killed her?" Micah asks.

Sam struggles to his feet and shrugs. "I don't see any external wounds, so the disease, I reckon. Fever, sunstroke, seizure when her brain swelled. Nothing to do for it."

"Poor girl," I say, shivering despite the heat.

"It's easy to feel pity when they're already dead," Curtis says, quietly. "But alive, she would've killed you soon as looked at you, and felt nothing for it."

"I know," I tell him. "Believe me, I know. But she was somebody's daughter once, and she never asked for this."

She looks sad. Sad, and confused. I've always wondered how much they understand. They feel pain, but what else is in their fever-cooked minds? Something drives them, fear or anger or hunger. Do they know what they are, what they've become? Are they still in there somewhere, trapped and unable to get out? That would be the cruelest joke of all.

And what if they are aware? What if it isn't the fever that sends them lunging at the healthy, teeth snapping and fingers tearing? Maybe we have it wrong. Maybe this is what humans are truly like, when you take away reason and control and hope. Maybe the shakes aren't sick; maybe they're just honest.

We leave the woman where we found her. It feels disrespectful, but we have no shovels and no time for grave digging. I comfort myself with the thought that whoever she was, that girl died a long time ago. This heap of teeth and finger bones is no more a person than husked-off snakeskin; it's just meaningless leftovers shriveling in the sun.

We only make it a few steps before we hear the growling.

33.

The coyote stares at us with black eyes, his mottled gray fur bristled and his shoulders hunched forward. His ears lie almost flat along his skull, hackles raised, and I don't need to see the old blood and spit around his muzzle to know what's wrong with him.

"Nobody move," Curtis says in a whisper. His knuckles are white on Nana's lead, he's gripping so hard. "Everyone stay very, very still."

The coyote wrinkles his lips back and growls deep in his throat. The sound raises the fine hairs along my arms. My muscles clench, preparing to fight without my direction.

"Easy, boy," Ben says, keeping his voice low.

The coyote snarls, loud and sharp, and everything in

me screams to turn and flee. My mind knows it would be on top of me in a moment, shredding me with those teeth and those claws, but my body just wants to run, run, run. Does it ever get to be too much, when your body can't take it anymore and stops reacting? Even now, with poison making its slow way through my veins, my body is fighting to stay alive.

There's a soft click, and it takes all my focus to not whip my head around. I take a deep breath and turn my head unhurriedly. Curtis is pulling his gun from his belt, so slowly I have to keep watching to make sure he's moving at all.

The coyote shifts, his shoulders arching. He takes one step forward, and then another, his eyes focused on Curtis.

"Curtis," Ben says, hissing at his brother. "Shoot it."

"Quiet," Curtis hisses back.

"Now, Curtis."

With a loud curse, Curtis yanks his gun free just as the coyote lunges at him. A shot goes off, I think I scream, and there's blood on the ground. The coyote drops back, twisting his body, and I see a long streak of red against his ribs. The shot just grazed him, and once my brain catches up with my eyes, I pull out my own gun.

The coyote licks at his wound and bares his teeth, his growl turning into a high-pitched whine. The sound eats at my heart; I make a bad daughter for a trapper, I hate to hear animals in pain.

I aim at the coyote's head, wanting to put him out of his misery. I pull the trigger and hear echoing shots from Curtis. The coyote yelps and falls to the dirt, his legs scrabbling at nothing. Poor thing; what chance did he have against humans with guns?

The blood slowly stains his fur and pools into the dirt. His eyes start to glaze over as he gives up whatever it is that makes him a coyote.

"I think it's dead," Micah says when the animal stops breathing.

"Right. We're done here," Ben says. "Nobody touch it," he adds, glancing in my direction.

"Everyone keep your wits about you," Curtis says. "Seems to be that kind of morning."

I don't touch the coyote, even though I wish I could close his eyes. Even though it couldn't hurt me. I sigh to myself as we move away; I'm tired of watching things die.

34.

A hot wind starts to pick up in the early afternoon. It's rare to have any kind of breeze out here in the flatlands, and I'm thankful for it. The wind buffets my cheeks like a warm breath, drying my sweat and spitting bits of dust and gravel into my eyes. Cockleburs skitter across the dirt purposefully, snagging on unwary bits of cotton and hair. I pull a sticker off my sleeve and flick it away, doing my part to spread the weeds.

"Move in," Ben calls, and the wind snatches up his words and throws them back to me. He points to a marker by the road; Curtis nods, but it means nothing to me. He motions for Micah and Sam and they trot up from the rear.

Ben waits for us to come level to him and Curtis

wraps Nana's lead firmly around his wrist.

"Stay close now," Curtis tells us. "We're gonna be passing by Silver."

Sam's eyes widen and I suck in my breath. Silver. The name is a warning, a threat parents use to scare unruly children. Be good or I'll send you to Silver. Count your blessings we're not in Silver. I used to have nightmares about it, what feels like forever ago.

It wasn't always a ghost story. Before it was a cautionary tale, it was a town. Nicer than Glory, bigger than Best, twice as many folks as Hide Town. They had a dress shop and a bank, a dance hall and a gin mill that was famous for its sour mash whiskey. Of course the sickness hit them first. And that many people, all packed together; there was no stopping it. The shakes spread like wildfire, and the whole town was sick in a handful of days. Afterward, folks figured out pretty quick to set up fences around the towns. As for Silver, it was too late to do anything but keep a distance.

"Stay together and stay sharp," Curtis says. "We're gonna give the city a wide berth, but there could be shakes out roaming."

"How many are still in there?" Micah asks.

"Enough," Curtis says.

A chill creeps up like a cold finger along my spine. The sickness kills your brain, but there's something about Silver that calls to the shakes, drawing them in like moths to the memory of a flame. They know the town is theirs now. Who knows how many are in there, feeding off the dead and hiding in the shadows.

"Eyes open and guns close," Ben says. "Understood?"

He looks at each of us in turn, and I swear he takes longest with me. Does he still not trust me? If fighting side by side won't convince him I belong out here, I don't know what will. It shouldn't sting, but it does.

"Ben, I'll be point man," Curtis says.

Ben nods and Curtis moves up to the front of our grimy group. The wind whips thin blades of ocotillo and they lash against my legs. As we get closer, I can make out the crumbling walls still standing in Silver and slight movement in between. There's a howling in my ears, whether from the wind or from Silver I cannot tell.

"Guns out," Curtis says, just loud enough for us to hear him, loosing one of his long-nosed revolvers from his belt. I pull my own revolver from its holster and cock it and I immediately feel surer with its weight in my hand. Micah slings his rifle off his back, and Sam produces a small pistol he was hiding somewhere. Ben opts for his smaller gun, too, leaving his rifle in place. We move forward, and I feel invincible with all this hardware glinting in the sun.

We reach the outskirts of the ghost town, and even at a distance my confidence starts to fade. It's one thing to know a place is abandoned, but it's another to see the outline of a single boot decaying in the sun and know that a foot used to wear it, used to live in it. The houses are hollowed-out shells now, sand-swept and overgrown with tarbush. This is the future that waits for Glory, if things keep up. Whether we go one by one or all at once, the end result is the same. At least I won't be around to watch it crumble.

We fan out along on the road, keeping Silver to the left. A high wail comes from somewhere inside and I shudder. I can't keep my eyes off the skyline of the town, dark walls jutting up into empty air. The sky has turned sour, bruised gray and green. This whole place feels ill, like the sickness sunk into the ground and spit into the sky. It doesn't take long to pass the town, but it still isn't quick enough for me. Time must move slower the more alert you are, every second stretching out painfully. When we clear the last sunken building, the minutes snap back into place and my shoulders start to ache as the tension leaves them.

"We're clear," Curtis says, smiling over his shoulder. "Not so bad, right?"

A dust devil whips up in the distance, doing its lonesome spinning dance. The dust swirls and separates, evaporating into the air like it was never there at all. But I saw it; that counts for something. I risk a look back at Silver, and from a distance it looks harmless, sad even; all those empty houses suspended in time. I pity the unmade beds still waiting to be slept in, the overturned chairs that will never be righted.

"What's wrong?" Micah asks me, nudging me with his arm. "You look more grim than usual."

"Just spooked, is all," I tell him. "Everything we hear about Silver, and there it is. It's like seeing a ghost."

"How hard did you get hit in the head?"

That makes me smile, like he knew it would. "Those stories scared you right enough, if I remember."

"Not as much as Doc Kincaid's story about the grass widow who wanted to marry him," Micah says, nodding to Sam.

"Oh, her," Sam says, shuddering. "That woman was

a terror. I don't think I ever saw Pa hide from anyone before."

"How come you're not hitched, Curtis?" I ask him.

"You offering?" he says with a smile.

"I already got two boys to look after, I don't need another. But I can find you a nice yellow-haired woman if you're interested."

"Thank you kindly, but my heart belongs to another. I'm just waiting for her to come around."

Ben snorts. "You'll be waiting a long time, brother."

"Anyone we know?" Sam asks.

"It's not for me to say," Curtis says.

Ben mouths a name at me, and I start to giggle.

"Elsie?" I repeat, and Sam and Micah break out laughing.

"What's so damn funny?" Curtis asks.

I take a breath and choke back my laughter. "Curtis, Elsie runs the Homestead. Do you know how many men spend all day in there drinking?"

"So?"

"So there's not a hunter in Glory who hasn't propositioned her at least once. It'll take more than time for her to come around."

Curtis sighs heavily. "Then I'll just have to prove I'm

worthy. Always did like red hair."

Sam and Micah make kissing noises at him until he swats them away.

"Curtis," Ben says, his voice strange.

"Just y'all wait until you're heartsick and see how kind I am."

"Curtis!" Ben yells, and we all look at him.

"What?"

"That." Ben points behind us. I whip around, hand on my gun, ready for a fight. There's nothing there, no shakes, no nothing. But I'm staring at the wrong spot; I lift my eyes higher and see a reddish-brown wall rising into the sickly sky.

There's no need to say it, but I do anyway. "Dust storm."

35.

The last dust storm I remember was right before the twins were born. Ma was huge, her belly like a perfectly rounded egg. The storm didn't hit us directly, but the sky was green and foul for days. Ma made us stay inside and stuffed rags into the cracks in the windows. I remember her squatting by the door, trying to plug the gap in the sill. Even locked inside, the air turned our eyes hot and bloodshot and made us cough up red dirt and spit.

"What do we do?" Sam asks, his voice tight. When no one answers, he looks at Ben insistently. "What do we do?"

"How far to the next box?" I ask, my mind racing. It's got to be at least five miles since we left the station; it can't be that much farther.

"Two miles," Ben answers. I can see the muscles of his jaw working beneath his beard.

"It'll hit us before we make that," Micah says, his eyes calculating the edge of the storm.

"Curtis?" Ben asks.

Curtis still has his sight on the dust cloud, a deep wrinkle between his eyes.

"Curtis?" Ben asks again, loudly, and Curtis jerks his head to face his brother.

"Run," he says, simply. "We run for it."

Curtis checks his grip on Nana and starts to move.

"No, stop," I call out. "Stop."

"What is it?" Micah asks.

"Keep moving," Curtis orders.

"But Curtis—"

"We can't stop, Willie," he says.

"We came this way," I tell him. "We're retracing our steps."

"We have to get to shelter."

"The hotbox is that way," and I point in the opposite direction.

"We ain't gonna make it to the box."

It takes me a heartbeat to understand.

"You can't be serious," I say. "We can't go to Silver," and I hate how childish my voice sounds.

"It's moving too fast; we can't cover two miles. We get caught in that storm we won't be able to breathe," Curtis says. "We'll be blind, and that sand can strip the skin from your bones."

"But—" I don't even know where to begin; this is madness. You run away from danger, not toward it.

"Will, he's right," Sam puts in. "We'll suffocate."

"Come on, Sis," Micah says, pulling me forward. "We gotta go."

"But it's Silver, Micah," I tell him.

"I know. We still gotta go."

And so we do; we start to move at a pace somewhere between walking and running, an awkward stride that pains my joints. Every step sets the bones in my knees grating against one another, and I bite the inside of my cheek to stop from groaning. We follow Curtis, who pulls Nana along in a series of sprints and stalls. None of us can keep this up for long, not in this heat. The sun glares down at us balefully and the hot blasts of wind sear my lungs. Sweat pools at my collarbone and the small of my back, soaking my shirt. My breath comes hard and fast, rattling in my chest; I lower my head to stop sucking in the dusty air. I'm staring at the ground, my eyes watering so that everything looks like gray smudges. It's better this way, that I can't see the town coming closer. Somehow I've found myself in one of my nightmares, and I can't even pretend I'm dreaming because my side is aching too sharply.

"Faster," Curtis yells back at us. "We have to reach the town before the storm hits."

He lets us stop only to drink hurried gulps of water, and each time the edge of the storm looms closer. I start to think it's not a dust storm, but a mountain, and we're the ones moving toward it. My body feels close to its breaking point when from the corner of my eye I see Micah stumble, his foot caught on a burroweed branch. He falls, his hands and knees slapping the dirt. I run over and hoist him up easily; he's distressingly light.

"I'm fine, Sis, keep going," he tells me, panting.

"Don't be stupid, I ain't going anywhere." I have to shout to be heard over the wind.

Micah gingerly tests his weight on his foot; he winces, but it holds. I give him my arm to lean on and look for the others.

"Over here," Curtis yells, barely visible through the haze. Behind him walls rise up out of the dust, more ominous because I can't see where they start. My hands tremble, and I can't tell if I'm afraid because I know I should be, or because I really am. Micah squeezes my arm and we make our way to the others, their figures strange and blurred.

"Stay as close as you can," Curtis shouts, clapping his hand on Sam's shoulder. "When the storm hits, the shakes won't be able to see any better than we will. We'll hole up in a house and wait it out."

The wind pulls out strands of my hair and whips them back across my face. I squint and tug my hat farther down my head.

"Keep a hand on the person next to you," Curtis goes on. "I'll go first. Ben, you're at back. Try and protect your face. Understood?"

Micah tightens his grip on me and grabs Sam's free shoulder. Another hand settles on my own shoulder, heavy and warm, and I tilt my head up.

"Brace yourself," Ben says, his voice muffled. I reckon he pulled his shirt over his mouth and I wish I could see him more clearly and then I realize I can't see at all; we're inside the storm.

36.

Everything is gray and murky, like my eyes are wrapped in gauze. The sun's gone black and the air feels like it's on fire, spitting and sparking in the dark. The wind whips and howls around me, an angry and vengeful thing; it freezes the sweat at my back and I start to shiver, cold and raw and frantic.

A tug on my arm brings me to my senses and I hurriedly raise my shirt to cover my nose and mouth. I can breathe, just barely, but the air tastes sour and sickly on my tongue. Micah pulls me forward, one painstaking step at a time. The wind screams and claws at me like I am insubstantial, like only the weight of Ben's hand on my shoulder is keeping me grounded. Without it the wind would snatch me up and toss me around like so many cottonseeds.

It takes us forever to move forward, the wind fighting us for every step. I keep my mind away from where we are and think instead of what we must look like: five tall children playing red rover in a dust storm. I have a sudden and wild urge to laugh, and then something solid and warm slams into me and I go flying.

The ground rushes up to meet me and I land hard on my hip and shoulder. A beat later something lands on top of me; I try to push it off and meet cloth and hot skin. Then fingernails are clawing at me, scraping against my shirt and ribs, trying to tear through to my skin. I open my mouth to scream and a rush of dirt and sand and clay shove their way into my throat. I choke and cough and flail my legs out; one of them connects and I kick again as hard as I can and dislodge the shake from my body. I scramble away, crawling on all fours and gasping, and I can't see or hear or breathe. This is what it feels like to drown in the desert.

I reach out blindly with one hand, desperate. But there's nothing; there's nothing weighing me down, there's nothing to cling to. There's dirt in my lungs and sand in my eyes and the storm rages on, unrelenting as life. The wind spits at me, pushing in from all sides like it's trying to crush me. I dig my heels into the dirt and curl in on myself, lost and blind in the dark. Above me the air keeps to its crying, and below me the sand fights to escape. I am nothing at all to this storm. Just a piece of debris caught in her path, like an ant or a stone. I've never felt so insignificant, and all I can think is that I don't want to be alone.

I struggle to my feet while the wind fights to keep me down. I spread my arms out wide, reaching for anyone, anything to hold on to. I move forward, or maybe back, or maybe in no direction at all. I think I hear shrieking and I feel my way toward it, not caring if it's only the wind or shakes. Halfway through a step my hand hits something soft and warm and I desperately cling to whatever it is. A hand grips my arm and pulls me forward. I don't know how, because I can't see him or hear him and there's no real reason for it, but I know it's Ben. I grab a fistful of his shirt and twist my fingers in it, as much to keep ahold of him as to make sure he's real. I'm so grateful I have to stop myself from crying.

He moves his mouth next to my ear and the coarse hairs of his beard itch against my skin.

"Don't do that again," he shouts, and I elbow him in the stomach for ruining the moment.

I lift the collar of my shirt to cover my nose and mouth and close my eyes to the sharp grit. I can't hide the rest of me, and the wind sends wave after wave of dirt and debris to pummel my arms and legs and sting my cheeks. I brace myself, hunching my shoulders and leaning into Ben. We stagger once or twice but he pulls me along, sure of where he's going. The world boils down to just this: the wind in my ears and sand in my face and Ben's arm around me.

A whistle pierces the roar of the air, and Ben whistles back, high and sharp. He turns to the right a bit, and Curtis, because it must be Curtis, whistles again. This time it sounds much closer. My foot scrapes against wood, and then we're being pulled through a door into a dark room, blessedly free of the wind and sand.

"I got her," Ben says.

"I got Micah," Curtis answers.

My eyes are crusted with dirt, and I blink to clear them. It takes a moment, but slowly I make out that we're in someone's house, the main room by the look of it. Nana stands in one corner, looking out of place and unconcerned. Curtis shoves the wooden bar across the door into place, and then Micah slings an arm around my shoulders in a feeble hug.

"One hit you too?" I ask him, pushing him back so I can check for injuries. My voice comes out strange, muffled by my shirt and caked with dirt. He nods, and a cloud of dust comes out of his hair.

"I'm fine. You all right?"

I nod; my skin is raw and red and chapped by the sand and my ears are ringing, but that's the least of my worries at this point. I'm just happy to be inside and out of the storm.

"Check the windows, make sure they'll hold," Curtis says, his voice thick with sand.

Wooden planks are nailed across both windows; whoever these people were, they must've tried to wait out the sickness. One window is completely blocked, but some of the planks have rotted through on the other. I'm exhausted, so I let Sam and Micah flip the table and place it upright against the wall, covering the exposed area.

"This'll work," Curtis says, nodding. "Stay away from the door, but we should be safe enough till the storm passes."

"How are we gonna get out?" Micah asks. "We can't stay in here forever."

"The storm should daze the shakes, some," Curtis

answers. "Even they can't survive that sand. They'll hole up somewhere, same as us. We might be able to leave without too much notice, if we stay quiet and out of sight. Either that, or we shoot our way out." He sighs and runs a hand through his hair, dislodging a cloud of dust. "Look, I know it's not ideal, but we're making the best of a bad situation. One problem at a time, all right?"

The house is bigger than ours, and well kept, though the furniture is nothing fine. There's a large threadbare rug covered with sand blown in through small cracks in the walls. Everywhere I see signs of former life: a broken mug, a tarnished and cloudy silver mirror, a bowl turned on its side like an unfinished thought. They left in a hurry; there's a pot of something now thick and black sitting on the stove. There are three shelves with rusted pots, a pile of shriveled firewood stacked neatly, four sagging chairs pushed back from the missing table. Ratted curtains may have been lace once, and a rotted ladder leads up to what I suppose is the attic bedroom. The house feels lonely, pining for its family; the waste of it sickens me.

"Here," Curtis says, passing around water. "I'll check the shelves, see if there's anything worth taking. Ben, check the lamps, will you?"

The water dislodges the grit from my throat, and Sam finds a quilt that smells of mold to wipe the dust from our faces. He takes his glasses off to clean them, leaving two perfectly round dirt-free spots around his eyes.

There are two kerosene lamps, both painted prettily with flowers. The first is empty, but the second still has a full fount. Ben tries to light it, but the fire won't catch.

"Give it here," Micah says, and Ben glances at me.

"Micah knows what he's doing," I tell him, and he shrugs and hands the lamp over.

Micah pulls the blade from his belt and digs something oily and black out of the lamp, then cuts off the top of the wick.

"Try it now," he says.

Ben flicks his lighter again, and this time the wick catches and holds. Once the dust burns off it glows steadily, though he turns it low to save the oil.

"I reckon these might still be good," Curtis calls, holding up two cans with the labels long since peeled off. "Y'all may as well get comfortable. Nothing left to do but wait."

37.

The storm lasts minutes, or maybe hours, or maybe days. Inside the house, I lose track of time. It's dark, the storm sucking all the light from the sky. Or maybe there's no more light; it could be midnight or high noon for all I can tell, the lamp casting long shadows on the floor. My back aches from bracing against the wind and my cheeks still sting from the sand.

The cans turn out to be stewed carrots, which we eat cold with some biscuits and hard cheese from the way station. My gun is packed with sand, and I hand it off to Micah for fixing; he's better with the fiddly parts than I am. Outside the wind beats against the walls, throwing fistfuls of debris with a determination that feels personal.

The waiting is the worst part. Ben throws his knife at the floor, where it lodges in the wood, upright and defiant. He tugs it out and tosses it again, and again, making a rhythmic thumping until Curtis glares at him to stop.

I sit on the old rug, away from the others, wanting only my own company. I cross my legs and I'm tempted to pull my boots off to give my feet some air, but when I try and tug them off they won't come. My feet are swollen from all the walking, so I give up on the boots and just let them rest. Curtis and Sam poke around the room until they're sure there's nothing of interest, then they flop down on the chairs, noisily and gracelessly, stirring up plumes of dust. The swirls lift into the air, and for a moment I see shapes in it. A cat jumping, a ship with a sail; is this what people see when they look at the stars? I've never been able to see the constellations, to find the plow or the bear in the tangle of lights. It doesn't make sense to me, to single out one bright spot in the spiderweb. I can't see anything but everything, all at once.

For a while no one says anything, and in a way it's peaceful. Or it would be if everyone weren't thinking so loud I swear I can almost hear it. Sam is thinking about how much longer the storm will last, how much water we'll need, doing the calculations in his doctor's brain. Micah is fussing with the barrel of my gun and wishing he had a different life, one where nothing is uncertain and everyone has a future. Curtis is planning, checking his watch, running scenarios in his head and weighing the results. I know what it's like to have people depending on you, looking to you for guidance; it's a lonely state, one I don't begrudge him. And Ben, Ben the gruff and taciturn; him I just can't read. He stares at the gashes his knife made in the wood, I would swear he's not thinking anything if I didn't know better. Maybe he's scared; I'm scared. I'm scared I won't leave this house, that I'll become one of the ghosts haunting it. I'm scared because it's not enough to have a plan. I had a plan, and look where it got me.

My hand hurts. The pressure is building up, the blood and the disease packed tight beneath my skin. I try not to think on it, but it throbs along with my pulse. Every heartbeat only serves to remind me that my heartbeats are numbered. I don't want to be stuck in this house, I don't have the luxury of time. My backside goes numb from sitting in one spot on the frayed rug, counting down the hours I'm wasting.

And then, when I'm starting to forget how time passes, the wind dies without so much as a good-bye. Light breaks through the cracks in the walls, spilling faint and yellow onto the floor.

"Is it over?" Sam asks, getting to his feet.

Curtis holds a finger to his lips and crosses over to a window. He presses his eye to the slit between two planks of wood.

"Looks clear," he whispers, stepping back.

After the noise of the storm, the silence is deafening. It takes a moment for my ears to adjust, and that's when I start to sense it. It's nothing I can hear, not voices or the din of people living, but it's there, on the edge of my awareness. A presence made up of shallow gasps and drawn-out sighs, the thousand tiny creaks and moans of shifting bodies.

"They're out there," I breathe.

"They don't know we're here," Ben says, his voice low. "Curtis, how do you want to do this?"

Curtis shakes his head. "I'm not sure." He pulls out his watch, looking down at it and frowning. "All right, listen up." He sits back on his chair and we gaze up at him, like he's about to tell us a story. "We've only got a few hours of light left. I'm putting this to all of you: we can stay the night here and leave in the morning, but the shakes are gonna be rowdier by then. Or we can leave now, while they're still shook up from the storm, but we won't make it to Best before sunset. That means we'll have to stay out through the night, find a hotbox to hole up in. I leave it up to y'all to decide."

Micah looks contemplative, but I don't need to think about it; I don't have a night to spare.

"I think we should go now," I say firmly.

"I don't know, Willie," Sam says. "We'll be blind at night, we won't be able to see any shakes."

"Better one shake at night than dozens in the morning," I counter.

A wail comes from outside, piercing and long. The hairs on my neck stand up, and then other voices join, shrill snappings and low moans. It's like some horrible song, all discorded and jangled, and then the howl cuts off in a choked gurgle.

"What are they doing?" Micah whispers, nervously handing my clean gun over.

"Eating their dead," Curtis answers, his face stone.

I shudder, my stomach turning over. They have to eat something to survive, but I don't want to hear it; I don't want to have to picture the torn skin and broken bones. At least they wait until one of them is dead; it's the only civil thing shakes do.

Over the awful noises comes a panicked bray from the corner, loud and startling; Nana's eyes are large and white with fright.

"Easy, girl," Curtis says, running over to her. "Easy."

Nana screams and shakes her head, pawing at the floor. Curtis strokes her neck, but she jerks away.

"Curtis, shut her up," Ben hisses at him.

But the mule is beyond help. She kicks her back legs out, smacking the wall and leaving two huge cracks. Curtis grabs for her reins, but he's too late; Nana jolts forward, half mad with fear, and strikes at the door with her front legs. It splinters and breaks, the wood bowing out and light coming in.

"Stop her," Curtis cries, but she rears up and we can't get between her hooves and the door. She brings it down with an echoing crash, then leaps over the frame and she's gone, out into the sunlight and whatever lies in wait.

38.

I stare at the empty doorway in shock, half expecting her to come back. She can't really be gone; if we lost Nana, we lost everything she was carrying. All we have left is what's on our backs. Curtis takes a step toward the door like he wants to go after her; his face is as drawn as I've ever seen it.

"Everyone back," Ben says, urgently. "Get back. Curtis, help me," and he grabs the legs of the table, dragging it away from the window. "There's no way they didn't hear that."

Curtis blinks, like he doesn't understand what Ben's saying.

"Curtis," Ben shouts at him. "I need you here, brother."

Curtis stirs himself and runs to help. "I'm sorry, I'm here."

They shove the table against the gaping hole in the door, and Ben drags a heavy chest in front of it. There's a loud thud as something bangs against the house.

"I guess they're here, too," Curtis adds, and my stomach drops.

Ben goes to the window and squints outside.

"I can't make out—there's at least three. More coming, but I reckon they'll mostly be aiming for the front."

Something slams against the broken door and I let out a startled yelp. The table shudders and Micah and Sam scurry back, as far from the door as they can get.

Curtis swears and frees his gun from its holster. He braces one arm against the table, holding it in place. "Ben, get over here. If we keep the door blocked, it should take them some time to get through."

"But they will get through?" Micah asks.

"Eventually, yes. It won't hold forever."

Ben pulls out his smaller gun, leaving the rifle on his back and going to stand next to his brother with the same resigned expression. He shoves his shoulder into the table, looking relaxed, like he just wanted to lean against it.

"When they get through, we start shooting. We can bottle up the door with bodies, that oughta slow them down," Curtis says.

But not stop them. There's five of us, and who knows how many of them. We'll run out of bullets before we run out of shakes.

"Make every shot count," Ben says. "Maybe we can last."

My hand wraps around the butt of my gun and it feels cold. Maybe this is for the best; better to go out in a hot blaze of gun smoke and grit than to wait for my body to turn on me.

"We need to get out of here," Sam says, turning in a panicked circle, looking like a cornered animal.

"We can't, Sam," Micah tells him, his lips tight.

The sharp creak of breaking glass whips my head around, and a shake's face and arm thrust through the exposed window.

"Micah, windows," I yell, and run forward, pulling my gun free. I carefully aim for the head and shoot, and the bullet finds its target. The shake slumps over, its blood dripping down the wall. Maybe this would be a good end for me, but not for the others. I can't let Micah die like this, I can't let go just yet.

A crash from behind me signals the end of the other window. I turn around and see a shake launch its body through the shards of glass. Micah's there, but the shake rushes him before he gets a shot off. I scream and raise my gun, but I can't shoot it with Micah underneath. He grabs the shake by the wrists, keeping its teeth out of range. The shake snarls, biting the empty air in front of Micah's face.

"Willie," Micah yells, struggling to keep the teeth away.

"Shoot it," Curtis shouts at me.

"Hold on! Sam, chair," I order him. "Get that thing off him."

Sam, quick as ever, understands right away. He grabs one of the chairs and with a grunt he swings it at the shake, knocking it clean off of Micah. It lands with a growl and I put two bullets in its chest before it has a chance to get up again.

"Thanks," Micah gasps, sitting up.

A loud bang from the front door ends my relief.

"Hold those windows," Ben says, grimacing as he repositions himself against the table.

"You two take that one," I tell Micah and Sam. I retreat to the other window, the blood now pooling in a large circle on the floor. A stray arm tries to shove its way past the dead shake. I shoot once and it recoils.

They're going to get in; I should prepare myself. It's only a matter of time now. I thought I would be scared. I mean, I am scared, but more than that, I'm angry. I flash back to McAllister at my door, barging in and threatening my family, to Dollarhide sneering in my face, trying to steal what little I have. I'm tired of being pushed around and bullied, I'm tired of losing. I didn't come all this way only to get trapped in this house with shakes at the walls, and I'll be damned if I'm just going to sit around and wait for them to kill us. If I'm going to die in a rundown house, at least it's going to be *my* rundown house. I didn't think I would ever miss it, but I do; I miss my bed and the stove that smokes and the patched-up roof and most of all the twins, dirty and sweaty and always underfoot. Or under—

"Micah," I yell. "Cover this window."

"Why?" he asks, confused but obliging.

I lean over and rip the rug aside. "The floor."

I kneel down and dig at a floorboard, my fingers scraping for purchase against the rough wood.

"What about it?" Sam asks, but Micah catches on

quickly, having chased the twins under the house often enough.

"Knife, Will," he orders, pulling out his own and wedging it between two planks of wood. "Sam, keep on the windows."

I grab my knife and jam it into the next slat; it's a tight fit, and I stomp on the handle to push it in farther.

"What are you doing?" Ben asks.

"I'm getting us out of here," I reply. "I hope." There's a bang from outside, and I swallow hard.

When my knife reaches as far as it will go, I use it as a lever to pry up the board. One side comes loose, and I dig my fingers underneath it, hoping with everything I can muster that they built the foundation high enough. I grunt and yank the board free and crouch down to look underneath. I reach one arm out, my fingers trembling, and I don't touch the ground until my entire arm disappears beneath the floor. I let out a triumphant cry and grin up at the others.

"We can fit," I say.

After the first board, the others tug out easily, and with Micah helping it only takes a minute to make a large-enough hole. I jump down and land with a jolt that pains my knees. I fall to a crouch, then push my legs back until I'm lying flat on the ground with my elbows propping me up. It's dim and musty smelling, and my face immediately catches on a spiderweb. I wipe the strands away and focus on the gaps between the stones the house rests on. Ahead is a tangle of legs and feet, a swarm of shakes clamoring to get through the front door. At the windows, too, all of them so packed together I can't count how many. They feel closer somehow, with no wall to protect me. I scoot back involuntarily and turn my head to look toward the rear of the house; I see three, maybe four pairs of legs. That's as clear as it's going to get, I reckon.

"Willie?" Micah lowers his head down and spots me. "How's it looking?"

I wiggle my way closer and throw out an arm; Micah clasps it and hauls me up out of the hole. Jagged pieces of wood scape my back as I stand, and I wipe dirt and cobwebs out of my hair.

"I think we can get out if we head out the back way," I say, breathing heavily. "There's not as many over there." I look up at Curtis and Ben, trying to keep the pleading out of my eyes; I want them to take charge, tell me this is the right thing to do.

The brothers exchange a quick glance, straining to

keep the door blocked, and Curtis nods sharply.

"Let's do it," he says. "Y'all go ahead, we'll hold them till the last second."

"Come on," I say, motioning at Sam and Micah. "You two first. Wait for us once you're down there."

Sam squeezes my arm briefly and climbs down, his face disappearing as he stretches out flat. He moves forward until I can't see his feet, and I wave to Micah.

"You next."

"You should be—" he starts, but I am in no mood.

"Micah, just go," I say, ready to shove him into the damn hole if he doesn't cooperate. Maybe he can see that, because he jumps down and crawls out of sight in no time.

I follow Micah, stepping both feet into the hole. I look over at the Garretts, not wanting to leave them. Curtis turns so his back is flat against the table.

"Go," is all he says, and Ben moves away from the door, grabbing the lamp on his way toward me.

"Get down," he tells me as he swings his feet over, and I reluctantly lower myself. Micah and Sam wait a few feet away, their faces shadowed. I keep close to where Ben stands, angling my head so I can see his face.

"Come on, Curtis," he says. "We're ready."

Boots run on wood, and then there's the thump of the table falling down just as Curtis's feet appear. I can't see them, but I can hear the shakes pushing their way in, scraping and snarling at one another, and I shudder at how close they are.

"Do it," Curtis says, and Ben raises the lamp. I don't understand what he's going to do until it's too late, and I cry out as he throws it. The second it takes to fall stretches out interminably, and then the crash comes and my eyes fill with flames.

39.

I back away from the Garretts, flat on my stomach and feeling ill. From the house come screams and the sigh of fire and the smell of charred wood and singed hair.

I crawl toward Micah and Sam quickly, my gun digging into my hip, trying to outrun the stench of burning bodies I know is coming. Ben and Curtis are behind me, but their size makes it slower going.

"What the hell was that?" Micah asks me when I get close, his forehead beaded with sweat.

"The house is on fire," I answer.

"Damn. They don't play around, do they?"

"Guess not." Smoke is trickling in through the floorboards, stinging my eyes. "Let's just get the hell out of here before we burn, too."

"Agreed," Sam says wryly.

We inch forward to the edge of the house, intent on the sunlight. I don't see any of the shakes I saw before; maybe they moved to the front, or the fire scared them off. We wait a couple feet back, close enough to reach and stick an arm out but not so anything standing can see us. Ben and Curtis finally pull themselves alongside, both breathing heavily; it's a tight fit for them, and the guns can't have been comfortable.

"It looks clear," I tell them, jutting my chin forward.

"All right. Hold back a minute," Curtis says, and with a grunt he slithers out from underneath the house and rolls to his feet, gun in hand. His boots turn in a quick circle and then his face appears as he crouches down. "Let's go," he says.

We crawl out quickly and get to our feet, all of us red-faced and streaked with dirt. I squint, the light bright after the dimness beneath the house, and take my first real look around Silver. There's a large chunk of the roof missing from the house that we couldn't see from the inside; smoke billows out of it, dark and ashy. We're in between a number of small houses, all with damaged roofs and broken or boarded-up windows. I reckon those are the first to go; eventually the walls and the floorboards will sag and then all of these houses will crumple in on themselves.

Curtis motions us to follow him and he leads us down an alley of sorts between two rows of houses. We move quickly, and I count four places down when he calls a stop. Curtis ducks his head out of the alley and looks both ways.

"All right, we should be just off the road. Once we clear these houses, we turn right and then keep going till we make it out of town."

"Everyone keep as quiet as you can," Ben says. "If you see movement, call it."

"Guns out," Curtis says, and I pull my revolver, heavy and familiar in my hand as I reload.

"Ready? Let's move."

Curtis heads straight for the gap between two houses. We turn right and pop out on the main road, the lane stretching wide and overgrown with sticker grass. Curtis turns to face us and holds a finger to his lips. He points to where the road continues straight through the town, then holds up one finger, then two, then three. On three we move, as quick as we can without losing sight of our surroundings, all of us fanned out to face the town. Small houses give way to larger houses, many of them with smashed-in doors and black streaks of fire damage; they must've started looting the rich when everything went to hell. I glance over my shoulder to find the smoke spiraling into the sky; I guess we did our part, too.

The houses turn into shops, dilapidated with dark interiors, paint peeling from signs on the windows. We pass the law offices and the gin mill and I reckon we must be getting close to the edge of town. I glance inside a drooping building with a red door, and a face stares back at me. I halt, my eyes frozen on the sunken mouth and hollow cheeks. My gun is aimed straight at the shake, but he, I think it's a he, only stares blankly.

"Sign!" someone yells from behind me and a gun explodes, the blast echoing sharply. I flinch and look around wildly as another shot rings out; smoke trickles from the end of Curtis's gun, and a body slumps against a storefront. I spin back, but the shake I saw is gone, disappeared somewhere into the shadows.

"Keep moving," Curtis calls, and I tear my eyes away. We're almost running now, and my heart is pounding painfully in my chest. Micah is in the lead and I stay close, keeping him on my right while the Garretts take the rear. Long minutes pass without any noise, and I can see the last buildings of Silver and just beyond, the desert looms wide and empty.

"Behind you," Ben yells, and I spare a moment to look over my shoulder: three shakes tumble out from behind a corner, separating Micah and me from the rest. I shove my brother forward and speed up, but the shakes are doing that lurching run they do, their eyes mad and roving. Ben fires and hits one of the shakes in the shoulder; it spins and screams in pain and rage, but he can't shoot at the others without hitting one of us. Those two don't even pause, their minds long beyond reason.

"Micah, keep going," I order. I bring my gun up and take aim behind me, stopping for a long moment to get one in my sights. I breathe out and pull the trigger; the crack pierces my eardrums and the kick jolts my shoulder. The shake on the left goes down with a hole in his neck. I cock the trigger to shoot again when the second shake takes a running leap and slams me to the ground.

When my back hits the dirt the air goes out of my lungs and time slows down to a crawl. I can feel my chest struggling to rise with the weight of the shake on top of me, his knees digging into my abdomen. I blink, and it takes forever for my eyelids to make the journey.

I stare up into the sunken face of the shake, and he stares back at me with dull eyes. But then something flickers across his face, an expression so fleeting I can't put a name to it—recognition maybe, or regret? Time stretches between us, and as I finally manage to take a gasping breath I realize he's not attacking me. The shake cocks his head, the gesture half animal and half human, and then there's the familiar crack of a rifle and blood splatters across my face.

I scream and the shake slumps on top of me, his head a wet mess of hair and skin. Blood gushes from the wound, more blood than I could imagine fitting inside something so emaciated. I turn my face away as I struggle to get out from under him, his dead weight pinning me down.

"Get him off me," I beg, "get him off me!"

Micah grabs my arms and pulls, and Ben uses his boot to roll the shake over. I stand up, trembling and covered in someone else's insides.

"Did he bite you?" Micah asks, scanning my face and neck intently. "Did it get in your eyes?"

"No," I say, wiping blood from my cheek.

There's a shriek in the distance and we snap to attention.

"Later," Curtis says, and we keep moving. My ears are ringing, my lips are numb, and the air is hot with gunpowder and fire smoke. I'm afraid; a tremor starts in my stomach and veins out through my body. It's not the fear of dying, it's not the blood or the pain or the loss. It's the fear of knowing the truth, knowing it in my bones; this isn't some paltry infection from a dirty penknife. The last small shred of hope I had is gone. That shake looked at me, looked at me like he knew me. Like I was one of them. Like I'm already gone.

All around eyes watch me, eyes of the sick and the eyes of the dead. All over I feel them, the old ghosts and the bad dreams, all of them that haunt this place. We turn a corner and run past a hollow building, and then we burst into the open desert, and safety. I keep going, wanting to outrun those eyes, but the ghosts stay with me; I reckon they know I belong with them.

40.

Curtis finally calls a halt, long after my lungs start to scream and my legs start cramping. I brace my hands on my knees and wait for my ears to stop ringing.

"We can slow down. They won't follow," Curtis pants, "not when they got dead to eat."

I grimace and clench my teeth. My heart is pumping so fast it feels like one long burning beat, and I bend my head down to ease the pain. My hand cramps and I realize I'm still holding my gun, my fingers white from gripping so hard. I have to peel them back, one by one, until my revolver comes free and I can holster it. The hand starts to tingle something awful, and I stretch it out gently.

I look back at Silver, at the black smoke still spewing

into the air. How long will it take for the house to burn to the ground, and what will be left when it does? How many bones did we leave in our wake?

"Willie," Curtis says, looking me over. "You sure he didn't get you?"

I shake my head, too tired to even mouth no. I can still see the blood, can smell it on my skin, coppery and hot. I scrub my face with my hands, wishing I could do the same to my mind. My fingers come away stained red.

"Careful," Sam says, "don't get it in your mouth or eyes." He hands me a handkerchief.

"Then maybe," I say, wiping my hands, "y'all shouldn't shoot shakes when they're on top of me."

"Sorry about that," Ben says. "Didn't have a chair handy this time."

I toss the handkerchief on the ground where it flutters sadly.

"Everyone else in one piece?" Curtis asks.

"I think so," Sam says. He stares down at his hands like he's unsure they're still attached to his body.

"We got lucky, then," Ben says.

"You call that lucky?" Micah asks, incredulous. "We get caught in a dust storm, lose our packs, and get chased outta town by shakes?"

Ben shrugs. "No one died."

"Day ain't over yet," Micah grumbles.

"You're right about that," Curtis says. "We still got a ways to go, and little left to help us along."

We do a quick inventory, and it's not reassuring. I still have my coat and the pouch around my neck, and Sam held on to his doctor's kit, but we lost most of our food and drink. Between the five of us we have three and a half canteens of water, some crackers and crumbling cheese, one mottled apple, and a scad of bullets. Too bad we can't eat lead.

Curtis surveys our paltry supplies and runs a hand through his hair. "It'll get us to Best, at least. I know y'all are dragging, and I know we've been through the mill here, but we have to push on while we have the light. It's two miles to the next box, that'll have to do for tonight."

We each take one swig of water and save the rest for later. I don't remember ever being this weary before. My body goes through the motions, one foot after the other, and I'm not walking so much as trudging, trying not to fall too far behind. My hair smells like smoke and gunpowder, the back of my neck is tight with sunburn, and my skin itches with sweat and grime. At this point

I'd sell my soul for a bed and a bath.

We're walking straight east, our backs against the lowering sun. The sky looks split, half orange and half blue, like it can't decide if it's day or night. We head toward the night, or maybe it's coming for us, stretching out purple and black tendrils to eat the last of the light.

The stars blink on, first one and then another, and then the sky is scattered full of them. The moon hangs slim and long, frowning down at us from a great height. My eyes are heavy and starting to blur, doubling my vision and smearing the ground. I stumble over something I can't see and catch myself, pinching my arm to stay sharp.

"There, up ahead," Curtis calls at last, his voice weary. "I see it."

"Longest two miles I ever walked," Ben says. "I'm baked."

We drag ourselves to the hotbox, dead on our feet. It looks small in the night, a dark shape in a sea of dark shapes.

Curtis reaches the box first and hauls himself up the ridged side. The rest of us watch; I sway slightly trying to stand in place, and Micah drapes an elbow over my shoulder to prop himself up. Curtis pulls at a latch and swings open the hatch at the top, ducking his head down to check inside.

"All clear," he says, sighing. "It's gonna be a tight fit. Good thing none of you like to eat. Find some kindling and we'll get a fire going."

The ground cover is sparse, but I pull up some tanglehead grass and Micah and Sam collect whatever brush they can find that will burn. Curtis and Ben find a spot to dig a bowl into the dirt.

"Is it safe to build a fire?" I ask, throwing my heap of grass into the pit. "Won't the shakes see it?"

"That's the point," Ben answers. "They don't like fire, mostly stay away from it. Some animal thing, I reckon."

"I reckon," I say, soot from the last fire still on my skin.

"Besides," Ben adds, "even if they see it, least this way we can see them, too."

It doesn't take long for the brush to catch, and soon the air fills with the crack and spit of burning branches. It's so dry that the fire hardly smokes. It casts a small glow, enough I reckon to see the shakes just before they kill us. I should be scared, out here at night, but I'm so tired. I used up all my fear today; I don't have any left.

"You look beat," Micah says to me.

"So do you." Streaks of dirt and sweat run down Micah's face, and Sam's hair is thick with dust. Ben has it worse; his beard is two shades lighter and dripping sweat that's soaking into his shirt collar. I can't see my own face but I can picture the dark circles under my eyes and my lips are so cracked and dry that they sting when I lick them.

"I reckon we've all seen better days," Sam says, wiping his face with a dirty sleeve.

"I bet that Hide Town feller don't seem so bad right about now," I tell Ben.

He runs a hand through his beard, shedding dust. "The fix is worse, but the company's better. Least y'all can shoot worth a damn."

Somewhere along the way, Ben dropped the gravelly voice, too tired or too scared to keep up the act. More and more he's looking to Curtis to take the lead, just like the rest of us. I feel a pang of guilt; Curtis is trying so hard to keep us safe, and I've already brought danger among us. I look over at him; he's standing alone and apart from the rest of us, the price of being a leader. I swear the wrinkles on his forehead are deeper than they were a day ago.

"That should last awhile," Curtis says, poking at the

fire. "Let's get some rest."

Sam and Micah climb up first and I wait for them to drop into the box before I head up. I dig my fingers into the grooves, the wood still warm from the day. I reach the top and take a moment to look out across a desert made murky and remote by the starlight. It's dark inside the box but I can make out the top of Sam's sandy head, and I try not to land on him when I drop down.

"Ow," Micah hisses at me when I knock him with my elbow.

"Oh, hush," I say. "I barely touched you."

The air inside is warm and close, and I can hear Micah and Sam breathing like they're inside my head. The box clearly wasn't meant to hold many people; I have to stoop a bit or my head bangs against the tin roof.

"I'm coming down," Ben says from above us, and I press myself against a wall but still get a boot in my face.

Ben lands with a grunt and suddenly we're face-to-face and standing very close to one another. I'm all too aware of the dirt on my cheeks and I sincerely hope the sour smell in here isn't just me. Of all the things for me to worry about, it's stupid to care what Ben thinks of me; it shouldn't matter, it shouldn't bother me, but it does.

"Room for one more?" Curtis asks from above.

"Not really," Ben answers.

"Too bad," Curtis says, and lowers himself down. There's not much room to maneuver, but he manages to squeeze himself in.

"Well," he says, pulling the hatch shut and fastening the latch, "I'll take first watch. Make yourselves comfortable."

Ben snorts and Sam gives a tired laugh. We have to sleep sitting up, but we're tired enough I doubt anyone will care. I lost my blanket and my ripped-up shirt, but I still have my coat; I pull it off and scrunch it on the ground and crawl on top. Micah sits next to me, his head tilted back against the wall. From Sam's deep breathing, he must already be asleep. I rest my head on Micah's shoulder, my knees pulled up to my chest.

"You think we'll find Pa in Best?" Micah asks me, his voice close to my ear.

"I hope so."

He pulls something out of his pocket, and I squint in the dark to see it. His pocket watch, the broken one that he's kept all these years. It spins lazily, and I can't see them, but Pa's initials are engraved on the back: JHW.

"You know, this is the only thing he ever gave me," Micah says. "And he only let me keep it 'cause it's broke and he couldn't sell it."

"You still carry it, though."

"Yeah. Don't know why. What are you gonna say to him?"

"I don't know. I ain't got that far yet," I admit.

Micah puts the watch back in his pocket and sighs. "You might want to think on it."

"You always were the smart one."

"True enough. 'Night, Will."

"'Night."

I stare up at the tin roof and even though it's there to keep us safe, I wish I could see the sky. It's a strange thing to miss, because it's not really gone. I listen to Micah breathing and shift my head so his boney shoulder stops poking into my cheek. He needs to eat more, if only for my own comfort.

I want to stay awake; I need these moments, I want to have every thought I can possibly have before my mind burns up and spoils. It's useless, though, to fight against sleep, and my eyes shut against my will.

41.

In my dream, everything is on fire. I would move, but my feet are glued in place, and all I can do is watch as the flames start to lick at my ankles. The heat races up my legs, burning away my clothes and then starting in on my skin. I scream as my flesh starts to bubble and turn black, and then the fire is at my throat and pouring into my open mouth.

A gunshot wakes me and my eyes fly open; I cough and fight to catch my breath, still feeling the flames on my tongue. The warm stale air confuses me until another shot rings out and I remember where I am.

It's still full dark in the box; I must've only slept a few hours. I blink, and see a pair of eyes shining back at me.

"It's Ben," Micah whispers, his voice tired but scared. "Think he needs help?"

A breeze brushes across my cheeks and I look up to see stars; the hatch is open. I glance at the others and find Curtis and Sam still asleep. I reckon Curtis is used to sleeping through gunshots, and Sam is too exhausted to care.

"I'll go," I tell Micah quietly. "Go back to sleep."

He nods and gives my arm a brief squeeze. I reach for my gun and wrap my coat around my shoulders. My lips are dry but my eyes feel hot, and I shiver despite the temperature. The fever is starting to set in. I guess I was expecting it, but the reality is somehow crueler.

I carefully poke my head through the opening, my breath catching in my throat. Across the box Ben is sitting on the edge of the roof, his rifle across his lap and his face softly illuminated. With a grunt I haul myself up, my feet dangling and trying to catch on something that's not there.

"Did I wake you?" Ben asks quietly, his teeth flashing in the dark.

I make a noise that could be taken as a yes and sit down next to him but not too near. The fire has burned low, but the embers give off some heat and light.

"How many were there?"

"Just one. Been a slow night so far."

"How long have you been up?"

"Not long. I let Curtis take a breather."

"Isn't this dangerous? Being out like this?"

He nods toward the open hatch. "Time enough to get in if trouble comes calling. And I ain't so good with small spaces."

"I think for this one you'd be forgiven," I say. "I felt like a chicken in a coop."

I stretch out my arms and legs, enjoying the space.

"Is Curtis gonna be all right?" I ask. "He seemed awful upset about Nana."

"Yeah, well. Curtis gets attached too easy."

"And you don't?"

Ben shrugs, picking at a nail. It irks me, that I can't get a read on him.

"It didn't bother you," I ask, "setting that house on fire? Leaving all those people to die?"

"They ain't people," he says, still cleaning under his nails. "Not anymore, not really. They don't even know the difference, if they're alive or dead."

I shake my head; he heard those screams same as I did. "I guess it's easier, to think of them that way. To do what you do."

"Go ahead and judge me, Willie," he says, and I don't like the stress he puts on my name. "You know the sickness will kill them sooner or later. Drifting around the desert, eating scraps or each other—that ain't no kind of life. I won't weep for 'em."

"No," I say softly. "I don't expect you would."

Chills go along my arms and I tug my coat tighter. I don't want Ben's tears, but I do want to be remembered. I want to be remembered as me, as Willie, not as a shake, not as something disposable that's better off dead. So I guess it's my responsibility to remember those shakes in Silver as something more—as people, real people, with desires and regrets. People with names and shoes, sorrows and babies and hats; solid things that existed, proof their lives were real and familiar. I'll keep their memory if someone will only do the same for me.

Ben moves suddenly, lifting his rifle to his shoulder. He aims across the desert, at a dark and lonely shape.

The shot makes me flinch as the darkness swallows up the figure.

"They scream," I say softly, and he turns to look at me, his face shadowed. "So they must feel pain. There must be something still in there."

Ben gives me a strange look.

"I reckon," he says. We stare at each other for a long, tense moment, and then he lets out a breath and lowers his gun slowly.

"You should go back to sleep," he says, his voice flat.

"I've slept enough," I tell him. "I want to watch the sunrise."

"There's plenty of those to see," he says.

"Ain't you heard? It's never the same twice." I tuck my knees up and hug them close. "I don't want to miss this one."

He blinks at me and finally shifts his gaze away and it feels like I've lost something. "Whatever you say."

I'd like to think that I confuse him as much as he confuses me. I can never tell what he's thinking, or where I stand with him. We sit in silence, but it's not uncomfortable. I rest my chin on my knees and look up. Yesterday the night felt rich and soft, but that was a world ago. I find no joy in the darkness, only the cold certainty that the stars do not shine for those of us watching.

42.

The sky starts to lighten to pale blue streaked with gold, and the sun glints into view from behind a low mesa. I squint my eyes nearly shut and watch it rise beneath the shadows of my lashes. It's strange, but I feel calm right now, even with the sickness raging inside me. I know too well what's coming; at the end, Ma was mad with the fever, fighting ghosts only she could see. The room stank of dirty hair and her hand was just bone wrapped in gray gauze. This is only the calm before the storm, but I'll take whatever small bit of peace is offered.

The others start to stir, their breathing going from even sighs to short gasps as they wake up. Micah pops up from inside and blinks blearily, looking so much like a prairie dog that I smile. Ben gives up his watchful position and starts to walk a bit, getting his legs moving. The fire's gone cold, leaving nothing but a few blackened, cracked branches.

My stomach feels hollow, like it's been scooped out. I've been spoiled these last days; I'd almost forgotten what it feels like to be hungry. The pangs are familiar, an old enemy come calling. I reckon I should be used to it by now, but it doesn't really work that way.

I stand up and stretch my arms out, ignoring the throb of my hand. Being hungry makes me focused, makes me sharp. Dawn's a good time for rattlers, they'll still be sleepy from the cooler night. I scan the ground until I see a larger rock that looks promising.

"Micah," I call, and he yawns at me, still sleepy. "Rifle."

"What for?"

I jerk my head at the rocks. "Breakfast."

He nods and pulls his rifle from his back. With a grunt he tosses the gun at me and I catch it and swing it around to grip the barrel, ignoring the pinch of my cut. I free my knife and hand it to Micah and we approach the rock quietly, our movements familiar. Unless I miss my guess, there'll be something underneath.

"What are you two doing?" Curtis asks.

"We need food, right? Ready?" I ask my brother, and he nods. "Go."

Micah kicks over the rock with his boot, and the rattlesnake hisses at me, surprised and angry. I keep just out of its reach, and when it lunges at me I pin it behind the head with the butt of the rifle. Its tail thrashes around, the rattle a constant low buzz. Micah crouches down and with one swift slash he slices off the head. I let up with the rifle and we wait for the body to stop twitching, just like we have a hundred times before.

"Feels like home," I say to Micah, who pokes at the snake's head with his foot. I trade him the rifle for the knife and pick up the body to examine it; it's not the longest snake, but it's thick.

"What do you think?" I ask, holding up the snake for the others to see. "It's not Elsie's bread, but if you get the fire going again I'll do my best."

"Works for me," Curtis says.

I make a small cut down the neck and get a good grip, then yank the skin off in one long strip, like pulling off a sock. I cut it off at the tail, just before the rattle, which I break off and toss to Sam. I usually let the twins have the rattles, and they see which one can annoy me the most with the noise. Sam catches the tail and gives it a shake, setting it buzzing.

I focus on cutting up the snake, happy to have a task; I let my mind empty of everything but the simple act of pulling out the entrails. The morning sun beats down on the back of my neck, and my skin prickles with the heat. With my hands covered in snake guts and my stomach empty, I feel more like myself than I have since I left home.

We each get a chunk of snake meat on a stick or a knife tip to roast over the fire. I prefer snake when it's fried, but we're hardly in a position to be picky. Without any seasoning the meat is gamey but mild enough, and soon we're all scraping the last scraps off the ribs. It feels wrong to toss the skin away; I resist the urge to clean it and hang it to dry.

When we finish eating, Curtis quickly covers the remains of the fire with dirt, then passes around a canteen of water.

"Just one drink each," he tells us. "We gotta make it last."

I pick up a scoop of sandy dirt and scrub the blood and guts from my hands. Making sure no one is watching, I untie my filthy bandage. It sticks to my palm and I wince as I peel it off. The skin around my cut is swollen hard and weeping pus. I rewrap my hand with the same dirty cloth; it's not as if it can cause more damage. I tie the bandage tightly, and the pressure sends a tremor up my arm. I pull my sleeve down as far as it will go, but with shakes roaming around, no one is looking at my hands anyway.

When the water comes my way I reach for it with my good hand and take a long swig. It's warm and stale but I have to fight to keep from drinking more. The water sticks in my throat and I struggle to swallow. I finally get it down when my left arm spasms, then goes completely numb.

I freeze and school my features into a blank mask. I try to move my fingers, but my hand stays alarmingly still. I take a deep breath, and another, attempting to calm myself while my heart races. This is all in my head, it is not happening, I tell myself, while my arm dangles uselessly, heavy and immobile. And suddenly I know that this is not my arm, but a dead snake hanging from my shoulder. I don't know how it got there, but it is punishment, I think, for all the rattlers I've killed.

"Will," Micah says, nudging me. Why isn't he screaming?

"Give it here," he says, and I blink and everything

falls back into place. I hand the water to my brother, trembling. I flex my bad hand and stare at my curled fingers. I don't know if what I see is real anymore, but these are the only eyes I have.

"Micah," I say, my lips stumbling over the familiar name.

"What?"

"I—" I have to tell him. I have to, because if I can't trust myself, he's the only one left.

"Let's go," Curtis calls, and the words die on my tongue.

"Will?" Micah asks, frowning, but I shake my head.

"Nothing," I say, turning away. "Just a headache."

We have nothing to pack, so we simply stand up and begin to walk, all of us determined. Soon. I'll tell Micah soon.

"Not far now. It's uphill from here," Curtis says. "We should be able to see the wall from the top."

I focus on his words. Somewhere up this road is Best, and Pa, and the end of this journey. If I can just keep it together a little longer, this trip won't be for nothing. I need to get my head straight; there is still work to do, and I need to do it. I can't go all to pieces, not yet. Not yet, I repeat to myself. Not yet.

PART FOUR:
THE DARK

The good die first,
And they whose hearts are dry as summer dust
Burn to the socket.
—William Wordsworth

43.

Ben spots three shakes before we hit the second mile. Micah and Sam scramble for their guns while Curtis barks orders; I wait for the fear to hit me, but I'm too sluggish to feel much of anything except resignation. It happens quickly this time, workmanlike and grimly common. Curtis fires the first shots and the shakes come running; we all fire and one by one they fall down screaming with bullets in various parts of their bodies. The last gets close enough for me to see his eyes are a lovely dark blue. Ben yells at me to get back, but I stay in place and watch as the light goes out of them, watch as that lovely blue begins to cloud. I don't know which bloody holes belong to me, my aim is so unsteady that I reckon not even one. At least I was right to hire the

Garretts; I would never have been able to shoot this many shakes dead with only my gun. I make up my mind to practice shooting at moving targets, until I remember that it's pointless.

I'm starting to feel like I've been walking forever, like everything else is simply a dream, a life I imagined for myself while I keep walking. One foot goes in front of the other, the movement repeated infinitely. I can't remember not walking, I can't remember my feet not aching.

It's strange not to be able to trust myself, not to know if my mind is still mine, or if it's starting to break apart. If I'm not sure, if I doubt myself, does that mean I'm still sane? If I'm worried, am I still me? I can only hope.

We pass another mesa, the flat ridge even with the horizon. We pass a clump of long-dead shakes, too decayed to even smell, their bones riddled with bullet holes from some other hunters in some other nightmare. The land is rockier here, more uneven, the dirt redder. The road slants uphill over a small crag and shale crunches underneath our boots. It's slippery where the rock is crushed fine, and I turn my feet to keep from skidding. We reach the crest of the hill and Curtis pauses, pointing ahead as if we can't see the massive walls rising up.

"Best," he says.

Sam whistles low, impressed. The wall is nothing like the fence we have in Glory; the reach isn't as high, but it's made of stacked stones, not wire choked with tumbleweeds. It looks like it would hold against cannon fire, let alone shakes.

"They ain't fooling, are they?" I ask, staring at the thick iron and wood gate set into the stone. This place is a fortress, not a town.

"No ma'am," Curtis answers. "You stay in Best, you stay safe."

"Come on," Ben says, pushing forward. "We ain't getting any younger."

I've never been to another town, and only now do I realize how little of the world I've seen. It's pathetic, really, that I've spent seventeen years in one small spot. Pathetic, and unfair, because I never had a chance. There are so many places I never got to see, cities built wider and taller than I can imagine, oceans stretching farther than I could see. If things were different, would I have actually done it? Packed up and moved north, after the twins were grown? I'm not so sure anymore. Underneath it all, maybe I'm just a coward, too afraid of anything new or different. Who is to say I wouldn't have spent the rest of my life in Glory, till I was old and blind and full of could-haves and what-ifs. Maybe I was never meant to leave.

The walls look even sturdier up close, the stones fitting snug against one another. I put a hand out and let my fingertips graze along it, the rock rough and warm from the sun.

Curtis approaches the two-door gate, reaching for one of the heavy iron knockers. It makes a loud bang that sets the whole gate ringing.

"At the gate," he calls loudly, his voice half drowned by the banging.

"How many?" someone calls back from behind the gate.

"Five," Curtis answers. "All well."

There's a scraping sound, and a grunt, and then the gate starts to open inward, revealing a young man standing between the doors. He has brown skin and a smattering of freckles, and he balances a long rifle against his shoulder.

"Garrett," he says, surprised. "What the hell are you doing here this early in the morning?"

"Long story. How you been?" Curtis and the man shake hands briefly while we file in past the wall.

"Aw, you know. Can't complain. Ben," he says, nodding.

"Hey, Levi," Ben says, tipping his hat up so he can see. "Now y'all folks I don't know," he says, turning his attention to the boys and me. "And I never forget a face."

"Levi, this is Willie and Micah Wilcox and Sam Kincaid. We brung them up from Glory."

"Glory," Levi repeats, and whistles. "What the hell you want to live in Glory for?"

"Y'all, this is Levi Mason, one of Best's finest gunmen."

"Only one of?" Levi laughs. "I'm a better shot than you, Curtis. Nice to meet y'all."

Sam and Micah mumble some pleasantries and I give a quick nod.

"You work the gate often?" I ask him.

"Now and then."

"We're looking for someone in particular, Harrison Wilcox."

Levi chews on his bottom lip. "Name sounds familiar."

"He woulda been coming through here the past couple days."

Levi shakes his head. "I only got back from Savage

yesterday, but I ain't seen anybody leave since then. You might want to check with Yao or Clarence. Hunters usually keep to the bars, that's where you'd find them most like. Sorry I can't say more than that."

I nod and give him a tight smile. "That helps. Thank you kindly."

My eyes fix beyond Levi, on the city spread out before us. I've never seen the like; even walking through Silver didn't prepare me for a town this size. I can't see where the streets end, they crisscross and turn into further roads. Like Glory, many of the shops are boarded up, the lumber yard empty and the mill quiet. But the banquettes are crowded with displays of dry goods and dress forms draped in patterned cloth. Even early there are people in the streets, not hunters but normal folks just going about their day, ducking out of the drugstore and smiling at one another. There's life here, real life that makes my jaw ache with want.

"You ready to find your pa?" Ben asks me.

"I reckon so," I tell him, my mind racing. He's here; I need him to be here. But I've got a question for Ben, too. "How the hell am I supposed to find one man in a city choke-full of them?"

44.

I stick close to the others; it's too much for me, the sounds of wheeling carts and striking hammers and the smells of sour mash and smoked meats threaten to overwhelm my senses.

"Would you settle down?" Micah whispers to me out of the corner of his mouth. "Stop twitching every time you see something new."

I punch him lightly in the shoulder; he's as wide-eyed as I am, he just cares enough to hide it. I can't help staring and craning my neck up; none of these structures are less than two stories high.

"This way," Curtis says, leading us through a series of turns. "We always stay at Mrs. Keen's when we're in Best. You'll like it, she's—" he pauses, trying to find the right words. "Well, she's the best cook in the south, though I'll thank you not to mention that to Elsie."

"Why would you ever leave here?" Sam asks, his eyes following a girl with ribbons in her hair and a basket full of apples in her arms.

"Have to, to work," Ben answers. "Supply runs, patrols, fares when we can get 'em. So many folks turned hunter, there ain't always enough jobs to go around."

"Don't it bother you, always bein' on the move?" I ask, but Ben just shrugs.

"It's that or stay in Glory, doing whatever dirty work the Judge needs doing."

I snort in distaste and Micah frowns.

"So you don't got a place you call home?" he asks.

"Ennis, I reckon, though we ain't been there in months and it's barely more than a patch. Part of the life." It doesn't seem near worth it to me, but then I'm no hunter.

"Here we are," Curtis says, stopping in front of an older but cheerful-looking house. The front porch is swept clean and bordered by five columns, each one framing a window in between. The windows are repeated on the second story, these ones outlined with dark shutters.

We follow Curtis up the porch, the worn steps slick beneath our feet; the wood is old and sagging and smooth, sanded down from dust and boots making the same journey over and over.

The door opens even before Curtis knocks, and a plump woman wearing a patterned shirtwaist and a dark green skirt clasps his hands delightedly.

"Mr. Garrett," she says, beaming at him. Her smile takes up half her face, her eyes disappearing into her cheeks. "I'm so happy to see you again."

"It's good to see you too, Mrs. Keen," Curtis says, carefully extricating his hands from her grasp.

"And now where's—oh yes, there he is, hiding behind you," Mrs. Keen goes on, wagging her finger at Ben. "As if I wouldn't see you there."

"Hello, Mrs. Keen," Ben says, staying safely out of her reach.

"Well, come in, come in, y'all are all welcome," she says, bustling us inside. I catch Micah's eye and he bites his lip, both of us trying not to laugh.

"Mrs. Keen, this is Sam and Micah, and that's Willie there," Curtis says, pointing us out to her.

"Well, don't that beat all? It's so nice to have young'uns in the house again. Now sit down and I'll bring y'all something hot. Are you hungry? We've had breakfast already but I always make extra in case of stragglers." Mrs. Keen doesn't wait for us to answer; she ushers us through the entrance hall and into the parlor and disappears through a door, still talking.

I glance around, feeling slightly dazed by the woman's energy. The parlor is small but well furnished, with a number of plush chairs and a long divan set around a polished wooden table. I sink down into one of the chairs, wishing I fit into this pretty room.

"Well, she's . . . something," Sam says, flopping down onto the divan.

"Aw, she's a good woman and charges fair," Curtis tells him. "Even if she could talk a donkey's hind leg off. We'll get some food in us and then we can figure out where to start looking for your pa."

"Well I doubt he'd be staying at a place like this," I say, looking at the heavy clouded mirror on the wall.

Micah lets out a bark of a laugh. "Pa? He'd stick out like a sore thumb."

I wince at his choice of words and tug my sleeve down to make sure it's covering my hand. The swelling is getting worse, and I don't know how long I'll be able to hide it from the others. I need to find Pa before that happens, and before the delusions get worse.

"Then where do you reckon we should start?" Ben asks.

"The saloons first. Or any gambling halls." I suck on the inside of my cheek, considering. "He used to sell to a man here, I think the name was Allen. Might be worth checking with him, if he's still around."

"We should split up," Curtis says. "It'll be faster, we'll cover more ground. I need to take some time to buy supplies anyway, since we lost most of them. I'll take Doc Junior with me, he knows what your pa looks like. Willie and Micah, you go with Ben."

"Here we are," Mrs. Keen interrupts, backing into the room with a tray balanced in her hands, the bright smell of coffee following her. "Now it's nothing fancy, but it should set you to rights."

Curtis jumps up and tries to take the tray, but Mrs. Keen shoos him away.

"Don't be silly, dear, I can handle it. Y'all just sit and rest awhile."

She sets the tray on the table gently and plants her hands on her hips. Along with the coffee, the tray is stocked with biscuits and a fat pat of butter, a bowl of thick jam, and a plate of sausages.

"There. Now eat your fill, and when you're finished leave the tray. How many rooms should I set up?"

"I think three will suit us just fine," Curtis answers. "Mrs. Keen, do you know a man named Allen by any chance?"

She wrinkles her brow, considering. "Can't say that I do, but there's an Ellis as runs the feed store."

"We'll ask around," Ben tells me.

"Dinner's at two, like usual," Mrs. Keen goes on. "Tea you can take before you retire for the night. And I'll get those rooms aired. Is there anything you're wanting especially?"

"No, Mrs. Keen, thank you," Curtis says. "This looks mighty fine. We'll have a look about town, but we'll be back shortly."

"Oh, bless your heart, it does me good to have company." Mrs. Keen smiles at us contentedly from the door, then she's gone in a puff of green cloth and coffee.

"Well," Curtis says, reaching for a biscuit, "eat up. Time's a-wasting."

45.

The city looks much kindlier with a belly full of coffee and grease. We walk from the Keen house back to the street we came through, and then Curtis and Sam split off, headed left while the rest of us go right.

"We got till dinner," Ben reminds us. "Then we meet back up."

It doesn't seem like enough time, but Ben knows the town and it's not like I won't recognize my own father.

"We might not find him today, Will," Micah says softly to me, trying to prepare me for disappointment.

"We just have to keep looking," I say, my mind on my hand. I can't spare a day, I can't waste the heartbeats. "There are only so many places a man can hide."

The banquettes rattle under my boots, the wood old

and shrunken around the nails. I stare inside the shop we pass, impressed by the order of it; here holsters, lanterns, pails, and ropes are hung neatly on a wall for all to see. My full belly allows me to simply admire the jars full of candy, frosted and glowing like colored glass.

"We'll try the Occidental first," Ben says, directing us toward a squat brown building with a bright green roof. "It's a hotel, but they got a barroom where folks like to gamble."

We follow Ben into the hotel, and he stops to talk with a man at a desk while I admire the lobby with its shining tin ceiling and embossed wall coverings.

"This way," Ben says, motioning to Micah and me. "Through here."

Micah has to pull me away, my head still tilted up to see the patterned ceiling. "Come on, Sis, we ain't staying here."

Ben walks us down the hall and into the barroom, which has a number of deer heads that must be at least ten years old mounted on the wall. Maybe more; I don't remember when the last deer died out, but I've never seen those pale, branching antlers in my life. There are only two men in here, one on each side of the counter. Maybe it's too early, or maybe folk in Best don't lose themselves in drink like we do in Glory.

"'Scuse me," Ben says, rapping his knuckles on the bar.

The bartender looks up and makes his way over to us, smoothing his moustache.

"Can I help you?" he asks.

"We're looking for someone. Harrison Wilcox, he's a gambler. You seen him?"

"Can't say I have. No one name of Wilcox in here."

"Right," Ben says. "Well, we're staying at the Keen house. If he does show up, we'd be obliged if you took note of where he goes."

The bartender nods and fiddles with his moustache again. "Anything else I can do for you?"

"No," Ben says. "Thank you for your time."

We file out of the barroom and back through the lobby.

"Well that's one down," Micah says, letting the door swing behind him. "Where to now?"

We try the feed shop and a general store next, and they both yield the same answer. At least the woman at the last stop is nice about it; from her we get a smile and a headshake, but the result is still the same: Pa's not here, and no one's seen him.

"We'll try a saloon next," Ben says.

"You think they're lying?" Micah asks him as we're directed toward another door.

"Could be," Ben says. "Best folk are closemouthed, but I don't see what cause they'd have to lie."

"Maybe Curtis and Sam are having better luck," I say, my gut tightening. Pa's always been good at weaseling out of tight spots, but there's five of us and one of him.

"Fourth time's lucky?" Ben asks, holding the door open for us.

"I don't think that's the saying," I tell him, ducking under his arm.

We follow him into the saloon, and I wait for my eyes to adjust to the dimness. I wrinkle my nose; it smells rancid in here, like old milk mixed with the sharp fumes of alcohol. Spittoons are scattered around the ground, but from the state of the floor it seems most folks have chosen to ignore them. There's some quiet chatter from two hunters at a corner table, and one sitting alone, looking full as a tick. I can't tell if he started early or if he's still drunk from last night.

The bartender takes his time acknowledging us,

giving a glass a few extra wipes. My temper rises as he slowly walks over to us.

"Can I help you?" he asks grudgingly, folding his arms across his chest.

"We're looking for Harrison Wilcox," Ben says.

The bartender sucks on his teeth, looking from Ben to me and then to Micah. "I ain't seen him and he ain't welcome here," he says.

Ben glances at us and I shrug.

"Pa has that effect on people," Micah says.

"Anything else?" the bartender asks, and he doesn't give us time to answer before he walks away.

"This is getting us nowhere," I say, impatient. I glance at the drunk sitting on his lonesome; he looks too addle-headed to lie.

"You," I say, weaving around a chair to stand in front of him. "I'm looking for someone."

The man looks up at me with bloodshot eyes set in a shiny face. "I don't know 'im," he says, pouring whiskey into a cup of coffee, sloshing some down the side of the mug.

"I didn't give you a name."

"I don't know 'im," he says again, and he spits out a gob of tobacco juice and sputum that lands squarely on my chest.

"You—you—" I stutter. I'm so hell-fired mad I can't even think of something bad enough to call him. "This was my last good shirt, you lily-livered bastard!" And I grab his mug and throw it in his face. He yelps and sputters, falling back in his chair, and I watch in satisfaction as the hot liquid drips down his chin. He tries to get up, cursing at me, and Ben swoops in, taking me by the shoulders.

"Time to go," he says, steering me out of the saloon.

"Willie—" Micah tries to chide me, but it's hard to do when he's snickering.

"Why don't you let me do the talking, from now on," Ben says. "As a matter of fact, maybe you should wait outside."

"Fine by me," I say, disgusted, wiping at the brown stain on my chest. "Look at my shirt. Disgusting. At this rate I'll be walking home nekkid."

Ben and I lock eyes for a second, and I glance away quickly, feeling my cheeks go hot.

"Damn shame, is what it is," I say, keeping my face down.

"Look, just cool your heels for a while," Ben says. "It's almost time to head back, anyway. Don't wander off."

I snort at him. "I got nowhere to go."

46.

I lean back against a half-rotted hitching post, with only my thoughts to keep me occupied. I don't mind; I like my own company, for the most part. Although lately I've been too quick to give in to self-pity and melancholy; a side effect of dying, I reckon.

My head hurts. It's not a sharp hurt, but a constant dull throbbing; it's the kind of hurt where if I don't think on it, it recedes into the background, like someone humming softly. I rub my temples and focus on the people walking past, trying to make up lives for them. This woman with the straw hat and the brooch at her neck, she's in an awful hurry. She's almost skipping, and I bet she's going to meet her fellow. He'll be young, and handsome, but too poor for her folks to approve of. She doesn't care about the money; they'll marry this month, in secret, before anyone can tell them not to.

And this man here, with the bowler hat and only the top button of his coat fastened, he looks like a lawman, or he would if we still had lawman around these parts. The man walks past, his eyes alert and focused, but I lose sight when someone stumbles past me and trips stepping off the banquette.

It's the hunter that spit on me, and he's so drunk he doesn't even notice I'm standing here. I glare daggers at his back as he weaves his way across the street. I push myself away from the post and debate whether to follow. Ben told me not to wander, but I doubt this fellow can go too far in the shape he's in, and I owe him for my shirt. I look over my shoulder, but Ben and Micah are still wasting time somewhere inside, trying to get answers from the most unhelpful people as ever lived. I grumble to myself and hurry across the street, following the man as he turns a corner. I lose sight of him for a moment and then see him duck into a storefront marked Alameda. I frown at the sign, the name ringing a bell; this has to be the place Pa sold to. What are the odds the fellow came here by chance?

I open the door and the smell of hides hits me like

a solid thing, that mix of rank meat and bitter smoke. The back wall of the store is half covered with a giant black and brown buffalo skin, the fur dense and shaggy. I reckon that one's for show; the wares are about what I'd expect, some calf and sheepskin, but mostly smaller hides. I see jackrabbit and coyote pelts slung over tables, and enough snakeskin to cover the rest of the walls. I run my hand over the cold scales absentmindedly, wondering how many of these Pa skinned himself.

The spitter is talking heatedly with an older fellow, his voice slurred and too low to overhear. The older man looks uncomfortable, but he nods briskly and after a moment the hunter claps him on the back and staggers past me out the door, not even looking at my face. When he leaves, I turn my attention to who I assume is Mr. Alameda.

"You got a nice store here," I tell him, petting the soft fur on a rabbit pelt. "You do these yourself?"

"Most of 'em," he says, smiling at me. At least I think he's smiling; he has a droopy gray moustache that covers most of his mouth and hangs down over his chin. "Not so much lately, of course."

"Of course."

"Looks like you're wanting a new shirt," he says.

"What I want and what I can afford rarely align," I tell him. "Are you Alameda?"

"I am. You have me at a disadvantage, young'un."

"My name is Wilcox," I say, watching him closely. "I think you may know my father."

Mr. Alameda blinks at me slowly. "I do," he says. "You'd be his oldest, then?"

"Yes, sir. I've been looking for him, came all the way from Glory to find him."

"And you want to know if'n I seen him."

"Please, sir. It's mighty important."

Alameda sighs, sending his moustache waving. "Time was, your pa used to come by often. Most of those snakes are his, you know. And I paid him proper, never tried to fleece him or nothing. If he wanted to spend his money on drinking and gambling, well that was his business."

"Mr. Alameda—"

"I ain't seen him," he says, meeting my eyes. "Last time he came by was months ago, claiming I owed him for all the times I stiffed him over the years. Now, I swear to you I never did."

"I know, Mr. Alameda; my pa cheats people, not the other way around. I just want to find him."

Alameda nods, looking relieved. "I wish I could help you, but I don't know where he is."

I press on my forehead, wishing my head would stop pounding. "You sure about that? You sure that fellow there didn't ask you to forget you seen him?"

Alameda draws himself up. "Miss Wilcox, I don't answer to anyone but myself. That's the truth."

I look him in the eyes and he doesn't flinch. "All right," I say, discouraged. "Thanks anyway."

I head to the door, my shoulders stooped. I pause, considering, and turn around once more.

"Mr. Alameda—if by any chance you do see him, could you give him a message for me?"

"I could that," he says.

"Could you tell him—just tell him his family needs him to come home."

Mr. Alameda nods solemnly at me. I give him a thin smile, the best I can offer under the circumstances, and leave the smell of dead animals behind.

47.

"There you are," Micah calls as I step outside. He looks relieved; he and Ben hurry over from across the road.

"I thought I said not to wander off," Ben says.

"I wasn't wandering," I tell him. "I had a very real purpose."

Micah rolls his eyes at me.

"I did," I insist. I point at the sign behind me. "Look, Alameda. That's the man Pa sold to."

"Well, I hope you found out more than we did," Micah says.

"No luck," I say. "He says Pa ain't been there in months. I left a message, but . . ." I trail off, feeling hopeless.

Micah swears softly. "I swear a rat would leave a bigger trail."

"Let's take a break," Ben says. "We need to get back for dinner anyway. We'll try again later, folk might be more inclined to talk once the sun goes down."

I doubt it, but I keep my grumbles to myself. There's a meal in my immediate future, and that's enough to look forward to.

We get back to the boardinghouse and Mrs. Keen makes a fuss over us, bringing out a tray of switchel to cool us off. We sip on the ginger-water in the parlor, waiting for Curtis and Sam to come back.

"I have your rooms ready if you'd like to clean up before dinner," she says, looking pointedly at Ben.

"I ain't shaving, Mrs. Keen," he says, crossing his arms.

"Well, I'm sure I didn't tell you to," she says, nose in the air.

Micah snorts into his glass, and I shoot him a look before Mrs. Keen can take offense.

"I'd greatly love a wash," I tell her. "And if there's somewhere I can clean my shirt—"

"Sakes alive, did one of these boys do that? No regard, I tell you," Mrs. Keen tsks. "You give that to me, dear, and I'll have it scrubbed and wringed in no time."

"Um." I lower my voice. "It's the only one I have."

"I have shirts aplenty, dear, there's no shame to be had. I'll send a girl to your room with water and something clean. Now stand up, let's see you."

I stand up awkwardly, and Mrs. Keen plucks at my shoulders and narrows her eyes. "Well, you're a skinny thing, and long, but I'm sure I can find something to fit. Won't be but a moment," she says, and bustles out of the room.

I sit back down and finish my drink, and now that it's been offered I'm longing for a bath. I look at my fingernails and grimace; even the twins' hands aren't this bad.

"What's taking Curtis and Sam so long?" Micah asks.

"They'll be here," Ben says. "I've never known Curtis to miss a meal."

"You really think we'll find out more tonight?"

"I reckon so. The harder drinkers and gamblers don't come out till late. No offense, but your pa seems the sort who keeps that kind of company."

"Ain't that the truth," Micah says.

The front steps creak and I motion to the boys. "Here they are," I say, as the front door bangs open and in come Sam and Curtis.

"You're late," Ben tells his brother.

"Hogwash," Curtis says, collapsing into a chair.

"Any news?" I ask, not expecting much.

"Yao didn't notice him at the gate. We got one 'maybe I seen him' and the rest don't bear repeating," Curtis answers.

"What about you?" Sam asks.

"Same," Micah says.

"Not to worry," Curtis says, grabbing some switchel and propping his feet on the table. "We'll try again tonight, and if that don't work, well, Ben and I can be very persuasive." He gives me a wide grin that's somehow both friendly and wicked.

"You need any help convincing, you let me know," I tell him, picking at my fingernails. I don't have the time for these folks to be dancing around our questions like this. I don't know what I expected; it's not like I thought we'd walk through the gates and Pa would be standing right there. I guess I didn't think this far ahead, or maybe I never really thought we'd get this far. But I'm here now, and mine is not a patient nature.

Mrs. Keen swoops back into the room and clucks at Curtis to get his feet down.

"Here we are," she says to me, holding out a soft creamy shirt. "It'll be a bit big on you, it was my late husband's, but it'll suit your purpose."

I hardly want to touch it with my dirty hands, but I take it from her. "Thank you, ma'am."

"It's nothing, dear," she says, patting my arm. "Now up the stairs with you, second door on the right. There's water waiting, just leave your dirty things outside the door."

I try to thank her again, but she waves it away.

"Go on and get," she says, shooing me until I start moving. The stairs are down a hall just off the parlor, and I scurry up with my clean shirt in tow.

"I'm only suggesting," I hear Mrs. Keen say, her voice carrying, "but in my experience, a lady likes a smooth face."

I laugh to myself as I climb; she might be right, but there aren't any ladies here. There's only me, and I like the beard just fine.

48.

The room is warm and full of light, the sun spilling in through one tall window. It's simple and cozy, with a small iron-framed bed with a thick quilt and a wooden nightstand with a kerosene lamp. There's a chair in the corner with a folded towel and soap, and best of all, sitting on the floor is a tin washtub filled with steaming water.

I pull the curtain across the window and then shuck off my clothes so fast I get stuck in my pants and have to hop around on one leg till I can free myself. I shove my soiled shirt outside the door and close it, checking twice to make sure it locks.

I step into the water slowly, one foot at a time. It's blessedly warm, and I ease myself down, taking care not to splash over the sides. The washtub isn't large; I could almost circle it with my arms, but I tuck my knees up under my chin and mostly fit. For a while I just sit with my eyes closed, listening to the soft lapping of the water against the tin. I wish I could make this moment last; why is it that the best parts of life are the quickest over? Water always gets cold, food has to be swallowed, and even the best dreams end when you wake up.

When the water starts to lose heat, I take the brick of soap and work it into a washrag and start to scrub the layers of dust and grime off my body. I untie the wet bandage from around my hand and let it fall to the floor. My palm is swollen red and tight around my cut; it's getting hard to move my fingers. I gently wipe the dirt away, taking care not to bump anything. Even that small pressure makes it throb, and the pain travels from my hand up to my shoulder.

I scour every bit of me I can reach, until my skin is bright and pink, some part of me thinking if I can get the outside clean enough, maybe it will make a difference.

Only when my skin starts to smart do I finally let the soap drop. The water has turned a murky gray with white suds skimming atop the surface. I take a deep breath and heave myself out of the tub, grabbing the towel before I drip too much on the floor. I wrap the towel around me and lie down on the bed, not caring that my wet hair is soaking into the quilt. I smell like soap and wet skin and I want to keep feeling clean as long as I can, before I have to put my dirty clothes back on. I could easily fall asleep right now, but life insists on moving forward, and I still have so much to do.

I reluctantly sit up and start to wring out my hair. When I'm dry I pull on the shirt Mrs. Keen lent me; it's soft and roomy and smooth against my scrubbed skin. The sleeves are too long, so I roll them up to just past my wrists. The fingers on my left hand do not want to cooperate, and I look at them grimly; I need my hand, I need to able to use it. For that I need the swelling to go down.

I get dressed quickly, tie my wet hair back and grab my knife and the dirty bandage before I lose my nerve. I crouch next to the washtub and rinse the snake guts off the blade, though the dirty water will hardly help. I take a few rapid breaths, grit my teeth, and position the point of my knife against my swollen palm, just at the corner of my scabbing cut. I press down, at first gently and then with more and more pressure until I puncture my skin.

Blood wells up around the tip of my knife, and I set it down beside me. I hold the bandage against my palm and with my good hand I press around the cut I made. It hurts, badly, and I hiss as more blood leaks out. I move my fingers and press on a different spot, and then, like someone cracked an egg, thick grayish-yellow pus gushes from the wound. I gag at the rotten smell, but I keep pressing to drain the wound, letting the blood-streaked liquid run down my hand and soak into the cloth. Already the swelling is going down, and still more pus seeps out, foul and runny and sickening.

I push at my skin until no more pus remains, until only clear pink fluid runs from the cut. My hands are covered with blood and infection, and I scrub them down with the washrag and soap. My palm feels normal-sized again, though my scabbed-over cut is still red and inflamed. The small tear I made at the corner is hardly visible now that it's stopped bleeding, and at least this time the wound served a purpose. I run my fingers lightly over the scab; it slices diagonally across my palm, making a path from my thumb to my pinky. If things had gone differently, I doubt it would even leave a scar.

My vision blurs, and when I blink the cut is split open, the two sides gaping wide. I watch, horrified, as the cut starts to grow. It streaks up my wrist and along my arm, the skin ripping apart and sloughing off in pale sheets. I can see the tissue underneath, only something's wrong with it; the inside of my arm is all black and lumpy and writhing with scores of white maggots. I open my mouth to scream, but no sound comes out. How long has my body been like this? How can I still be alive and have something so rotten inside me?

Bile rises in my throat, hot and sour. I barely make it to the tub in time to vomit up stomach acid and ginger into the water. I wipe my good hand over my mouth and force myself to breath in deeply through my nose, shutting my eyes tightly so I can't see the putrid mess my arm has become. I count to ten slowly, taking long even breaths, waiting until my stomach stops rolling and settles.

"It's not real, it's not real, it's not real," I repeat to myself, rocking back and forth. It's only in my mind; it has to be. But I still can't open my eyes. I don't know which is worse, that I imagined the whole thing or that it could be real, that there's dead flesh lying just beneath my skin, crawling with filth and disease.

Someone knocks on the door and I jerk violently.

"Willie," Micah calls. "Dinner's ready, come down."

I open my eyes just a crack, afraid of what I'll see, but my skin has grown back, clean and pink and whole. I lean back and gasp with relief, making a sound that's half laughter and half groan.

"Willie?"

"I'm—I'm here," I say, my voice breaking.

"Will? Are you all right?"

I get to my feet, trembling and exhausted. I'm really starting to lose it, but right now I don't even care, thankful my arm is in one piece again. Whatever that was, that darkness inside of me, I never want to see it again.

Micah pounds on the door but I don't answer. It's time, long past time I told him. He's going to be so angry with me. I don't know which will upset him more, that I let myself get sick or that I lied to him. Knowing Micah, it will be the lie.

"Willie?" His voice is rising, loud through the wood. "Open up right now."

I reach for the handle and slowly open the door. Micah stares at me, his brows a flat line of worry. And I look back at his eyes, my eyes, our father's eyes, and my throat closes up.

"What the hell, Will?" he asks. "What's going on?"

I open my mouth, but the words burn and die on my tongue. I can't form the thoughts, can't find my voice. I cradle my injured hand in the other and look away.

"I'm sorry," I tell him, and I am. I'm sorry for everything. I'm sorry for failing, I'm sorry for lying, and I'm sorry for being weak. Because maybe Micah could take the truth, but I can't take him hearing it. "I was asleep. Bad dream, I reckon."

His lips curl down at the edges. "Why do you bother lying to me when you know I can tell?"

"I'm sorry," I say again.

Micah looks over my face, my wet hair, and he takes a step forward. I throw my good hand out, blocking his path, and he stops.

"You can talk to me, you know," Micah says. "I just—I wish you would trust me."

"I do," I say quietly. It's me I don't trust. "Go on and start without me. I'll be down directly."

Micah is still staring at me when I shut the door. I listen until I hear his footsteps fade and brace my head against the wood, as cold and heavy as all the words left unsaid.

49.

I don't have a clean scrap of cloth for my hand, but I reckon the air might do it good now that it's drained. My new shirt is too big and I let the sleeves hang down to my fingers, low enough to hide the cut. My dirty bandage and the washrag get stuffed into my pockets; they're covered in blood and pus, and I don't want anyone else to handle them. The rest I think is safe, the water will get dumped and the towel will get washed with harsh lye soap. It's reckless and weak to let it go this long, but at least no one here will get sick because of me; I don't want that on my conscience.

I head downstairs and through the empty parlor, following the sounds of chatter and the clink of forks. The parlor leads me to the entrance hall, and I go through the opposite door into the dining room.

I pause at the entrance, unsure of myself; there are unfamiliar faces sitting around the end of the table, two men and a woman, and they all turn to look at me. The woman has a scar cutting across one eyebrow, and I stare for a moment until she scowls at me.

"Down here," Curtis calls, waving at me from the other end. I nod at the strangers and quickly make my way over to my group, which now includes Levi, the hunter from the gate. The table is long, almost the length of the room, and covered with steaming platters.

"We saved you a seat," Sam says, his mouth full of food.

I sit down between the two boys gratefully.

"Thanks."

Ben, Levi, and Curtis are sitting across from us, and I sneak a look down the table as I tuck my napkin in my lap.

"Who're those folks?" I ask in a whisper.

"Other hunters," Curtis says. "Don't pay them no mind."

"They're here for the food," Levi says. "Mrs. Keen always outdoes herself."

"Try the corn pudding," Sam says, spooning a lump

of the yellow mash onto my plate.

I'm slightly overwhelmed by the amount of food laid out on the table. In addition to the pudding, there's a thick pea soup, roast chicken with some sort of sauce, currant jelly, and small boiled onions. I pile my plate with some of everything, but as I start to chew on a bite of onion I realize I'm not even a little hungry. In fact, the smell of the food is making my stomach turn, and the burnt edges of the meat remind me too much of my rotting insides.

I force myself to swallow what's in my mouth and take a long drink of water to wash the taste away. I put my fork down and stare at my plate, at the mound of food I have no appetite for. It looks more like a challenge now.

"Not hungry?" Micah asks, glancing at me.

"No, I just—I think I'll start with the soup," I say. I can manage that much; I have to eat, I need to, to keep my strength up. I shovel the soup into my mouth, spoonful after spoonful, before my stomach has a chance to reject it. It goes down easy enough, but it might as well be watered-down broth for all I'm enjoying it. All these years spent eating grits and beans, and now here's a wasted feast in front of me. I would laugh, if it were at all funny.

"Well ask Levi, then," Ben says to Curtis, carrying on a conversation I missed most of. "Someone's gotta have a mule for sale."

"I heard tell Rivera brung a couple animals down from Rath City," Levi says.

"Rivera's a good hunter, but he don't know horseflesh," Curtis says. "I ain't paying a dime unless I see the animal myself."

"You're a hardfisted bastard," Levi laughs. "Beggin' your pardon," he says to me with a wink. I roll my eyes, and he laughs again.

I listen to them argue and eat as much of the soup as I can keep down, and then I just move the food around on my plate some. Mrs. Keen brings out spice cake and stewed fruit for desert, and I take a small slice to be polite.

"I'm too full," I tell Micah, rubbing my belly. "You want the rest?"

"Since when do you turn down food?" he asks.

"You want it or not?"

Micah narrows his eyes at me, but he jabs my cake with his fork. I push my chair away from the table and lean back. My eyes feel heavy, and the day is barely half over.

"Will," Micah nudges me.

"Hm?" I look up, and he points toward the door, where Mrs. Keen is motioning to me.

"Darling, do you have a moment?" she asks. "I hate to interrupt your dinner, but there's someone asking for you."

I get up from the table immediately to follow her, glancing back at Micah. It's Pa; it has to be. How did he find us?

"He said it was urgent, or I would've sent him away," Mrs. Keen tells me apologetically.

"It's fine, Mrs. Keen, I was finished anyhows."

She leads me through the parlor and into the entrance hall, where a man is standing with his back to me.

"Here she is, then," Mrs. Keen says, and the man turns around and I brace myself to see my father's face. Instead, I see a gray moustache and it takes me a moment to place it.

"Mr. Alameda," I say, confused.

"Ah, Miss Wilcox," he says, and he looks nervous. "I was hoping I could speak to you in private."

Mrs. Keen looks from him to me, and I shrug.

"Well, I guess I'll let you two alone," she says, giving

Mr. Alameda a warning look as she leaves.

Mr. Alameda stands awkwardly in front of me, rubbing one hand with another.

"What can I do for you, sir?" I ask him.

"Miss Wilcox, what I said to you before, that were the truth—I don't know where your pa is."

"I believe you, Mr. Alameda," I tell him, frowning. "You didn't need to come all this way."

He swallows, and his throat moves up and down. "I don't know where he is," he repeats. "But—" and he pauses.

"But?"

"But I can guess," he finishes, looking down.

"Please tell me," I say, my head starting to pound.

"Grayson's—the saloon—there's an old stable out back that's empty now. Grayson lets him sleep out there sometimes." Mr. Alameda shifts uneasily, edging back toward the door. "That's where I'd check."

"Mr. Alameda," I say, and he stops moving to look at me. "Thank you."

"I'm sorry I didn't tell you sooner," he says. "Good luck to you."

I watch him leave from the hallway, considering. The saloon isn't far from here, if I can remember the way.

The others are talking in the dining room, laughing and eating cake. Standing here in an empty room, I feel as far removed from laughter as I can be. I'm miles from them, and they don't even realize it. I don't belong with them anymore; I'm already gone.

50.

I set out purposefully, retracing our steps from earlier. I have a few choice words in mind to say to that bartender, and none of them are "thank you." The nerve of that man, lying to our faces. I conveniently forget the many lies I've told over the past few days; my righteous anger won't be dampened.

I turn right and look for the hotel; I'm pretty sure this is the street I want. I scan the buildings for the green roof, but I don't see it. I swear under my breath and keep walking; maybe it's the next clump of buildings.

Footsteps suddenly pound fast behind me, and I duck around a corner, pressing myself flat against a wall.

"Nice try," Ben calls, slightly out of breath.

"Damn," I say. So much for doing this alone. I peel myself away from the wall and turn to face Ben, who approaches me with an annoyed expression.

"You know, you hired us to guard you. You running off like this, it kinda defeats the purpose."

I cross my arms. "This is Best, not the open road. I think I can manage."

Ben shakes his head. "Oh, no you can't. Someone spits on you again, you're likely to get killed in a bar fight."

I snort, half amused and half aggravated. "Fine. Come on, we're going back to that saloon."

"Hold up," Ben says, looking over his shoulder.

"What? Who else did you drag along?" I look past him and see Micah hurrying toward us.

"I didn't drag him, he wouldn't stay put."

I give an exasperated sigh. "Yeah, he's like that."

We stand in silence, waiting for Micah to catch up. I glance sidelong at Ben, squinting against the sun.

"Killed in a bar fight, I ask you," I mutter to him. "I would never die in a bar fight. Undignified."

"We'll see," Ben says.

Micah stomps up on the banquette and glares at me. "Can't you sit still for one minute?"

"No," I tell him. "Alameda says Pa's in the old stables behind the saloon. Can you take us there?" I ask Ben. "I forget which way it is."

Ben takes the lead, just like we're back in the desert. Micah grumbles under his breath, but he falls in with us. Ben takes us across the street and to the left, and we turn and there's the green roof of the hotel. I wasn't that far off, but I reckon it's better Ben found me than let me wander around the town for who knows how long.

The saloon is right where we left it, sitting small and quiet; I glare at the door like it personally insulted my looks.

"Alameda said the stable's out back," I say.

"Probably best to avoid going inside," Ben says, raising his brows at me.

"Good," I tell him, jutting my chin out. "Then I won't hurt my fist on that bartender's teeth."

"Come on," Micah says, shaking his head.

He tugs my arm and we head toward the small gap between the saloon and the shuttered horse tack shop next to it. We squeeze by a wagon wheel that's leaning on its side and pop out behind the saloon. I consider kicking over one of the whiskey barrels stacked against the wall, but they look heavy and it may take some time. Instead I focus on the stable, or what used to be a stable. Even when there were plenty of horses to keep, it couldn't have housed more than two or three of them; now it's a hollowed-out shack that still stinks of horse and moldy hay.

We approach warily, not sure of what we'll find. The afternoon sun glints lazily off the nails and hinges in the wood. One of the stalls is open, the gate hanging wide, the wood too warped to close properly. The empty stall is filled with matted-down hay and rusted cans, all mixed with horsehair and piss. I purse my mouth, disgusted; of course this is where Pa would be sleeping.

A rustling comes from the next stall, and Micah and I both reach for the closed gate. He gets there first and unlatches it, letting the heavy door swing open. Slouched against the corner on a bed of rags is a greasy man with a whiskey bottle in his lap. His head hangs down to his chest, his eyes closed and his mouth half open.

My heart is like a fist in my chest. "Pa."

51.

He looks like he's dead. For a moment I let myself think it, let myself think how it would be easier, and then a low snore comes out of his mouth.

"Pa."

He doesn't move, and I say it again, louder.

Still nothing. I reach down and shake him, more violently than I intend. He snorts loudly and flails an arm out and I step out of the way.

"Pa, wake up."

Pa stares at me with bloodshot eyes and looks around the stable, disoriented.

"Willie—where am I?" His voice is slurred, but it's still the same playful drawl that used to sing us to sleep. It brings back memories I don't want or need right now.

"We're in Best, Pa. We been looking for you."

"Oh." Pa slumps back against the wall, his mouth drooping open. His eyes start to close and anger washes over me, prickly and pointless. It's not as if I was expecting Pa to change, but it still smarts; we've been through hell and back while he's been snoring here, drunk out of his mind.

"Micah," I say, glancing at him, and he nods once, his mouth tight and mad. He doesn't say anything to Pa, barely even looks at him. I grab Pa's whiskey bottle and splash the alcohol on his face.

"Hey, what—" he sputters. He lurches to his feet, swinging out wildly with his fists. Micah and I each grab an arm but Pa goes limp in our grasp.

"You want some help?" Ben asks.

"No, we've got him," I say, straining under Pa's weight. He's half conscious and cumbersome and sweating whiskey, and it's embarrassing enough without Ben having to carry him.

Micah and I ease Pa down until he's in a sitting position, propped up against the stable wall; he rolls forward, his limbs spilling over like boiled rope.

"Just like old times, huh," I say bitterly, wiping sweat away from my eyes.

"Yeah," Micah says. His face is blank, removed. "This is the last time I'm doing this, Will, I mean it."

"I know." I bite the inside of my cheek and glance around until I find a crate that looks like it may hold my weight. "Um, Ben—"

"Coffee? Food?" he supplies.

"Yes, thank you."

Ben walks away as I settle down on the crate. "Pa," I say, nudging his shoulder, and he grunts at me.

Micah bangs the butt of his rifle against the stable wall, over and over. I grit my teeth, and Pa raises his head and clutches it with his hands.

"What in the sam hill—"

"Sorry," Micah says loudly, with one last thump.

I sigh, but he's not doing anything I'm not tempted to do. There's a long, uncomfortable silence as Pa and I stare at one another; it's been a long time since I met my father's eyes.

Pa finally breaks the quiet by hacking; he coughs loudly and spits something on the floor, then wipes his mouth with his sleeve. I wrinkle my nose.

"Well, you found me," he says, breathing heavily.

"You look awful," I tell him.

"Yeah. You ain't wrong about that." He gives a hollow

laugh that dies as Micah stares at him stone-faced. Pa rubs the back of his neck and the silence resumes, a heavy and suffocating noose around our throats.

"Here." Ben returns and places a plate of stew and a cup on the ground in front of Pa.

"Who's this?" Pa asks, tilting his head up to see Ben's face.

"Benjamin Garrett. He's a—he's a friend."

"Then hello, friend," Pa says, putting out a hand.

"Sir." Ben makes no move to shake it, crossing his arms over his chest and standing next to Micah. Pa lets his hand drop and picks up a spoon.

"Well, I thank you for the vittles." Pa shovels the food into his mouth quickly, like he's afraid someone will take it out from under him. He starts to sit up straighter as the food hits his stomach; I doubt he's had anything but whiskey today. "I seen you before, ain't I?" he says to Ben, mid-chew.

"I reckon you seen me at the Homestead," Ben nods.

"You a hunter, ain't you?" Pa frowns at me. "Since when you keep company with hunters?"

"Since I need to," I answer. "You know why we're here, Pa."

He blinks at me, and it hits me how much he's aged

from my memories of him. The lines around his mouth are deep, pulling his face into a permanent frown, and his skin sags down from his cheeks to hang over his chin.

"I think I'm done," Pa says, pushing the plate away. "Nice of y'all to stop by."

"Pa, don't," I start, but he's already taking a long swig of whiskey. I reach down and grab the bottle and turn it upside down, letting the alcohol splash into the dirt.

"Hey," Pa yells at me, struggling to get up.

"Where's the money?" I ask him, done with being polite.

He slumps back against the stall and avoids my eyes.

"They came into our house." I struggle to keep my voice even. "McAllister and his man, they came in and they threatened us."

"Give us the money and we'll leave you be," Micah says flatly.

Pa raises his head and blinks watery eyes. "It's gone," he says. He sniffs hard and clears his throat. He digs a hand into his pocket and pulls out a few rumpled bills. "Tha's all I got left," he whispers, holding it out to me.

I take the money, look at the bills, and close my eyes briefly. It's less than twenty dollars. "Where's the rest of it?"

"Washburne took it and ran. Didn't even feel him lift it off me."

Micah scoffs angrily. "That's a surprise."

"I'm still your pa," he snaps at us. "And I woulda sent y'all some of that money. It were for all of us."

"Do you know where he went?" I ask, ignoring the lie.

"No. Could be anywhere by now."

"Then what good are you?" Micah says. "You couldn't even hang on to money you stole."

"Micah, enough," I say. I breathe out slowly, telling myself I'm prepared for what happens next. I knew it would come down to this; I knew that money was as good as gone when Pa took it. "Pa, get up. We're leaving."

Pa shakes his head. "I ain't going anywhere. I'm staying right here."

"Like hell you are," Micah says, erupting. "Those men were looking for *you*."

"I never meant for that to happen," Pa starts.

"What did you think was gonna happen?" Micah yells. "You thought they would just let it go? You knew damn well they'd come after you, and if they couldn't find you they'd come after us."

Pa looks down, and from the shame on his face I can tell Micah spoke right. I thought I was long past getting hurt by Pa, but here it is again, fresh pain on an old wound.

"I'm sorry," Pa says, lamely, as if that makes a difference.

"It's too late for that now," I tell him. "If the money's gone, then McAllister wants you. If you plead, maybe he'll let you work off your debt. So get up and get sober, 'cause it's a long walk back to Glory."

"They'll hang me." Pa looks at me with red-streaked eyes. "They'll hang me for sure."

"They might." My throat feels tight, and it's hard to speak. But Pa made his bed, and now he has to lie in it. "They might not."

"Willie, I'm your pa."

"You don't care what happens to us," Micah says. "Why should we care what happens to you?"

Pa ignores Micah, struggling to his knees. He inches forward and puts his hands on my arms. "Willie, come on now. You're my good girl."

"Don't you dare," Micah says, pushing Pa away from me. "Don't you dare try and act like you give a damn."

"I ain't going to McAllister," Pa says, pointing his

finger at Micah. "You can shoot me yourself, I ain't gonna be hanged."

"Fine." Micah pulls out his rifle, and Pa takes a step back. My mind goes white and blank, and for I moment I think I'm going to see my brother kill my father.

"Easy," Ben says.

"Micah, stop," I say, moving in front of him. "Just. Stop."

"Why?" Micah asks, and his eyes are too bright. "This is what we came here for, right? Come on, Will, be honest for once. We both knew he wouldn't have the money. We both knew he wouldn't come home. We came out here to kill him."

I open my mouth, but no words come to me.

"See?" Micah laughs. "You're not even gonna deny it."

"Micah, stop this," Pa says from behind me. "Think about your ma."

"Shut up," Micah yells. "You don't get to talk about her, you lost that right a long time ago. You wouldn't even help her . . . Willie had to do it. It should've been you, Pa. It weren't supposed to be her."

I flinch, feeling the memory bite. It was the last thing she asked of me, the only thing I had left to give her. I didn't even look away when the gun went off. I owed her that much. It eats at me, every day it gnaws at me, even though it's what she wanted. And that's why I can't allow this to happen, not because I can't lose Pa, but because I can't lose Micah. It would tear him up inside, and I won't let that happen.

"Micah," I say, and he looks at me with dead eyes.

"It weren't supposed to be you," he says hollowly.

"And this shouldn't be you," I tell him. "This ain't on you, Micah." I pull the rifle out of his hands, very gently. I look beyond him, to where Ben stands. He meets my eyes and nods at me, just once, before I turn and aim the rifle at Pa.

"Willie," he says, putting his hands out.

"Give me a reason not to," I say.

"I'm your pa."

I shake my head. "Not good enough."

Pa swallows hard, and gives me a ghost of a smile. "Your ma wouldn't want this. You look just like her now," he says.

After all this, that's what undoes me.

"No, I don't," I say. "I don't look anything like Ma. I look like you. I'm just like you, in fact. Bad luck follows me and I blame everyone but myself. And I'm a coward, like you. Because I can't even do what I oughta do."

I lower the gun, my hands trembling.

"That's my girl," Pa says.

I turn the rifle in my hands and smash the butt into Pa's forehead. He drops like a stone, falling face-first into the dirty hay.

"Find some rope," I order Micah.

Micah complies wordlessly, and I roll Pa over onto his side so he doesn't die in his sleep. A line of blood trickles down his forehead, and I try to pretend he's not my father, that I didn't do this to him.

"I'm sorry, Pa," I say to his sad, gray body. "You're coming with us, one way or another."

52.

We leave Pa where we found him, his hands tied and the rope looped through a hook. Even if he wakes up, he won't be sober enough to get himself out of it.

Micah leads the way back to Mrs. Keen's, taking long, angry strides that leave me lagging behind with Ben.

"He all right?" Ben asks me, watching Micah push past a stranger and turn the corner, his shoulders tight.

"I don't know," I say. "Pa has a way of gettin' to him."

"I can see that," Ben says. "What about you?"

I shake my head. "I just wanna get this done."

We get back to the house and I slowly climb up the steps, my legs heavy and uncooperative. I trudge through the parlor and into the dining room, where

Micah is picking at the food still spread out on the table. I'm so tired, but I sit down across from him while Ben goes to find Curtis.

"You want to talk about it?" I ask.

Micah drops a piece of chicken and rubs his greasy fingers on his pants.

"Oh, now you wanna talk?" he asks, reaching across the table for the decanter in the center. "'Cause earlier you slammed the door in my face."

Micah pours himself a sizable glass of what stinks like whiskey and I frown.

"I said I was sorry."

"Yeah, you're sorry, Pa's sorry, everyone's sorry."

"I know you're upset," I say, gritting my teeth. "But you don't understand."

"Of course not," he says, taking a huge sip and grimacing. "I'm only your dumb little brother, how could I ever understand?"

"Micah—"

"It's all up to you, right? You make all the decisions, and it don't matter what anyone else thinks or who you're gonna hurt." His voice cracks on the last word and he lifts his glass again.

"That's it," I say, shoving myself up. "You want to sit

here and bellyache, fine. I'm going to bed."

"Go ahead," Micah calls after me. "Run off and leave again, Will, just like Pa."

I storm past Curtis and Ben as I go, ignoring their questions and concerned faces. Micah can tell them what happened if he's feeling so damn chatty. I barricade myself in my room, making sure the door is locked before I curl up on the bed and wrap my arms tight around my shoulders.

Micah's words eat at me. Because here's the truth, sober as sunlight, final as a shut door: I am leaving him. I've got one foot in the ground already, and there's no fixing it. I don't know how to tell him, how to make him understand. I wanted to get out, but not like this. Never like this.

Now all I want is to go home. More accurately, I want to go home two years ago, when everything was simpler. Maybe we weren't always happy, maybe the floor sagged and we struggled to get by, but Ma was alive and I didn't have to worry about making the wrong decisions. I didn't have to level a rifle at my pa and lie to my brother. I don't want the life I have now, and fate, ever agreeable, will make sure of that.

There's a soft knock at my door, almost hesitant.

"Go away, Micah," I call, and roll over onto my back.

The knock comes again, more insistent this time. I let out an exasperated groan and get up.

"What?" I ask, flinging the door open to find it's only Sam, Sam with his perpetually hunched shoulders.

"Micah's in a rotten mood," he says, like we're already in a conversation. "Guess it didn't go so well with your pa."

I sigh. "Come in."

I sit back down on the bed, pulling one leg up and resting my chin on it. "Is he still mad at me?"

"He's always mad at you," Sam says, smiling a little. "Besides, you know it ain't about that."

"You know, the stupid thing is I missed Pa," I surprise myself by saying. "I ain't seem him in months, he causes this whole mess, but somehow . . ."

"He's your pa." Sam shrugs.

"Yeah." I pluck at the threads in the quilt absentmindedly.

"He was always nice to me," he says. "I'm sorry for what I said about him the other day. And I'm sorry he don't wanna make things right."

"He weren't always this bad, you know. I mean, he always went off to drink and play cards, but he would eventually come home to Ma. After she died, it's like—I don't know, it's like she took a piece of him with her. And every time he went off after that, less and less came back, and now all that's left is what I saw today."

"That ain't your fault, Will."

"It's nobody's fault. It just is."

"Some folks aren't meant to be parents." Sam looks off, like he's seeing something far beyond the walls of this room. "My ma took off when I was four."

"I remember," I tell him.

"She left a note, saying she loved me and she'd come back for me when she was settled. It took me two years till I was able to read it, and another three to figure out she was lying."

I've never heard Sam talk about his ma; I look at his face, concerned, but he stares at whatever he sees in the distance. I don't say anything, because there's nothing to say that will make it better. Glory's full of stories like Sam's, like Ben's, like mine. Just 'cause it's common doesn't mean it hurts any less. We're all orphans out here.

"People have a way of disappointing you, if you let them," I tell him.

Sam shakes his head, breaking his reverie. "They can surprise you, too, if you let them." He smiles wanly at me. "You want to come down? I hear there's calves' feet for supper."

My stomach rolls, and I press my lips together. "I think I just want to go to sleep. Long day tomorrow. Tell Micah to take it easy with the whiskey."

"All right. I'll tell him."

"Hey, Sam?"

He pauses by the door. "Yeah?"

"What you said at the station, about fixing up a cut . . ."

"Is your hand worse?" he asks, stepping back.

"No," I say quickly, angling my palm away from him. "No, it's healing. But if an infection did get bad, is there anything I could do?"

Sam frowns. "Mostly keep it clean, maybe try some heat or bleeding. If it gets too far gone, you're talking amputation. Or cauterization."

"What's that?"

"Burning," Sam says, his mouth twisting. "But I don't recommend it, not without a lot of opium. And once it hits your bloodstream, there's nothing can be done. Why are you asking me this, Will?"

"'Cause I'm clumsy, Sam, and I can't always come running to you."

"Sure you can," he says, grinning.

"Well, thanks. For that, and . . . for talking with me."

"Anytime. We'll be home before you know it, Will. Get some rest."

I listen to the door close and lie down on my side, staring at my hand like there's an answer hiding somewhere in the crisscrossing lines, if only I can find it.

53.

I can't sleep. I lie on my bed, staring wide-eyed into the darkness, watching shadows melt into other shadows and counting the hours down. I'm exhausted, but my body refuses to settle, jumping and twitching against my will. I finally drift into a sort of numb daze before dawn, and when I wake up my bed is soaked with sweat and all I remember of my fever dreams is that they were dark and full of twisted limbs.

I start the day off in a bad state, exhausted and shivering. I'm anxious to leave; I'm restless, my skin hot and jittery and my eyes like burning coals in my head. I want to get home, and I rush through our breakfast of hotcakes with fried potatoes and eggs. I take a few bites because I have to eat something, and then I sip on my coffee and watch the others eat, silently urging them to hurry.

Micah sits next to me, shoveling eggs into his mouth at a rapid speed. We don't speak, both of us awkward and stilted. His eyes are red rimmed and his face looks puffy, which should teach him not to drink so much. Maybe I should've come down to make up with him last night, but I don't know what to say to make it better.

"You missed cards last night," Micah says quietly. "Levi won three hands out of four." He takes a bite of potato and chews with his mouth open wide.

"Then I hope you weren't playing for money," I say, swatting him to close his mouth. He doesn't apologize, and neither do I, but we don't need to. I drain the last of my coffee, blanching a little at the sweetness. I have to ration our sugar at home, and I've grown used to the taste of bitter coffee.

"Still not hungry?" Micah asks, watching me closely.

"Anxious, I reckon," I say, and force myself to take a bite of eggs. "Pa's not gonna make this easy."

"No, he's not, but when has he ever," Micah agrees. "You think McAllister will really kill him?"

I look down at my full plate. "I don't know. I reckon

he'll try. But Pa's always been good at getting out of tight spaces."

"A family trait, I think." He smiles, just a little, and my shoulders ease.

"Do you think the twins are all right?" I ask him quietly.

"The twins? Sure, they're fine. Even McAllister wouldn't go so low as to hurt them. Why?"

"I don't know. I just have a feeling, like we need to get home. Like something bad is gonna happen."

I expect him to laugh at me, but he doesn't. "It'll be all right, Will," he says, meeting my eyes. I think the line between his brows is permanently etched in now. "We'll do whatever it takes, like we always have."

Breakfast ends, and I try not to push everyone out the door. Curtis loads up his new rucksack with canteens of water, rope, crackers, everything he managed to replace. Mrs. Keen is beside herself that we're leaving; I get the feeling that she likes a full house. I hope the woman has children who will give her grandchildren soon, she has so much love that it's spilling out her ears. She gives us each a small bundle of food for the road, and only Ben manages to escape without a hug, and only because he runs outside when he sees her coming.

"Thank you for loaning me the shirt, Mrs. Keen," I tell her, holding it out, but she presses it back to me.

"Keep it, dear," she says. "I've no use for it any longer, and lord knows Mr. Keen don't need it."

I won't turn down a free shirt, and it obviously makes her happy to give it to me. "Thank you," I say, and I allow her to hug me again.

"Come back and see me, Daisy. A soul gets lonely, on her own."

"I'll do my best," I say, gritting my teeth at my embarrassment of a name. I whip my head around to glower at my brother, but he holds his hands up in surrender. A snicker from Ben tells me who the real culprit is, and I do my best to ignore him as Mrs. Keen waves us off.

Curtis leads the way to the stable, and my cheeks grow warmer the closer we get. It's bad enough Ben had to see Pa like this, now Curtis and Sam get to see what kind of useless father I have. We push open the door where we left him, and it's as bad as I think it's going to be. Pa has vomit on his chin and shirt and he looks even worse in harsh light. I swallow hard, and almost take a step back.

"Come on, Will," Micah says, coming to stand next to me. "We gotta do this."

I take a deep breath, then open a canteen and douse water over Pa's head. Sputtering, he opens his eyes wide. He sees the ropes around his wrists and tugs, confused.

"What the—"

"Morning," I say loudly, and Pa glances around wildly, noticing the group of people staring at him.

"Willie? What's going on? Get these off of me."

"No," I say, hoping I sound steadier than I feel. "Here's the deal, Pa: you're going back to Glory."

"The hell I am—" he starts, but I cut him off.

"Don't talk. Just listen. Really listen, because I'm only gonna say this once, and it needs to get through that whiskey-addled brain of yours: you're coming."

"We're done asking, Pa," Micah tells him. "See, there's five of us, and one of you. You can walk with us, or you can be dragged by us. Up to you."

Pa looks at me, searching my face for sympathy that he won't find. He looks behind me, to where Ben and Curtis stand shoulder to shoulder and Sam has his arms crossed over his chest in an unsuccessful attempt at intimidation. He's lost, and he knows it.

"You're right," Pa says, his voice raspy. "You're right, this is all my fault. I'm sorry. I'll come with you, I'll turn myself in."

I don't believe that for a minute; Micah and I exchange a cynical look. We both know Pa's routine by heart, he'll act contrite and wait for us to let our guard down. Fine, I'll play along if it gets us moving.

"Great," I tell him. "Glad to hear it. The ropes stay on."

Pa scowls at me, but he doesn't argue. Micah unwinds the rope from the stable hook and wraps it around his own wrist. He tugs roughly and Pa staggers to his feet. No one helps steady him, and Micah doesn't wait for him to regain his balance before starting to walk off. You lie down with dogs you expect to get fleas, and Pa is getting a tight leash and no mercy all the way to Glory.

54.

Levi's not on guard this morning, so Curtis merely nods at the stranger while we wait for the gate to open. He barely blinks at Pa, but I reckon he's seen more exciting things than a man with his hands bound. We clear the wall and I breathe a sigh of relief; maybe things didn't work out the way I planned, but at least it's half over. I found Pa, for better or for worse. Now all that's left is the long walk back and a short good-bye to everything I love.

I step into the desert and take a deep breath of the hot air, letting it fill up my lungs like it could scald away the disease inside me. After a night in a strange bed, the desert almost feels like coming home. It's comforting, to see the barren land and the fat tumbleweeds doing their lazy roll. Things out here are simpler, purer. I know the danger in the desert, I know what to expect. A shake won't disappoint you, won't lie to you or let you down. They kill you because they're hungry, because their liquified brains tell them to attack. When they hurt you, it's clean, sharp, without malice or intent behind it. I can respect that. You can't hate the rawboned dog that bites you, only the master that starved him.

Curtis lets out a whoop that makes me jump, and he claps his hands together.

"Half done and then some," he says, smiling. "Let's get you folks home."

He sets a fast pace; the boys are burning on full stomachs and have energy to spare. Pa drags Micah back some, hungover and protesting. I lag behind, too; I should have eaten more at breakfast, but even thinking about food makes me feel nauseous. I push myself to keep up, but I'm so tired I don't know how long I can last.

We clear the crag and the rocks under our feet grow smaller and smaller until they're only dust. An ache starts to pound at my temples, and I drink some water to keep it at bay.

"Willie, darlin', give me some of that, there's my girl,"

Pa calls to me. "I'm parched."

He does look pretty pitiful, and I reckon his head is as bad as mine. Wordlessly I cut over and hold up the canteen to help him drink. Pa downs the water like he's dying of thirst, his throat moving rapidly.

"Thanks," he says, and wipes his mouth with his tied wrists. "How are the little ones doing?"

"Fine," Micah answers for me. "No thanks to you."

Pa glares at him and looks back to me. "You know, this ain't necessary," he says, holding up his wrists. "Where am I gonna go?"

"Shut up," Micah says.

"I'm talking to Willie, not you," Pa yells at him.

"You shut up or I'll gag you," Micah yells back.

"Both of you shut up," I order, pressing my fingers to my painful head. "Give him to me, Micah."

"Willie, he's trying to play you," Micah says quietly, like I don't already know that.

"Just give him over before you both do something stupid." I stare down Micah and Pa until they both look away. I hold out my hand, and with a huff, Micah throws me the other end of the rope. "Catch up with the others. I've got him for now."

Micah shakes his head and runs to catch up with

Sam. I start walking at a slower pace, wrapping the rope around my hot arm. My skin is burning, the fever inside me raging unchecked.

"Willie," Pa starts, but I won't look at him. "Willie, I don't blame you for doin' it this way. I know I ain't been a good father to you, or to the others. After your ma—well you know what it were like. I'm sorry for that, truly I am. But I always loved y'all. You believe that much, right?"

More than anything, I want to believe it. But it doesn't change anything.

"It's too late for sorry, Pa," I tell him. "And maybe you really do love us. But you love yourself more."

"I can make it right—"

"Just stop," I tell him. "I got nothing more to say to you and you got nothing I want to hear."

He still tries. He tells me he's sorry, he tells me he didn't have a choice; all the same lies and excuses I've heard from him before. I stop listening, letting his voice fade away until it's a soft buzz in the background. My head feels full of cotton and mud and the lack of sleep is costing me, making it harder to sort out my thoughts. I stare at the ground for so long that after a while I don't even see the desert anymore. Everything is indistinct, one mile of scorched sand interchangeable with another.

When Pa's voice grows loud again I pass him back to Micah, who manages only a few minutes before handing him off to Curtis. I don't know what Curtis says to him but it shuts Pa up quick enough.

I feel dizzy, like I've been spinning in circles. When they were smaller I would hold the twins by the arms and twirl them around until their feet left the ground. I watch my own feet and see it's not me moving, but the ground; miles of tarbush and grit pass under my boot heels, and my eyes grow hot and blurry as the desert flashes by.

The sun rises in the sky and the heat gets more intense. Micah takes Pa again and I keep an eye on them until my lids grow too heavy. My head droops over my chest, my chin almost touching my collarbone. I'm half asleep on my feet, somehow remaining upright and moving. I drift in and out of consciousness, snatches of dreams mixing with reality. A gaping chasm opens up in front of me and I'm too slow to jump back and I'm falling, falling, falling into the darkness inside the earth and it's swallowing me whole; I open my mouth to scream and realize I can feel the sun on my back and my feet are still moving, one boot in front of the other. I raise a trembling hand and slap my cheeks, just enough to wake myself up. My skin feels hot to the touch and dry, and I can't even focus my mind enough to worry that I've stopped sweating.

"Marker," Curtis calls, making me jump. He points to the red-tipped stake in the ground. "One down, more to go."

"How much farther to the station?" I ask. Time, I need more time.

"Eighteen miles," Micah answers, doing the math in his head.

"We should get there by late afternoon," Curtis says. "It's shorter from here to the station than it is from Glory."

We still have hours of walking left. What I really need to know is how much longer I can trust my thoughts. Sam would know, wouldn't he? I open my mouth to ask him and remember I can't. No one can know I'm sick, not yet. Right? Shouldn't they know? It feels wrong, that they don't. It isn't safe for them to be near me. But if they know, they won't let me go home. If they know, that means I'm really sick. It means it's the end.

"What?" Sam interrupts my thoughts.

"What?"

"You're staring at me."

"Oh. Sorry." I switch back to looking down at my boots and the endless stretch of dirt moving beneath them.

A mile or so after we pass the marker, Curtis calls a break. I'm so bent on putting one foot in front of the other that it's almost a physical shock to stop walking. Ben hands around some dry crackers, to Pa, too, but they stick painfully in my throat until I wash them down with water. Curtis stands apart from the rest of us, squinting into the desert.

"What're you looking at, Curtis?" Micah asks.

"Silver. We're gonna be passing it soon. Wish to hell I'd been able to find a new glass in Best." He sniffs loudly. "But it seems quiet enough."

"Think they're mad about earlier?"

"Mad about what?" Pa asks Micah. "What're you dragging me into, boy?"

Curtis ignores Pa and shrugs. "I don't think shakes remember that far. Guess we'll find out."

My stomach twists at the mention of Silver. I can't see any movement, but my eyes can't be trusted and I can barely make out the dark smudges of buildings. I don't want to go back by that town, the burnt walls or the blackened bodies. I've seen enough of it, the sea of pink sand, the bones rearranged into shapes that don't resemble any kind of animal. The bad memories are starting to bleed into one another, into one long parade of death and gore.

"Everybody ready?" Curtis asks, twisting his neck one way and the other.

"Guess so," Sam says nervously.

"Let him loose," Ben says to Micah, nodding at Pa.

"What?" I ask, sure I misheard.

"Let him loose," Ben repeats. "Anything happens, we all need both hands. We can string him up again after."

"He'll run off," Micah insists.

"No, he won't," Curtis says. He looks Pa in the eye. "Mr. Wilcox, you know where we are?"

"I know very well we're close to Silver, son."

"Good. Then you know it's not wise to go running off alone around here. Unless, of course, you're looking to turn shake?"

Pa stares at Curtis and his mouth twists down.

"Then we understand each other." Curtis pulls his knife from his belt and with one swift slice, cuts the rope from Pa's hands. Pa rubs his wrists, but stays in place.

"All right. Move out."

Curtis starts us walking again, but the closer we get to Silver, the more jittery I become. My limbs feel disconnected from my body, like at any moment I will lose my balance and topple over. Heat shimmers off the road, causing the air to ripple and distort. The town lies to our right, and I can feel it glaring at me balefully. The eyes are back, those prying ghostly eyes that see straight through to my rotten insides. They're whispering to me, and what they're saying is that I'm one of them now. Dread overtakes me, a sinking sense of inevitable disaster. Something bad is going to happen soon, and I think that bad is me.

"Guns out," Curtis says.

"Wait," Pa protests, looking desperate. "Come on now, you wouldn't leave a man unarmed."

"Shut up," Micah tells him. "You ain't getting a gun."

Curtis shoves his knife at Pa, who grasps it in both hands and holds it out in front of him. My gun quivers along with the tremor in my arms and feels as useless as that knife. I want to say something, tell everyone about the wrongness I feel, but what comes out is entirely different.

"Thank you," I say, and I hardly recognize my voice.

"Thank you all, for trying to help. For taking me in the first place, and for coming after me."

"None of that, now," Curtis says. "You don't get to say good-byes just yet. We get through this day, and the next, then you can thank us."

But I don't think I'll be getting through this day.

55.

"**W**ill, brisk up," Micah calls, and I snap my head up. I'm lagging behind, and I shake my head to clear it, which only makes it fuzzier. I stagger back to the rest of the group and try to keep close. I match my stride with Micah's, which is hard, his legs being that much longer.

"Quit looking at the dirt, Sis," Micah says. "You keep drifting off."

"Sorry. My head feels like a bag of nails."

"Yeah, well, mine too. I maybe had too much to drink last night."

"I would think you knew better than that," I scold him feebly.

"I do. I just—I needed to not think so much."

My boot shudders against a burroweed branch and I

stumble, reeling forward. Micah grabs my arm to steady me and his face swims in front of my eyes.

"Come on, Will, focus," he says. "Now ain't the time to daydream." He waves his gun toward Silver for emphasis.

I try not to look where he points, but my rebellious eyes move of their own accord and then I can't look away from the muddy bloodstains in the dirt and the streaks of soot on the roofs. I blink and my eyes lock on a lone figure, standing still deep within the town; I freeze in place, because the person framed by the empty buildings is my mother. It's so plainly her, and not the way she was near the end, not thin and wasted and gray, but the way I remember her. Her long hair falls down around her shoulders, framing a face like sweetness and warm cotton. She smells like rosewater. She always smelled like rosewater.

"Mama?" I whisper, and she smiles at me. I drop to my knees, my eyes filling with tears, and I blink them away as hard as I can because I need to see her clearly.

"Will," Micah says, but I won't look away. He'll understand when he sees her. Right now, nothing matters but the woman standing there.

"I miss you," I say, and she holds out her graceful

arms to me. More than anything I want her to hold me, but the hand that grabs my shoulder is not gentle. Micah yanks me onto my feet and tries to tug me away.

"No," I say, and I wrench out of his grip to look back at the town. It's empty, of course, and too far away to see anything, and it's like losing her all over again.

A sting across my face snaps me back to myself, and I look up to see Micah staring at me, his mouth hanging open.

"I'm sorry," he says. "I—I didn't know—"

"No," I say, raising a hand to my cheek. My skin stings where he slapped me. "I needed that. I thought—I thought I saw something."

Micah reaches his hand out to me. "We have to catch up with the others."

I look down the road, stretching long and endless in front of me.

"Too far," I say quietly. "It's too far."

I'm not going to make it back to Glory. The knowledge hits me low, and I sink into Micah, clutching his arms.

"Will, come on."

"I have to tell you something," I say.

"No you don't," he says.

I lean against Micah and take deep, gulping breaths, hoping the air will keep my head clear. I have to do this, have to make sure he understands.

"You have to get Pa back," I tell him, digging my fingers into his arms. "You have to. For the twins."

Micah pushes his face close to mine, his mouth thin. "Will, we're not doing this. Not now."

"Micah—"

"We're almost home," he says, his voice cracking. "Just—just hold on. It's not much longer."

My heart stutters and I finally understand. "You know," I whisper.

His eyes are red—I thought it was from drinking. How long has he known?

"You're a terrible liar, Will," he says. "Always have been."

"When—when did you figure it out?"

"I'm your brother. Did you think I wouldn't notice that you stopped eating? Or that you look like death warmed over? You think I don't know what vomit smells like, that I don't remember how it was with Ma?"

Something's building in my chest, a scream or a sob or a stone.

"I'm sorry," I say.

Micah looks away, blinking rapidly. "It ain't your fault."

"It is. If I hadn't left—"

"It don't matter," Micah says roughly. "All that matters now is getting home."

"I don't know if I can make it," I say.

"Yes, you can," Micah says, stepping close to me. "Just hold on a little longer, Will, and I'll get you home. And I'll take care of you, like—like you did for Ma."

I close my eyes. "You promise?"

"I promise," he says, because he has to. Because I would do the same for him, no questions asked. Because that's what it means to be family in Glory.

"I was wrong," I tell him. "I thought I could do this alone. I thought it was all up to me, but it ain't. I can't do this without you, Micah."

"Come on," he says, putting his arm around me. "Let's go home."

The pressure in my chest eases, and I sag against him. He doesn't cry, and I don't cry, because tears change nothing.

We keep moving down the road, shoulder to shoulder, and I keep my eyes fixed away from the town as we catch up to the others. My mind feels like it's made up of circles and coils, an endless loop with no straight lines. Somewhere buried in that mess is a small scrap of peace; Micah promised. I can be strong for him, if he can be strong for me. He'll do what needs to be done, and the twins will be safe. He'll take better care of them than I ever could.

"Almost past," Curtis calls from up ahead, his lips pressed thin and white. "Keep your eyes—sign!"

He yells the last word as one shake, then another, melts out of the shadows of Silver.

"Sign," Ben echoes as another shake comes running, and two more behind it.

Curtis swears and motions to Ben. "Keep going," he says to the rest of us.

We do, Pa cursing us all for his lack of a gun while Ben swings his rifle around. I look over my shoulder to watch him shoot; the gun goes off and a shake spins, its shoulder blossoming red. It falls to the ground and two shakes fall on it, but the others keep coming, and more follow behind.

"There's too many, Curtis," Ben says grimly. "They ain't gonna stop for one or two down."

"Get to the box," Curtis says.

"It's five miles," Ben tells him quietly.

"You got a better idea?" Curtis looks at the rest of us and I realize we've all stopped moving. "We got a good start on them," he says with forced calm. "But we're gonna have to run."

"Run!" Ben repeats, yelling, and I jump and start running.

Pa didn't need to be told twice, he takes off running with no backward glance. Micah keeps an arm curled around my waist, supporting half my weight. My heart beats erratically, shuddering painfully in my chest. Every time I look over my shoulder the shakes have gained on us; they're close enough now that I can tell some of them are burned and others have blood smeared on their faces. I have the wild thought that they're coming for me, to drag me back to Silver.

"Keep going," Curtis yells. "We can make it."

His gun goes off and he and Ben pull alongside me and Micah and there's smoke in the air and it's hard to breathe. My legs are heavy and my head is stinging and we're so far behind the others.

"Willie, hurry," Micah says. "We have to go faster."

My joints aren't working properly, but I push my knees up to run faster and for a moment it works. Then my stomach revolts and I twist away from Micah and throw up every bit of my small breakfast. My legs give out from under me and I fall into my own sick and sit there, stunned.

"Willie, get up." I look up at Micah, panting. "Come on," he says, grabbing my shoulders and trying to pull me up.

"I can't," I tell him, gasping. "You have to leave me."

"No chance in hell," Micah says, shaking his head. "We're in this together. Now get up."

The shakes are coming, but Micah doesn't move, his face set and grim. He's not going to leave and the shakes aren't slowing down. I grit my teeth and throw out my hand and Micah heaves me to my feet. There's salt on my lips and every muscle in my body is screaming, but I pull out my gun and start moving, Micah's arm wrapped around me. I push through the pain, through the burning of my lungs and the ache in my tendons, push until my bones start to creak.

"Almost there," Micah says in my ear.

I nod, and then a weight slams into my back and I go sprawling face-first into the dust. Micah yells and I roll over to tell him I'm fine, just in time to watch a shake jump forward and bury its teeth in my brother's neck.

I open my mouth to scream and nothing comes out.

The shakes are all around me, ahead of me and behind, surging forward. I crawl through them, knocking against feet and limbs, clawing my way toward Micah as the air explodes with distant gunshots and shrieks. My hand finds my brother's leg and his body is crowded with shakes. My gun goes off, again and again; I can't feel the trigger but I shoot until I'm out of bullets and the only shake left on Micah is the one at his throat. I drop my gun so I can use both hands to grab the shake's head away from Micah; he bites the air frantically, neck veins bulging. His hands scrape at my face and chest while I hold him off; he's so heavy and his breath is like rotting meat and fresh blood. I scream into his face and shove my thumbs into his eyes. The shake howls and throws his head back, blinded and enraged. I grab my blade from my belt and stab him in the chest. His own weight pushes the knife deeper; blood drips down my hand and wrist and I twist the blade until he stops thrashing.

Somewhere close I hear gunshots and Ben yelling and the stamping of boots, but I don't care about any of that. I roll the shake off me and crawl over to my brother. He's lying on his back, his chest moving rapidly up and down and one hand clutching his throat. His blood has soaked through his shirt and pooled beneath his head, a shining red halo. Dead shakes surround him, riddled with bullet holes I don't remember causing.

I crouch by my brother and cover his hand with my own. He's so pale that his blood looks shockingly red, like it's glowing. His neck is slippery and warm where I can feel it beneath his hand.

"I'm sorry," he says, his eyes finding mine.

"You're gonna be fine."

"Liar." Always, always the bone-deep truth.

"Just hold on, Micah."

"I can't, Will. I just wanted to say good-bye." His hand beneath mine goes slack and slips off his neck.

"No," I tell him firmly. "This isn't how it's supposed to be." I clamp my hand over his wound, feeling hot blood welling up between the rough edges of his torn skin.

"Let go, Will."

"I can't."

"Please. It hurts, and I'm tired."

"I won't let you die. This is my—this is because of me."

"Don't think like that." His breathing is slowing down, becoming ragged. I press harder on his neck, but the blood seeps out between my fingers.

"I see Ma." Micah's eyes are unfocused, cloudy.

"I saw her, too."

"Love." His voice is so soft I can barely hear it.

I press my lips together. He's waiting for me to say it, waiting to hear it so he can go. Micah's eyes meet mine.

"Love." My hand drops.

56.

There's a high-pitched keening in my ears that goes on and on. I take a sobbing breath and the sound stops and I realize it was me. I reach for Micah's hand and hold it to my brow, rocking back and forth. If I cry hard enough, if my heart breaks enough, it won't be true.

"It's not real. It's not real. It's not real." It's only in my mind; it has to be. My brother can't be dead.

"Daisy."

The name breaks through the haze. Sam must have been yelling for some time, or he wouldn't dare use that name. I lift my head up and find the others standing watch over me. Ben's chest is soaked with blood and Curtis is holding his arm awkwardly. Sam's shirt is torn and tears run down his face, leaving streaks in the dirt.

Pa stands away from the others, watching stone-faced and silent.

"Willie," Sam says thickly, and his face is a mask of anguish. "Are you all right?"

"It's not real," I say, in a reasonable tone. I smooth back my brother's dark hair, tucking it off of his face. Sam glances back at Curtis and Ben. They must have decided he would do the talking.

"Willie." Sam looks at me with pity and tears in his eyes. "He's gone."

"Don't." I close my eyes.

"Willie, we can't stay here."

"Give her a little longer," I hear Pa say. "Let her say good-bye." There's a rustle, and he kneels down next to me.

"This is your fault," I say quietly. "If you hadn't left—this is all your fault." I say the words to Pa, but I mean them for myself.

"I'm sorry," Pa says.

"Too late," I whisper. "It's all too late."

Pa reaches out to me, but I flinch away.

"Don't touch me," I snap at him.

His hand falls back slowly and comes to rest on Micah's rifle, half hidden in the dirt where he dropped it. I stiffen, staring at his hand.

"So that's how it's gonna be," I say, unsurprised and numb. Pa looks down, refusing to meet my eyes.

"You gonna shoot me, Pa? Leave us both here to rot?"

Pa swallows. "I didn't want this. I didn't mean for this to happen."

"It should've been you," I say bitterly. "It should've been you, not Micah."

"You won't get no argument from me," he says.

Pa's hand circles the rifle and he draws it to him. From above us I hear the unmistakable clink of guns being raised as Ben and Curtis level their weapons at Pa. I look at my father and I feel nothing; there's no love there, but no hate, either, just an empty sort of pity. He looks back at me with the dull eyes of a man who gave up on himself a long time ago, and I think I understand.

"No, you're not gonna shoot. You just want us to kill you. Is that it?" I ask him.

"Better to die here than hang in Glory," Pa says. "Let me go out with some dignity. Let me die by my son."

"Willie?" Curtis asks tentatively. I glance up, see them standing there, guns cocked and waiting for direction. Micah's hand is heavy in mine, made heavier by guilt.

"He ain't worth your bullets."

There's no point to killing Pa. His life is its own punishment.

"Just go," I tell him. "Take the gun and go. I'm done with you. Go drink yourself into the ground or die in the desert, I don't care."

Micah's dead. I'm dying. There's no one left to protect. The twins are young; they'll forget us, move on. None of it matters anymore, there's no point now. It's over.

I look at Pa, look straight into eyes that are just like mine. "Don't ever come back to Glory, not ever. Just disappear like you always do. Go and stay gone. Don't use your name, don't even think it. Harrison Wilcox is dead, you hear me? You're dead. I don't ever want to see you again."

I bend over my brother, clutching his hand to my cheek, feeling the warmth leaving his body. I don't look up, don't watch my father walk away from me for the last time.

"Willie," Curtis says when the soft footsteps have faded away. He puts his hand on my shoulder. "We have to go. More will come."

I slowly let Micah's hand fall away, tucking it gently

against his side. Sam helps me to my feet and I lean heavily on him and see for the first time the carnage spread out around us. There are bodies everywhere, strewn across the red dirt like some beast's innards. My knife is still sticking out of the chest of the one I killed; I pull it out and it's slippery in my hand. This can't be all the shakes left in Silver; Curtis is right, there are more out there and the smell of blood will have them running.

"I can't leave him like this," I say.

"Will—"

"I can't leave his body here for the shakes. They'll turn it inside out, Sam, I won't let that happen to my brother."

"We don't have time to bury him," Curtis says gently.

"Burn him," Ben says. I look up, but he won't meet my eyes. "It's all we can do."

Sam looks gutted, but I'm beyond that now. I'm beyond sick and heartbroken and I'm beyond help.

"Do it," I say.

The only thing I take is the damn pocket watch that doesn't even run. Micah's sleeve catches fire easily, like it was waiting all along for the flame. His clothes burn quickly, his shirt threadbare and thin from how often

I've washed it. He doesn't look peaceful; people always say that about the dead. Micah doesn't look peaceful, he doesn't look like he's sleeping, he looks empty and pale and strange. He looks lonely. He looks dead.

It's hard to stay standing, even with Sam's help, but I do it for Micah. I watch long enough to make sure he'll be safe from the shakes. Sam and Curtis stand on either side of me and Ben is close at my back, three attentive guards to watch over me. It's kind, their concern, but unnecessary; nothing can hurt me anymore. The feeling I had, the badness, it's over and done. All I feel now is hollow.

My face is tight with dried tears, but I don't remember when I stopped crying. I turn away from Micah's body, the smell making me choke back bile.

"We have to go now, Will," Sam says gently.

"I know," I say, and pat his shoulder. "Be safe."

He looks at me, confused, and I almost smile; he thinks I'm going with them. It's too late for that. Micah's gone, Pa's gone, it's all too late. I let go of Sam and reel back, my body folding in on itself. Ben catches me by the arms and slowly lowers me until I'm sitting on the ground.

"Willie, are you all right?" Sam kneels in front of me. "What is it?"

My brother is dead and it's my fault. I'm turning into what killed him. I don't know how to answer, so instead I blink at him.

"Give this to the twins." I hold out the pocket watch and the few paltry dollars from Pa. "Tell them that I love them and take them to Elsie. She'll know what to do."

"I don't understand—"

"You should go now," I say slowly, my tongue thick.

"Will, can you hear me?"

"What's wrong with her?" Ben sounds concerned, and it's sweet of him to care. I don't deserve that.

"I lied," I tell Sam. My voice sounds very loud in my ears. "I don't have any money." I lift my head up to find Curtis. "I can't pay you."

"That—that don't matter now," Curtis says.

"You were right about me," I say to Ben. "You were right from the get-go." He frowns at me, his mouth tight.

I wish they would just go. I don't want to get up. I can't walk anymore. I don't want anxious faces looking over with their pitying eyes and their worried voices. I want to be alone with my grief and my guilt.

"Will, come on now, it's time to get up." Sam pats me

on the shoulder twice, but I brush him off.

"No," I say, the word coming out slurred. No to getting up. No to pressing on. No to everything. This is my line in the sand; this where I stop fighting. My vision is starting to go gray and dim, like all the color is being washed from the world.

"I think she's in shock," Sam says, glancing back.

"That ain't it," Ben says, suddenly wary. He kneels down and pushes Sam out of the way. "Look at me," he says, grasping my chin in his hand. "Were you bitten?"

I try to focus on his face, but it's difficult. My eyes are blurring in and out, the world narrowing to two small pinpoints.

"Were you bitten?"

I find this outrageously funny, and I can't help but laugh. They don't get the joke; I peel back my sleeve and shove my hand out so they can see what's so funny.

Sam hisses in his breath. "You said it was healing."

"I told you I'm a liar." The Garretts back up, looking at me in horror, and that only makes me laugh the harder.

"Let me see it," Sam says, but Curtis grabs him by the shoulders.

"Don't," he says roughly. "Don't touch her."

The laughter dies in my throat.

"How long?" Ben asks, stone-faced.

"Long enough," I say.

"You should have told us," Curtis says.

"Would you have kept going if I did?" He doesn't speak, and that's answer enough. "Don't matter now, anyhows," I say quietly, watching the flames lick at my brother's body. "It were all for nothing."

"Willie—" Sam starts.

"There's nothing can be done, Sam. There's nothing left to say."

"Do you . . ." Ben clears his throat. "Do you want us to help you along?"

I meet his gaze, and his face looks pained. It's a kind thing to ask, a kind thing to offer, this small mercy. But I don't want that from Ben, I don't want his last memory of me to be bloody.

"Thank you," I say, "but I can take care of it well enough on my lonesome."

The three of them stare at me and the weight of their combined gaze presses me deeper into the sand.

"You should go," I say, swaying. "It ain't safe."

"No," Sam says. "Willie, we can't leave you—"

"Curtis, please," I say, closing my eyes.

"Come on," Curtis says, pulling Sam away. "There's nothing we can do."

I keep my eyes shut so I don't have to see Sam struggle against Curtis. When I open them, only Ben is there.

"Go," I tell him.

"I'm sorry," he says.

"Me too."

"I wish . . . I wish it weren't ending this way. But I'm glad to know you."

"Good-bye, Ben."

"Good-bye, Willie."

I lie back in the sand as he walks away, turning my face against the sun. The ground is hot beneath me and smoke drifts into my nostrils as I curl up on my side and wait for my brother to turn into ash.

57.

I'm cold when I start to move again. Nothing is left of Micah but charred bones and bits of buckle. I look at the mess of darkened sand and ashes, but it doesn't sicken me; that is not my brother. Not anymore.

I don't know where I'm going, only that I don't want to be in this spot anymore, where Micah stopped being Micah, where his blood is still soaking into the sand. It hurts my joints to walk, it hurts my chest to breath, but I drag myself forward, one foot in front of another. My skin is on fire and when I try to drink something my stomach rebels and I keel over, retching into the sand. My vision is dark and narrow, and I can't tell which direction I'm headed or if I'm still on the road until my feet bump up against something hard. I look up and my eyes piece together wood and tin into the shape of a hotbox. It's a little large for a coffin, but I reckon it's as good a final resting place as any.

My hands run over the rough wood until I find the notches and begin to haul myself up. I'm trembling when I get to the top, sweat beading along my arms and neck. I pull open the latch and try to lower myself in slowly, but my strength gives out and I land hard on the floor.

I lie where I fell, my breath coming in short, rattling bursts that only leave me more desperate for air. I never thought I'd die like this, alone in a box in the sun. I held Ma's hand at the end, waited until the last bit of warmth left her fingers. No one will hold my hand, no one will weep over my body. Maybe we get the deaths we deserve.

It's dim in here, and cool, and I wipe my damp face and prop myself up against a wall. The ache that's been building in my head starts to streak down my neck to dance along my spine, but the pain is nothing compared to the tear in my heart.

I slide my pack off my shoulder and pull my gun from my hip. I hope the Garretts and Sam are far enough away that they don't hear the shot. They must be almost to the station by now. I wish I could've have gone with them; I wish I could have held on just a little longer. Maybe if I'd told them earlier, maybe if I'd told Sam—but it's no use going down that road. I knew the odds, knew them the second I stepped outside Glory, and I risked it anyway. I'm as bad a gambler as Pa.

I check to make sure my gun is fully loaded, with no empty chambers. Mouth, I wonder, or temple? I shot Ma through the head, so maybe it's right that I end the same way. Temple will be cleaner, and I don't want to leave blood splattered on these walls. I wonder who will find me in here, and when; a hunter, most likely, but it could be days or months before the box is needed. I should have done this outside, I realize, but I don't have the strength to climb out now. And I don't like the idea of leaving my body unprotected, of pieces of me ending up in some shake's stomach. A hunter will know not to touch my blood, at least, to avoid the hole in my head when they move me. But my hand—they won't know not to touch my hand.

I glance down at the wicked slice across my palm. Such a little line with such a long reach. The cut has split open and blood weeps from one corner. This last small thing I can do, and I send a silent apology to the poor soul who finds me. I pull my matches out of my pack, tossing the rest aside. I won't need anything from it anymore. I take my knife from my belt and strike a match with unsteady hands, holding the blade over the flame. When the match goes out, I light another, and another, until the steel singes the tip of my finger when I test it.

I take a tight, raw breath, and I press the hot knife against my hand. My palm erupts in fire, and I scream, loud and long, out here where no one can hear me. It hurts, and I'm glad it hurts, because I've earned this pain. The blade sticks to my skin, like it's melting into me, and when I tear it away the ground drops out beneath me. A black wave rolls over me and I understand too late that I made a mistake; unconsciousness flutters and I fight it, fight with all I have left, because if it takes me, I won't wake up again. Not as myself. I need to end it, I have to end it—I reach feebly for my gun and my fingers brush the metal before my eyes roll back in my head. *Forgive me*, I beg, and I don't know who I'm asking. The last thing I see is a patch of sun through the hatch, and the searing, endless white of the desert sky. It's not so bad, I reckon, as last views go, and then the wave crashes and drags me under.

58.

I'm falling. I think I've always been falling, because I don't remember what came before this. I don't remember my name. I sink down through the sand and dust, through layers of forgotten bone and stippled rock, through hidden water and damp earth, until I come to rest in soft darkness. The pain is gone, or maybe it's my body that's gone, but I'm grateful for the respite. The darkness isn't bad, it isn't empty, it isn't anything. It's the absence of what came before. Except—I can hear voices. I frown, and I'm surprised to find I still have lips. I listen, but the voices are muffled, like they're very far away. They shouldn't be here. I strain to hear them, twisting what might be my head one way and another.

"Liar," a voice screams in my ear, and I jolt upright,

reeling in the darkness that doesn't feel soft anymore. It's sharp, and freezing, and I can't tell where my body, if this is still my body, ends and the cold air starts.

I don't belong here, in the cold, in the dark. I am blinding sun and dust, hot metal and chapped skin. This is not my home, so I start to climb. I scramble up what feels like dirt, my nails digging into crumbling earth and chipped stones.

The darkness doesn't want me to leave. If I stay, it promises, everything will be cold and nothing will hurt. All I have to do is let go. It would be so easy, and I have nothing left. Nothing but the small bits of my body that still count as me. Stay, the darkness says. Stay down. Stay quiet.

But I've been pushed down my whole life. And it's never stopped me before.

I scream and sand pours into my mouth, into my lungs. I choke and sputter, but there, at the corner of my eye, I can see light. I shove my hands into the dirt and dig, grit grinding between my teeth. Something is burning. The acrid smell fills my nose and mouth, and when I breathe I realize the smell is coming from inside me. My skin feels hot and stretched too tight, like diamondback skin pinned in the sun, and the blood is boiling in my veins. I keep climbing, even as my skin bubbles and blisters. I cry out as the blisters pop and wetness oozes over my hands, but I couldn't stop now even if I wanted to; I don't know how to back down from a fight.

Tears stream down my cheeks and blood runs down my arms, and still I climb. I dig through sharp, jagged rocks that tear my fingernails and sand that sticks to my blood and stings. And when I think I'll climb forever, I hear a deafening noise, and light, hot light, pours into my eyes until all I see is white.

"Oh my god," says a voice that I know. "She's still alive."

PART FIVE:
THE START

———

Home is where one starts from. As we grow older
The world becomes stranger, the pattern more complicated
Of dead and living.
—T. S. Eliot

59.

I'm hungry. It's the first thought I form, when I can think again. I'm so hungry that it hurts, that it's all I can think about. My stomach feels hollow and twisted, sucked up against my other organs.

"You're all right." A hand presses down on my shoulder and it feels like a knife slicing into muscle.

Light stings my eyes and I shut them, and suddenly I'm in Silver, I think I'm in Silver. I'm standing in the ruin of someone's home. Half the roof has caved in, and the house sags to one side. Rubble crunches under my feet, rocks mixed with chalk from the whitewash, broken boards and shards of glass. My ruined hands feel along the wood, searching for something, anything to eat, to fill up the vast emptiness that's yawning inside me. I hear a noise, a faint scrape against the sand, and I spin around. My eyes land on a man standing alone in the wreckage, and then my vision goes red.

"Breathe, Willie."

I start to run, and my body moves roughly, like it's new and unused. My feet come down hard and jar my teeth with every step. The man starts to run too, away from me, and it makes me angry. I'm so hungry and he's making me chase him, and I'll make him pay for it. I want to tear the flesh from his arms, let the hot blood fill my mouth and taste what he's like on the inside. It's easy to run him down, he's weak and he's faltering and I'm right behind him. I smell the sweat on his skin and the acid fear beneath it and when I jump on him he screams and the blood is pumping hard in his neck and when I bite it pours out like a faucet.

It's the sweetest thing I've ever tasted, warm and soft and pure; it fills me up and makes me whole. I bury my face in his neck and eat, eat until the emptiness goes away. I finally pull back, breathing hard, and I lock eyes on the face of the man. A boy, really, and one whose face I know as well as my own. I swallow my mouthful and I scream in a voice I don't recognize. Then I lean back in, knowing full well I'm eating my brother, but he tastes so good I can't stop.

I wake up heaving, my stomach in convulsions, and I choke up something wet on my chin. I can't tell if I'm awake or dreaming, everything is black and harsh and damp.

"Don't try to move."

A darker shadow moves across the sky, the outline of a person. I can't make out the features, but I know Sam's voice. Why is he here? He shouldn't be here, shouldn't be near me. I try to speak, but my mouth doesn't remember how to open properly.

"Just lie back," Sam says. The shadow comes closer, bending over me. Something touches my face, my wrist, and I flinch, expecting pain. It doesn't come; all I feel is a slight pressure, coolness against my hot skin.

I'm burning from the inside out. Help me, I plead silently. And maybe Sam can hear me, because his voice comes very close.

"It's all right, Will. Keep breathing. You had a seizure—a fit—and it's gonna take some time to recover. But the worst is over, I promise."

There's a sharp stinging in my arm then, and the shadow starts to fade.

"Go back to sleep," he says.

I try to fight it, try to make him understand. Don't make me go back there, don't let it take me. The words won't come, and the clouds are already starting to roll in and he sounds very far away. I can't stop it and the clouds pull me back into the soft place of dreams.

60.

When I wake up, actually wake up, I know it's real because of the pain. My joints ache; everywhere my bones connect it feels like they've been pried apart and hammered back together. I'm lying on my back, and when I try to roll over my body screams in protest. Even breathing hurts: my throat is tight and raw, and something in my chest pinches when it rises. Opening my eyes takes an effort, my lids flutter and twitch against my cheeks. It's dim, wherever I am, and my vision is hazy. Soft light comes from somewhere, and I move my head to face the bloom.

"Welcome back." Sam peels back my eyelids and his face starts to come into focus. He looks exhausted, deep circles beneath his eyes and a gray tinge to his skin.

"Sam?" My voice is a rusty hook, and it scrapes my throat as it comes out.

"I'm here."

"No," I say, struggling to push him away. I can still taste blood on my tongue. "You have to get away from me—"

"Willie, stop," he says, and I'm so weak I can't move him.

"I'm a shake, I'll kill you—"

"Look at me," Sam says, gripping my wrists. "You are not a shake. You won't hurt me."

I'm shivering, and I want to believe it so badly.

"Am I dead?" I whisper.

"No," Sam says, releasing my arms and easing back. "But you tried your damnedest."

I move my head slowly, trying to take in everything around me. I'm on a cot, and Sam has a stool pulled up next to the bed. There's a thick, clean bandage wrapped around my hand.

"What . . ." I have to stop and cough, and it sets my jaw aching. Sam stands up and fetches me a glass of water, and to my embarrassment he has to help me drink.

"What happened, Sam?"

He sits back down, his hands gripping the empty glass so tight his knuckles are white. I stare at him, not sure if he's real.

"We were almost back to Glory." He says it like he's been reciting this speech. "But I kept thinking about you out there, all alone and waiting to die. I knew I couldn't help you, but Micah would never forgive me if I left your body to the shakes. So I told the Garretts I'd pay if they helped me find you, so I could put you next to Micah."

His name hits me in the chest, a tight punch that has me curling in on myself. My eyes get hot and blurry, but the tears don't come.

"It took us a while to find you," Sam says. "I didn't know where you'd gone, or if you were still in one piece. We finally thought to check the box, and I saw you lying there, and I thought you were dead." Sam looks up at me with haunted eyes. "And then you moved. And I thought I'd have to kill you right then."

My injured hand throbs along to my heartbeat. I don't understand what he's telling me.

"Two days you were in that box, Will. Two days past when the sickness should've ended you. But when I went to get close"—Sam shakes his head, disbelieving—"you were sweating. Your fever was starting to break."

"I think . . . I heard your voice," I say to myself.

"We couldn't move you far, not in the condition you were in, so we carried you here to the station. Well, Ben and I did the carrying; Curtis couldn't, on account of his wrist being broke. It's set up nicely now. We told the guard you fainted from sunstroke."

"I'm not . . . I'm not going to become a shake?"

"No, Will, you're not. Once the fever broke, it was only a matter of keeping you breathing. I stuck you full of morphine and waited. Took four days, but you're finally awake." Sam smiles at me, tired but triumphant, and it's clear that he hasn't slept in those four days.

"I don't understand."

Sam laughs hoarsely. "Neither do I, really. But Curtis told me about the well. I think—I think the infection was weaker, on account of the sickness being in the water. It was thinned-like, easier to fight off. And whatever you did to your hand, it was enough to kill the worst of it."

I look at the white cloth around my palm.

"You made a real mess of it, by the way. I did what I could, but you'll have a scar."

"Sam." I reach out for his hand, even though it sends

a jolt of pain through to my shoulder. "I'm so sorry. Thank you. You saved my life."

"No, Will." He shakes his head. "You did that on your own."

Sam's eyes start to droop, and in a moment he's asleep, his head slumped over his chest. He's wrong, though I don't wake him up to tell him. He did save my life. They could have killed me; in fact they should have killed me. You don't bring infected people inside a fence and tuck them into bed. You kill them before the fever cooks their brains past reason, before they turn on you. No one survives once they've been infected. No one fights it off, or gets better. No one except me. Maybe I'm still dreaming, because none of this makes sense. Why me? Why not Micah, why not my mother? The unfairness of it stings. I'm not special, I'm not exceptionally strong or clever or lucky. I'm not nice, or deserving, or good. But maybe, just maybe, I'm alive.

61.

"Doc says you're awake."

My eyes fly open, and I don't remember falling back asleep. The light is different, brighter, harsher, and Sam's stool is now occupied by Benjamin.

"Easy, now," Ben says, as I try to sit up and fail. "I don't think you should be moving yet."

"Where's Sam?"

"Curtis had to drag him outta here to get some food in him. Kid's dead on his feet."

I didn't expect to find Ben still here. My fever memories may be jumbled and blurry, but I recall parts of what I said, how I lied about the money, about everything.

"You didn't leave."

"No. Thought about it." He shifts back on the stool. "You should have told us."

"I know." I lie back, try to find a position that doesn't ache. "I was afraid you'd kill me. Or make me turn back, and I needed to find Pa. I thought if I could just hold on long enough, I could make it home. Micah—Micah knew." I feel a stabbing between my ribs, and I close my eyes briefly, willing myself to forget. "But it was too late."

"You put us all in danger."

"I did."

"You could have killed us all."

"And you could have left me in that box." Ben's amber eyes watch me evenly. "You could've shot me, thinking to be merciful. You knew I lied to you, and you brung me here anyway."

Ben sighs and rubs his face. "Yeah, well, Curtis did promise not to kill you. Besides, I reckon we lied to you, too. The deal was to get you to Best and home safe. This ain't home, and we sure didn't keep you safe."

"You did your best. I have a—a knack for trouble."

"Seems like it. We had a hell of a time trying to figure out how you caught it till Curtis remembered the well."

I make a sore fist with my injured hand. "It was just a stupid accident."

"Maybe not so stupid, if you're still here. I don't know how, but . . . Doc Junior says people survived the plague, once upon a time."

"What do you think?" I ask, meeting Ben's eyes.

"I think you can take a punch." He stares at me evenly, with none of his mockery.

"How's Curtis's wrist?"

Ben huffs out a breath. "Worst thing to ever happen to man, to hear him tell it," he says. Ben doesn't look injured, aside from a bruise on his cheek that's still puffy.

"You don't have to stay here on my account."

"Sam hired us fair and square. Can't go breaking our word, now, bad for business. Speaking of," and Ben reaches down into a pocket. He pulls out a roll of bills and tucks them into my hand.

"What is this?"

"We didn't hold up our end of the bargain, so Curtis and I don't feel right taking your money."

The bills spread out in my hand like a fan. "This is more than what I paid you."

Ben averts his eyes. "It's your brother's share. I reckon it's yours now."

The pain hits me again, right between my lungs. I

close my eyes and take deep shuddering breaths until it passes. "I don't need your charity, Garrett."

"That's funny, coming from someone who can't sit up."

"Sam paid for Micah, this money is his."

"He won't take it. I tried, and he near bit my head off. Kid's got a stubborn streak," Ben says, admiringly.

"Just because you feel sorry for me—"

"Will you just shut up and take the money? This ain't about charity, it's about doing what's right."

I look down at the bills in my hand. It's more money than I've ever held in my life, and it will still only last me a matter of months. But those are months where I can feed the twins and pay our dues and survive enough to figure out the rest.

"How much would you charge to get me back to Glory?" I ask Ben. He raises his eyebrows at me.

"You know we'll do it—"

"How much?"

Ben sighs. "Twenty dollars."

"Fine, then." I peel off some bills and hold them out. "I'd like you to take me home, please."

Ben rolls his eyes, but it's a compromise we can both live with.

"Yes, ma'am," he says.

62.

The weakness of recovery frustrates me most. I can't walk. At least not well, and not far. The first time I try to stand, I'm embarrassed to realize that someone took my pants off to put me in bed. I hope it was Sam, who only sees me as a patient or a sister. After the miles in the desert, I thought I'd never want to walk again, but days spent lying flat have me itching for the freedom of movement.

Sam lets me hobble around the tent, but my legs are stiff and creaky and I get short of breath quickly. It's just as well I can't go far, since no one here knows I'm recovering from the sickness; the story, thought up by Sam, is that my sunstroke was brought on by a nasty case of pneumonia. I get a tent to myself and the other hunters steer well clear of me, but I'm desperate for distraction. Sam says I need to rest, that I need to get my strength back before I can move, but I'm sick of being in bed. At least I can feed myself now, which saves embarrassment on both sides.

I try not to think about Micah. When I'm awake I school my thoughts away from him, but I can't stop him from invading my dreams. They're sticky and suffocating, fueled by the drugs Sam gives me for the aches in my bones. Sometimes I see Micah the way he always looked, disheveled and thoughtful, and then sometimes his face is pale and blood-covered and I'm the cause. Those times are the worst, because the medicine keeps me sleeping, trapped in foggy nightmares.

My own face is hardly recognizable now. I look at my reflection in a spoon and a stranger stares back: raw-boned and pale, with sunken cheeks and hollow eyes and brittle clumps of dark hair. My lips are chapped and peeling, and if I smile they crack and bleed. Not that I feel like smiling much. I was never a great beauty, but the fever burned off the last bits of flesh I had, leaving nothing but dry skin on bone. Sam says I have to get some meat back on me, and he brings me bowl after bowl of clear salty soup that tastes of fat. I still look half dead, though. I still look like a shake. I go through the motions, lift the spoon to my lips, say please and thank you, but inside I can feel the anger building, a raw wound of resentment and rage.

"You have to give it time, Will," Sam tells me. I ask how much time but he can't or won't answer. I've missed my week deadline with McAllister, missed it by days. He's not one to forgive, or forget.

I worry for the twins; they must know by now something went very wrong. I didn't even tell them about the peppermint drops I hid. It seems terribly important that they know about the candy.

After four days Sam weans me off the drugs, and only then do I realize how much I need them. I take to the cot again, unable to stand without shaking. My neck and back throb when I move them, and my infected arm burns with heat as it heals. That night when my dreams turn dark and stained I wake up screaming, pouring sweat and chattering. Between my dreams and the noise of gunshots from the fence, I wake up more tired than I went to sleep. I beg Sam to give me something, threaten and cajole him, but he remains unmoved. I plead for Ben and Curtis to force him to listen to me, but those two defer to Sam in all things medical. When I call Ben a coward, he says I must be feeling better.

I'm being awful, I know. Maybe some part of me is changed, maybe I've become something dreadful. Not a shake, exactly, but not myself, either. There's a rottenness in me, something left over from the sickness. It's a darkness only my fevered mind could see, damp and vile smelling underneath my skin. Why else am I so furious, so pathetically weak and brimming with bitterness? I could scream until my voice wears out and never empty myself of the anger inside.

After five days of liquid meals and one day with no drugs, I finally throw a spoon at Sam's head.

"If you don't bring me some solid food, I will gut you." I breathe hard through my nostrils, my chapped lips pursed.

Sam bends down and picks up the spoon. It didn't even come close to hitting its target. He sighs as he rights himself, a sigh full of weary righteousness that sets my teeth grinding. "You are the worst patient I've ever had."

"You're not even a real doctor yet!"

Sam shakes his head and walks away, leaving me alone with a bowl of soup and no spoon. I lie back in my cot and curse at myself. I can't stand being stuck here, and I'm driving away the people who want to help. My mouth has always gotten me into trouble, but now I can't seem to control it at all. Compared to this, I was downright restrained before.

I sip my soup straight from the bowl, burning the roof of my mouth. My sore jaw craves something to chew, anything that puts up the slightest resistance. The soup slips down my throat, oily and hot. I can feel it sloshing around my insides, simply moving from one bowl to another. I'm not even hungry, I haven't been hungry since I woke up. I can't eat without remembering the taste of bloody meat in my mouth. I eat because people tell me to, because I can feel my body creak when I move and see my finger bones through the skin on my hands.

"Knock, knock," comes a voice from the opening of the tent, and Curtis peeks his head around. "Can I come in?"

Curtis likes to pretend he's just dropping by my house to say hello. "You don't have to keep doing that, Curtis. No one else does."

"Girls like their privacy," he tells me, like it's some great piece of wisdom. He sits down across from me on the stool I'm growing to hate, I stare at it so much. I know every knot and chip in the wood, just like I know every scuff on the wooden beams and each stain on the canvas of the tent.

"Did Sam send you in here to deal with me?"

"Now why would he do that, I wonder?"

I glare at him, but it has no effect. Curtis watches me calmly, his arm in a sling folded across his chest. The silence stretches long and heavy between us, and I start to fidget under his even gaze. I'm too restless to play this game, I have too much pent-up energy and nowhere to direct it. I break first, like he knows I will.

"What do you want, Curtis?"

"Thought you might want some company."

"What I want is real food. I want to sleep through the night, and I want to get out of this bed and I want to get home. If you can't get me that, then I want you to leave me the hell alone." My voice rises, until I'm almost shouting at him.

Curtis shrugs his shoulders at me, unmoved by my outburst. "I know you're mourning, young'un, but yelling at people ain't gonna make it better."

I press my lips tight together and refuse to look at him.

"You're gonna have to talk about him sooner or later."

"I won't."

"Why not?"

"Go away, Curtis."

"No."

"Go. Away."

"Talk to me, Willie."

"If you won't leave, then I will," I tell him, throwing my blankets off me. I swing my legs over the side of the cot, and even that small effort leaves me winded. After three steps I'm drenched in sweat and after four I'm falling; I clutch at the fabric of the tent to keep myself upright. Curtis just watches as I falter, making no move to help. Ashamed of myself, I let go of the tent and slowly slide down to the ground.

"I want to go home."

"I know."

"And I don't want to talk about him, Curtis."

"Why not?"

"Because it's my fault!" I scream at him. The truth echoes painfully in my ears. "It's my fault," I repeat, quietly.

I thought it was grief, the pinch in my chest, but it's not. Grief I've felt before, great and gray and lonely, but this is different. When Ma died, I thought the sadness would be too much to bear, but I now I find the grief is nothing compared to the guilt. It gnaws at the center of me, drags at my skin and sets my teeth aching.

It's my fault Micah's dead. He was following me, he always follows me. Followed. The past tense hurts, and I let it hurt.

I wanted a way out of my life. I wanted out of Glory, wanted to leave behind the sickness and the fences and the empty plates. I wanted Pa to come back and save me from all that, and it turned out he wanted the same thing I did: freedom. And now he's gone, and so is Micah. And I hate my brother for that, I think. For getting out when I couldn't. I hate him for leaving me alone.

I finally start to cry. And once I start, it's hard to stop. To his credit, Curtis stays until I'm done, until it feels like I've cried myself inside out. Then we just sit in silence.

"He was following me," I say finally, my voice thick.

"You didn't ask him to," Curtis says. "It weren't your fault."

"He wouldn't leave me. I told him to go, and he wouldn't leave me."

"What would you have done, if it were him falling behind?"

I look down at my hands. "The same," I whisper.

Curtis nods slowly. "You remember that. You didn't kill him, a shake did. And for that I'm sorry, Willie. I'm sorry we failed you."

"No. This trip was cursed from the beginning. Anything that could go wrong, did. I think sometimes there's something rotten in me, something unlucky. First Ma, then Pa, and now Micah. If I was you, I'd stay away from me."

Curtis gives me a lopsided smile. "Willie, you're the first person to ever catch the sickness and live to tell about it. That's the kind of unlucky I'll take."

That's part of my curse, though. I'm still standing, when all the people I love are dying, one by one. Is there anything worse than being alone in the world? If this keeps up, I'll be left with only the shakes for company.

63.

I fall asleep early, exhausted from crying, and then wake up halfway through the night with a stiff shoulder and a jaw sore from grinding. I don't remember my dreams, a small mercy. I spend hours alternatingly sweating and shivering, and finally fall back asleep sometime around dawn.

A hand on my shoulder jerks me awake, dragging me unwillingly into consciousness. I blink heavy eyes and look around, confused when I see morning light and Sam bending over me. He always lets me sleep as late as I can, going on and on about how I need to rest to heal.

"Willie," Sam says urgently. "Willie, you have to wake up."

"Mm?" My mouth feels mushy and has trouble forming words.

"Wake up."

I grunt some kind of agreement but my eyes close in protest. Water splashes my face, cold as a slap, and I sit up sputtering.

"Sam, what the hell," I say, glaring at him. I'm wide awake now, wet and angry.

"Get your stuff," Sam says, still holding a soaking rag. "We're leaving."

"What?" I focus on his face and see he looks grim. "What's going on?"

"There's a hunter here, just came from Glory last night. Curtis got to talking to him over breakfast."

My heart thuds in my chest. "And?"

"I guess McAllister got tired of waiting. He put a bounty on you and your pa."

The words ring in my ears and I wait until it sinks in.

"How much?" I ask, getting out of bed and feeling for my belt and gun. My legs are unsteady and I lean against the cot for balance.

"Two fifty."

I give a rough laugh. "Good. I'd hate to think I was worth a small amount." Inside I'm starting to panic, and my hand trembles as I put my gun on, the weight more noticeable after days without it.

"He musta thought you skipped off with the money. We just need to get you back to Glory and he'll call it off."

"I don't see why he didn't make it an even three hundred. I mean, for that price—"

"Stop it," Sam snaps at me. "This isn't funny."

"I know it's not, Sam." I take a deep breath, already winded, and sit down weakly. "You said I needed more time," I say, looking up helplessly. "I can barely walk. How the hell am I supposed to get to Glory?"

"Curtis has an idea, he's working on it. But right now we need to get you out of here and away from the other hunters."

"What about Pa?" I ask, thinking aloud. "You think someone will find him? If McAllister finds out I let him go—"

"We almost didn't find him," Sam says. "If he knows what's good for him, he'll stay hid."

I nod absently. Maybe it was stupid of me, to let Pa go. It didn't seem right, to kill someone that broken down. Not like that, not after Micah. But this is what being soft gets you: hunters on your tail. I put my slicker on—it hangs much looser now—grab my hat, and realize I have nothing else to take.

"Ready?"

"I reckon so," I say. I've been wanting out for days, but leaving the tent causes my back to knot with anxiety. Sam walks next to me, one hand on my elbow to help keep me standing.

Outside, the morning is coming along begrudgingly, pale and musty. Everything washes together, the sun and the sky the same diluted color as the ground, a milky gray that turns my stomach.

A whistle grabs my attention and I turn my head to see the Garretts walking toward us wearing guns, rucksacks, and severe faces.

"Sam explained?" Curtis asks when they reach us.

"I hear I'm worth a lot of money," I say. "You looking for some extra cash?"

"Not if it's blood money," Ben says, looking tired and worried.

Sam squeezes my arm reassuringly. "Don't worry," he says. "I know you ain't up to this yet, but we'll make it."

"I wanted to leave," I tell him with a bony smile. "Couldn't have planned it better myself."

"Let's just get out of here before anyone sobers up," Ben says. He offers me a handful of cold leftover corn dodgers from supper. It's the first bit of solid food I've had, and I fit three into my mouth before I start to choke. "Put your hair up and keep your head down," he tells me.

I raise one eyebrow.

"Folks are looking for you. Ain't that many girls to choose from out here."

Ben waits while I make sure all my hair is tucked under my hat.

"You really ain't gonna hand me over?" I ask him quietly.

Ben frowns. "You think we'd do that? After everything?"

"I wouldn't blame you," I tell him. "That's twice now you should've left me."

"You get dragged back to McAllister on a bounty, he'll kill you," Ben says. "And I already had to make my peace with you dying. I ain't interested in doing it again."

I tug the brim of my hat down low so it hides my eyes. "You're a good man, Benjamin Garrett. You and your brother. For all that you're hunters."

I can't see Ben's face, but I can feel his sleeve brushing against my arm.

"Yeah, well, go on and keep that to yourself."

We head to the gate, Ben and Curtis keeping me and Sam slightly hidden behind them.

"Morning, Lopez," Curtis calls to the guard. "We're heading out."

Lopez gives an impressive yawn, either bored or tired. I've never seen him before, or maybe I have; his features are outstandingly forgettable.

"All right then, on you go."

We file out past him, Sam still supporting my arm. As I walk by, Lopez gives me a sharp look. He opens his mouth to say something, but Sam coughs and quickly pushes me past him.

"Good hunting," Lopez calls after us, and just like that we're outside.

The road sweeps out in front of us, cutting through the expanse of the desert. It's a familiar sight, too familiar, and the memories flood into my head and suddenly I have no air in my lungs. I feel exposed, and the tremble in my hands has nothing to do with being weak. My heart sounds loud in my ears and my breath rattles in my chest. Ben and Curtis walk out ahead, but my feet refuse to move forward.

"Willie?" Sam is at my elbow, his brow knit with concern.

The desert smells like the sun hitting metal and old rotting paper, the smell of heat and dust. Nothing's changed out here, but I have; something in me is broken and bent. I thought the desert was immobile, a fixed place that I moved through, but that's not the case. The desert is a shifting thing; the cracks widen and the shadows shrink, burrs scatter and plant and grow. The sand moves itself from one spot to another, bones and bullets are covered and uncovered. Nothing is ever lost here, only buried; only waiting for the sand to shift, waiting to be found.

"I'm all right, Sam," I say. "Let's go home."

64.

It's slow going. I keep looking back at the station, half expecting to see a posse riding out to round me up. My boots scratch at the dirt, and it's that sound more than anything that calms me. It's steady, like a heartbeat, but more rhythmic than my own erratic heart. Every noise startles me, sends me skittering to one side like an insect under a turned rock. I'm not afraid, exactly; McAllister most likely assumes I'm dead or running, so I doubt anyone will think to look for me heading back to Glory. But I know what can happen out here now, and I'm wary. I scan the desert with wide eyes, looking for dark shadows against the sand.

"Relax," Curtis says when I glance over my shoulder yet again. "We got a good head start. And we ain't gonna let any hunters truss you up and carry you off."

I can't help but laugh.

"What's so funny?" Sam asks.

"Two hunters protecting me from other hunters. I never woulda believed it." I look down at my feet, feeling grateful and undeserving. All that time I spent hating hunters, and now I trust these two with my life.

"I told you, we don't go around killing clients if we can help it," Curtis says. "Bad for business."

"Speak for yourself," Sam interrupts. "I'm turning her in first chance I get. Gonna buy me a horse with that money."

I turn around to punch his shoulder and pause, fist midair; a cloud of dust rises lazily from the road behind us.

"We got company," I say loudly. A single gunshot echoes out, and Curtis swears.

"So much for slipping out early. Let's get this over with," he says, firing a shot back.

"Stay behind us, Willie," Ben orders, and he moves to stand shoulder to shoulder with his brother.

I hear the other hunter's heavy tread before I see him; he stops in front of the Garretts, bending over with his hands on his knees.

"Mornin'," Curtis says pleasantly.

"Y'all thought you could sneak out and no one would notice?" the man says, panting. I frown; his voice is harsh and familiar.

"That was the idea," Curtis says. "You look mighty beat. Up too late or drinking too early?"

I peek around Ben's shoulder as the man catches his breath and stands up.

"You," I say with a sneer, recognizing the hunter who stole my biscuits back in Glory.

"You know him?" Ben asks.

"His name's Grady."

Grady glares at me angrily. He rests his hand on his gun, but doesn't draw it.

"I don't want any trouble," he says, his eyes darting nervously. "Just give me the girl."

I open my mouth to give my own opinion but Sam puts a restraining hand on my shoulder.

"Why don't we let them handle it," he says softly, which is his way of asking me to not make it worse. I sigh and keep my thoughts to myself.

Curtis smiles blandly at Grady. "You're outnumbered and outgunned, friend. Now you go on your way and we'll go on ours."

Grady screws up his mouth in thought, which I'm sure is hard for him.

"I'll split the bounty with you," he says abruptly. "We take her to McAllister, split it fifty-fifty." I don't like the way he's looking at me, like I'm something to be eaten.

"You're not hearing us," Ben tells him, sounding annoyed and thoroughly unimpressed.

Grady licks his lips. "Sixty-forty," he says, getting desperate. His hand trembles ever so slightly on the butt of his gun.

"I don't think—"

"No," I interrupt Curtis. "It's a good deal."

"What are you doing?" Sam hisses at me, but I shrug off his hand to shoulder my way between Ben and Curtis. I face Grady squarely, drawing my neck up so I'm just as tall as him.

"I'll go with you," I tell him. "But I get the share. Sixty-forty."

"Willie—" Curtis starts, and I hold up a hand to silence him.

"We have a deal?" I ask.

Grady blinks wet and hungry eyes at me. He's calculating in his head, trying to figure out if McAllister will pay before or after he kills me.

"Deal," he says, nodding once.

I move closer and hold out my hand; he hesitates a moment before he moves his own off his gun to shake on it. Then I knee him, hard, in a place where no man should be hit. Grady grabs himself and drops like a stone, his face white. I bend down and pluck his gun off him and hand it to Ben, who doesn't try and hide his amusement.

"Geez, Will," Sam says, sucking in his breath. "You coulda just punched him."

I glare down at Grady, who's busy moaning.

"That's for eating my biscuits," I tell him.

Curtis claps me on the back and steers me back toward home. We leave Grady alone in the dirt, where I reckon he belongs. I lean heavily on Sam as we start walking again, tired but vindicated.

"Pleased with yourself?" he asks dryly.

"Yes," I say, and my lips crack as I smile.

65.

"**A**bsolutely not."

"Do you have another suggestion?" Curtis has his reasonable voice on, and I can tell Ben and Sam put him in charge of the talking.

Ben unrolls the litter they want me to ride in. "It's— it's humiliating. I don't want to be *carried* like some wounded animal."

"You are a wounded animal," Ben says under his breath.

"You're not helping," Sam tells him.

"Not trying to," Ben counters. I narrow my eyes at both of them, but they don't scare easy.

"Look, Will, stop being difficult," Sam says. "You can't make it back to Glory on foot; how else are we supposed to move you?"

I weigh my options, and they don't look promising. My legs are trembling and there's a fine sheen of sweat covering my face and arms. I suppose I could insist they let me sit here until I die, but that doesn't seem likely.

"If any of you ever tell anyone about this, I'll—I'll—" I can't think of a good-enough threat. "I'll do something horrible to you. Something permanent."

"Agreed," Curtis says. "Now get in."

The litter is fashioned out of an old saddle blanket and some rope. It's rough and it smells like horse, and I protest one last time purely for pride's sake. Then I climb onto the scratchy blanket gratefully, and with a grunt I'm lifted up, Ben taking the front while Sam helps Curtis on account of his arm. It's a strange sensation, to be lying down and carried; I feel like I'm floating over the desert. At first I try to keep scanning the ground, but it's too difficult to keep turning my head from side to side. I let myself lie back and just stare at the pale sky. The moon is still visible, just a thin splinter so light it looks transparent. The sun is starting to burn off the grayness of the early morning, a promise of a beautiful day.

I feel safer in the litter, which I know is silly; if anything happens, I'm at a disadvantage. Still, being wrapped in a blanket is always comforting, especially one carried by well-armed hunters. I start to relax, lulled by the movement, and close my eyes.

"You always this sweaty?" Ben rudely interrupts my reverie.

My eyes fly open to find him staring at my face. He's trimmed his beard recently, I guess at the station.

"I'm ill," I tell him. "And I have hunters chasing me. What's your excuse?"

"I'm carrying an ill person. Who's being chased by hunters."

I grin ruefully, because there's nothing I can say to that. I study the leather guard at his throat; it looks sturdy and well made. I wonder if I could make one out of snakeskin. There has to be some way for me to bring in more money. Under the sadness and the shame, the reality of losing Micah is starting to sink in. My brother is really gone, along with everything that entails. Who's going to keep me truthful now? Who's going to help me skin snakes and chase after the twins? I don't know how to survive without him. I don't know if we can survive at all.

"I don't mean you're heavy," Ben says, disrupting my thoughts again.

"What?"

"You're looking blue at me. I was only joking, you're not making me sweat."

I frown at him. "Oh, it ain't about that. I'm just thinking."

"'Bout what?"

"My brother. We always worked together, you know? Like you and Curtis. It was hard enough with the two of us, what am I gonna do now? I got nobody else."

"You'll think of something." Ben gives me a steady nod. "You'll find a way to get by."

"I reckon I must." My mind goes back to the conversation I had with Clementine. I scoffed at her then, still sore about the Judge. I never thought things would get bad enough I'd really consider joining up with Pearl; that's for girls with no other options. But I'm looking around, and my options are mighty slim. And one thing's certain; I didn't survive the sickness just to starve to death in Glory.

"Why did you become a hunter?" I ask him.

His eyebrows shoot up before he schools them back down. He pauses before he answers me, choosing his words carefully. "Our family were horse breeders, up in Ennis. Our granddaddy started the stables, and Pa took over when he passed. Only I don't need to tell you what happened—everybody knows shakes go for the animals first. Our horses got sick, or died on the road, and we had to shut down."

"So you decided to go kill shakes."

"Seemed like the thing to do. What else is there out here?"

"You could go north. I hear they got real cities there, with proper roads."

Ben shakes his head. "Ain't no way out. No railroads, no stations once you get past Llano. Judge don't want us leaving, and neither do the folks up north."

"He can't control y'all forever."

"Someone else will take his place. Don't much matter who's at the top when you're scraping the bottom. Look, I know you don't like hunters, but there ain't many ways for a man to make a living now."

"A woman neither," I say, trying to keep the bitterness out of my voice. "And I like you fine, Garrett. You done right by me, hunter or no."

Ben smiles at me, that rare lopsided smile of his. It makes my stomach turn over, but not in an unpleasant way. His smile's gone as quickly as it came, but I think I can still see a ghost of it hidden in the corner of his mouth.

66.

I sleep for a spell, a restless, impatient sleep. I wake up often, catching scraps of conversation and mumbled curses when the litter jostles. I throw one arm over my face to block the glare of the sun but it worms its way in, hanging over the edge of the litter like a pink ribbon. When the litter comes to a full stop, I wake up sticky and drowsy, my mouth tasting sour. The boys lower me carefully, and I clamber out like a newborn calf, groggy and disoriented.

"Where are we?" I ask.

"Maybe a third of the way," Curtis answers. He hands me a canteen, and I drink away the taste in my mouth.

"I can walk for a bit," I say, wiping water off my chin.

It's half question, half statement, and I raise my eyebrows in Sam's direction.

"If you feel up to it," he says.

"I do."

I reach my arms over my head, stretching out the last bits of sleep. Ben passes around apples, and I take my time eating one, enjoying the crunch and chew of it. I gnaw on the core while we start moving again, sucking at the last bits like a dog with a bone. I toss the remains far into the desert, watching for the cloud of dust when it lands.

Riding in the litter seems to have calmed my nerves some. Well, that, and getting back at Grady. I flex my calves, and they're sore but steady. The sun is hot on my neck and shoulders, soothing my achy muscles while sweat collects under my hair. I desperately need to bathe again, my shirt is stiff with fever sweat and dirt and I feel like I'll never get all the grit out from under my nails. When I get home, the first thing I'm doing is washing myself, and then these clothes. After I deal with McAllister and get the twins, of course. And after I tell them about Micah, and Pa. I don't know how much of the rest I should say.

"Sam?" I get his attention.

"Do you need to stop?"

"No, I'm fine. I'm wondering—are you sure it's safe for me to be around the twins? The sickness won't come back?"

Sam shakes his head. "I told you, once the fever's gone, you're not contagious. I wouldn't let you hurt anyone, Will."

I nod, chewing on my lip. "What are you going to tell your father? About what happened?"

Sam frowns, rubbing a finger under one eye. "I don't know. Some of it, I guess."

"About me getting sick?" I suppose I shouldn't mind if Doc Kincaid knows, but for some reason it feels private. "And what about you two?" I add, glancing at Ben and Curtis.

The boys exchange glances, and I can tell they've talked about this already. I'm slightly annoyed; when were they planning on including me?

"Willie, we're not going to tell anyone," Curtis says. "Nor should you."

"It's not something you want people knowing," Ben adds.

I scratch the scab on my hand, feeling irritated. "You're saying that like I did something wrong."

"Folks won't trust you," Curtis says bluntly. "No one's survived before, and they won't understand. They'll want to know why you."

"Why me, why not their husband or wife or child," I finish for him. It's the same thought I had, why me and not my mother. Why not Micah, who was so much better than me. I can understand their imaginary anger well enough.

"Right," Sam says. "And it ain't only about you, Willie. We're in it just as much. If the Judge finds out—well, he's gonna want to know how, and I don't know the how. And he won't take 'I don't know' for an answer."

"And we didn't exactly follow the rules on this one," Ben says. "If the other hunters find out we brought the sickness inside the station, we're done for."

I look at the three of them, pained at how much they risked for me, how many times they've spared me; I did nothing to deserve it.

"We'll figure this out together, Will," Sam says. "Figure out what happened, and if—if we can make it happen again."

"You think there's a chance?" I ask, my breath catching.

"I don't know. If you'd asked me a week ago, I'd

say you'd lost your mind. Now . . ." Sam shrugs. "Everything's different."

"One thing at a time," Curtis says. "Till we have answers, safest thing is to keep quiet."

"I don't want to cause you any more trouble than I already have," I tell him. "No one will hear about it from me, I promise."

I make another, silent promise to myself: no matter how long it takes, somehow, I will pay back what I owe these boys.

67.

I walk for as long as I can, and next time I don't argue when Sam tells me to stop. I get back in the litter and stare at the horizon without really seeing it. My mind is stuffed with too many questions and not enough answers. I don't know how to tell the twins about Micah; hell, I don't even know if they'll still be at Bess's. They thought we'd be home days ago and if Calvin gets anxious he's likely to run off back home. I hate to think what they're doing to the house unsupervised.

A scream pierces the quiet of the desert, a human-sounding scream; a second later a gunshot rings out. The litter stops immediately, and I scramble out, my heart pounding in my ears.

"Where did that come from?" I ask.

"Not sure," Curtis says, his voice clipped. "Ben, do you see anything?"

The boys drop the litter to the ground as soon as I'm clear, and Ben jerks his head around like a madman.

Another gunshot sounds, and I whirl around, straining to see anything.

"There, straight ahead," Sam says, pointing. I follow his arm and see a pale cloud of what looks like rifle smoke rising up.

"Damn," Curtis says, his eyes narrowed to slits, "it's on the road. I can't make out how many."

He throws a loaded glance to Ben, his good hand already on his gun. The brothers are coiled tight as snakes. Curtis looks at me, and I give him a sharp nod.

"Go. I'll keep up as best I can."

"Stay with her," he says to Sam, already starting to run. Ben has a head start, but Curtis gets even with him in a matter of seconds. Their boots pound the dirt solidly, kicking up huge billows of dust.

My hands are trembling something awful, but I help Sam quickly roll up the litter. I throw my pack on my back and we start after Ben and Curtis, Sam letting me set the pace. I grit my teeth and break into a run, adjusting my gun where it bangs against my thigh.

Another shot sounds and I push to go faster, but my legs start to quiver and my lungs are burning in my chest. I can't keep up this pace for long, but I focus on Ben and Curtis ahead of me, keeping my sight fixed on their backs. The gunshots have stopped, and now the only noise is my own labored breathing and Sam's feet next to mine. The distance diminishes step by step, and I realize Ben and Curtis aren't shooting. That, and the silence, means I should prepare myself for what we're about to find.

Ben is putting his gun away when we pull alongside him.

"Too late. Nothing's moving."

I use the last of the walk to catch my breath and steady my nerves. The land slopes up gently, and my legs protest even the slight incline. Sweat drips off my nose and chin, and I wipe my face with my sleeve. My eyes go immediately to the lumpy figures in the road, maybe three of them; it's hard to tell the shapes apart. I would take them to be piles of wood and dirt if it weren't for the red smears. The blood looks out of place, the color so bright against the sand. It is out of place, I remind myself; it belongs on the inside.

Curtis swears under his breath and stops a good

ways away from the scene. I can make out individual faces now, separate the bodies from one another. They're not from Glory or I'd recognize them. Hunters on a supply run, I reckon, judging from the bags scattered in the sand: salt, feed, nails, and the like. It's easy to tell how they died, but I try to keep my eyes off those mangled parts. One man still has his gun in his hand, so he must've gotten off a few shots before he bled out. The shake that did it is lying close, slumped against a large rucksack like he's just sitting.

Ben walks around to look at the shake more closely and his eyes widen. He looks up quickly and sniffs.

"We should go," he says, his voice far too casual, "before any more come."

I march up to where he's standing and make for the shake.

"Willie, don't," Ben says. He catches me by the arms but doesn't protest when I break away.

I smell the liquor coming off him before I even see Dollarhide's face. I give a quick, sharp inhale, not quite a gasp but more than a breath. His mouth is wet with blood and the skin over his eyes looks almost translucent. There are bullet holes in his shoulder and stomach, but I guess they didn't slow him down much. I bite my lip hard, fighting the rising nausea that comes with understanding. I did this. I bled on him, I infected him, and I turned him loose on these people. That's three more deaths to place at my feet.

"You couldn't know—"

"Don't," I say, cutting off Ben. "Just don't."

He held out longer than me. I wonder if I would have lasted longer, too, if I were stronger, if I always got enough to eat. Did he know what was happening to him, or was he too drunk to even tell how sick he was? I didn't like Dollarhide, but I wouldn't wish this on him. I wouldn't wish it on anyone.

"Should we move him?" Sam asks, rubbing the back of his neck. "He was one of y'all."

"He was a damn cur and a poor excuse for a hunter," Curtis says calmly. "He ain't one of us."

Sam shrugs, but he doesn't argue. He comes to stand next to me and puts a hand on my shoulder. I turn away, feeling sick to my stomach.

"Come on, Sam," Curtis says. "There's nothing we can do for him now."

I take one last look at Dollarhide, Sam standing over him, and only then do I see his chest rise.

"Sam!" I yell as Dollarhide lunges forward, Sam in

his sights, and everything slows down to a crawl. It all becomes very simple in my mind. All the wrong choices I've made in my life, all the mistakes, they lie out behind me like faulty footsteps. I can see it: every time I should have been kinder, or quicker, or better, every point I should have turned back or started over; it's all there, written in the dirt. I can't erase it, can't undo it or fix it. I can't go back to make things right, all I can do is go forward. And maybe this, this one thing, I can do right.

My feet move forward of their own accord, like my body knows what I'm going to do before I do it. It's only a few steps to Sam, but it feels like the distance is insurmountable. It takes forever to reach him and it takes no time at all. One arm shoves Sam out of the way as Dollarhide's teeth sink into the other.

68.

The pain snaps me back into reality, and everything is fast and loud and harsh. Sam is screaming at me from the ground, but all my focus is on the jaws latched on to my arm. Blood bubbles up around Dollarhide's mouth, staining his teeth red, but just as quickly he releases my arm. I don't stop to think about why he let me go, I pull my gun free and jam it against his temple. He stares past me, his eyes feral and uncomprehending, even when I pull the trigger.

The shot blasts Dollarhide sideways and his body hits the ground with a thud. More shots go off as Ben and Curtis make doubly and triply sure he's dead. Sam grabs me by the shoulders and pulls me away, turning me around to face him.

"Let me see it," he says, his voice shaking.

"It's not bad."

"Let me see."

I hold out my arm for him to see. The wound is jagged and bloody, but not too deep. Of course it's my injured arm, because I certainly need more scars on it.

Curtis and Ben are by my side now, making me sit down. Despite how much my arm hurts, I'm surprisingly relaxed, a strange peace sitting like a stone in my belly.

"I need alcohol," Sam says.

"From where?" Curtis asks.

"If Dollarhide's here, there's alcohol," Sam snaps at him.

"Right." Curtis runs begins to frantically search through the debris on the ground.

"Sam, please calm down," I tell him.

"Willie, that was so stupid. How can you be this stupid?" Sam looks angry and frantic, like someone turned him upside down and shook him.

"Hey, now," Ben says, "take it easy."

"Got it," Curtis calls, and returns grasping a bottle of whatever rotgut Dollarhide had on him.

Sam doesn't offer any thanks, he just grabs the bottle

and opens it. "Brace yourself," he orders.

"Wait—" But he doesn't, and I cry out as the whiskey burns into my wounds. My arm is on fire; everywhere the liquid burrows into my skin is a stinging spot of pain.

"Son of a bitch, Sam!" My calmness evaporates, especially when he tries to do it again. I yank my arm away and he grabs it back. "Let go."

"Will, I need to clean this."

"Like hell you do."

Ben grabs my other hand and holds it, and I look at him, shocked. Sam uses my distraction to pour more liquor on my arm, and I squeeze Ben's hand as hard as I can.

"Damn it," I say, gritting my teeth in pain. I keep my eyes locked on Ben, and he stares back and something stretches between us that I can't name, something sharp and bright and blinding.

"Drink this," Sam says, breaking my focus. He hands me the bottle and I frown at him. "I'm out of laudanum."

I let go of Ben's hand somewhat reluctantly and take a long drink. I have to fight not to spit it out; it burns going down almost as much as it did on my arm.

"How deep is it?" Curtis asks, bending over.

"She doesn't need stitches," Sam says, prodding at the wound gently. Now that the blood is rinsed off, I can see that the bite is a perfect circle of teeth marks.

"He let me go. I told you it wasn't that bad. But this is." I take another swig of the foul whiskey.

Sam starts to bandage my arm, rolling clean white bands around my bleeding and dirty skin. The spots of red bleed through, little blooms of color dyeing the cloth.

"Damn it, Will," Sam says. "Why did you—" he stops, his jaw working, and Curtis squeezes his shoulder.

"Sam. It wasn't stupid." I keep my voice low, but I want to make sure he understands. "I had to. This was the only thing that made sense. Why risk losing you when we know I can beat it? I fought it off once. I'll do it again."

"You can't promise that," Ben says. He looks at me sternly, his eyebrows almost meeting.

I try a smile. "I just did. No more lies, Ben. You have to trust me."

Ben sighs and takes the bottle from me.

"I thought you didn't drink on the road."

"I'm making an exception."

"How many times are you gonna make me patch you up, Will?" Sam asks, tucking in the ends of the bandage. He's still angry with me, but his bloody hands are steady.

"Don't scold. Give that here, Ben," I say, and take the bottle away from him. I crook a finger at Sam to hold out his hands and I pour enough whiskey over them to wash away the red. "You can't be getting sick, too. I'm counting on you to get me through this again, Sam."

He stares at his wet hands. "And what if I can't? What then?"

"Then we deal with it. Right now all I care about is getting home."

"I got something that'll help with that," Ben says, his eyes glittering as they alight on something beyond the road.

"Well I'll be damned," Curtis says, his voice awed. "Is that Dollarhide's horse?"

I stand up to get a look, and sure enough, standing on her lonesome half a mile down the road is Dollarhide's dun.

"She musta bolted when the ruckus started," Ben says. "Good thing he didn't turn shake when he was still on her back."

"Lucky girl," I say.

Curtis puts two fingers in his mouth and whistles a

high note and the horse leaps forward. She walks hesitantly, shaking her head every few steps.

"Easy, girl," Curtis calls, walking out to meet her. The horse stops and paws at the ground, and Curtis sidles up to her one small step at a time. He keeps his voice low and makes a grab for her reins. "It's over now."

He makes soft clucking noises at the horse, rubbing her nose like he's already in love.

"Well, how about that," Ben says. "Dollarhide was good for something after all."

69.

The horse is badly spooked, and it takes Curtis some time to calm her down. Ben empties out Dollarhide's saddlebags, keeping only more whiskey and some rope. I'm still working on the first bottle, and it's making me feel giddy and loose. My forearm is almost completely numb; it's an odd sensation, and I poke at the bandage before Sam slaps my hand away. He hovers around me like a cross mother hen, asking how I feel every few minutes. It would annoy me if I were sober, but as it is I just ignore him.

"What are you going to name her?" I ask Curtis.

He strokes her nose and the horse lips at his shirt, clearly smitten. "I was thinking Daisy has a nice ring to it."

I shake my head ruefully. "Well, I reckon that name is suited to a horse."

"Can you ride?"

"It's been a while." In truth I've only ridden once, and that was on a small donkey that McNab had behind the general store. I don't want back in the litter, though, so I keep my mouth shut and figure I can blame any falls on the alcohol.

"Need a hand up?" Curtis offers.

I grab his hand, telling myself I don't wish it were Ben's. I know enough from watching others mount up to stick my left foot in the stirrup, but the horse looks impossibly tall and wide from this close. I get halfway into the saddle before I start sliding down and Curtis has to shove me back up. I end up lying sideways over the top of the horse and it takes a fair amount of readjusting to get myself properly seated.

"Just relax," Curtis says. "Hold on to the horn there. She knows what to do, she'll take care of you."

"Are we all set?" Ben asks, taking a last look around. "Let's hightail it outta here before something else goes wrong."

Curtis loops the reins around one hand and the horse lurches forward, sending me swaying. I grab for

the horn and right myself, but it doesn't bode well for
the ride. I bounce up and down in the saddle, feeling
every jolt and bump; the horse can tell I'm not a good
rider and snorts with irritation.

"I'm doing my best," I whisper into her ear. "Just get
me home and you never have to see me again."

Maybe she can understand me, because we reach
some kind of compromise; I find the right rhythm and
stop bouncing, and she doesn't dump me on my rear.
We make much better time now that no one has to
carry me, and the saddlebags lighten our loads consider-
ably. Daisy—I make a face at her name—follows Curtis
without hesitation, matching the pace he sets exactly.

"How you feeling, Will?" Sam asks.

"The same as I did the last time you asked. And the
time before that." I don't mean to snap at him; the whiskey must be wearing off. I give and a sigh and muster up
an apology. "Sorry, Sam. I know you mean well. I'll tell
you soon as anything changes."

"You swear? 'Cause last time . . ." Sam shrugs and
trails off.

"All right, I get it. I shoulda told you straight off I
was sick. But honest, I didn't even start feeling poorly
till the next day. The only thing that hurt was my hand,

and right now my arm is so numb I could put it through a wringer and I wouldn't feel a thing."

Sam narrows his eyes at me, and I sigh again, this time with exasperation.

"Sam-I-swear-I-will-tell-you-when-I-feel-something," I rattle off. "Happy?"

"Yes ma'am," he says, and he smiles. I haven't seen him smile since I woke up, and a sudden rush of concern and affection floods me.

"I'm sorry, Sam," I tell him. "I'm sorry I keep putting you through all this madness."

Sam gives a rough laugh. "I should be the one apologizing. I don't think I thanked you yet for saving me from Dollarhide."

"Well, we're even now. Seems only fair." I look down at my bandage; I'm lucky he got my arm and not someplace more tender. I wonder how much worse it was for Micah, how much it hurt to feel those teeth rip into his neck. Thoughts like that will keep me up nights.

"Why do you think he let you go?"

I frown. "I don't know. I would say he remembered something, but Dollarhide never showed me any kindness. Maybe he thinks I'm one of them. Maybe I smell like a shake now."

The shakes in Silver, it was like they knew me. Like they could tell. I'm not a shake, but I'm not the same; I'm something in between.

"I guess that could be a good thing," Sam says. "But you smell fine to me. I mean—well, we all could use a bath."

"Gee, thanks, Sam."

He smiles at me again. "You know Micah would be furious you let a shake eat up your arm."

"I know," I say. "I'm awful mad at him, too."

70.

We're almost home. I would hold my breath until we go through the gate if I could; every mile we pass safely seems to tempt fate. Part of me didn't think I would really get home again. Maybe the desert decided it's taken enough from me; it's a different me that's going home, anyway.

The closer we get to Glory, the closer the boys get to the horse; they huddle around me, Curtis in front, Ben in back and Sam flanking my side. From this height I feel like someone important, a queen surrounded by her guard. The thought makes me laugh to myself; it's a sorry kind of queen with hand-me-down pants and knotty hair.

The numbness wears off after a couple hours, and

now the skin of my arm is sore and hot. I don't worry until the itching starts, and then I keep good on my promise and tell Sam.

"How long has it been itching?" he asks.

"It just started. I wouldn't think much of it, but it happened like this last time, on my hand. It got all red and puffy and wouldn't stop itching."

Sam gives a jerky nod. "All right. Keep the bandage on and don't scratch it."

"What does it mean?" Ben asks him, but I already know what he's going to say.

Sam pauses, then lets out a long breath. "It's a sign that a wound's infected."

He glances at me and I shrug; it's what I expected. I suppose I should act more concerned, but there's no point. I'll fight it off or I won't, and either way I'll do it on my own terms. I've used up all my capacity for grief and anger, I have nothing left to give. It's easier this way, not to feel so much, to let it all drain away. This is what Ma meant, when she told me to be hard. It's not about being strong, like I thought. It's about giving up what makes you weak. The fever burned the fear out of me and the desert burned out the last of my softness. All that's left is grit.

When the gate comes into view, it feels unreal. I've been imagining it for days and it looks too solid, too tall to be true. I fight the urge to whip the horse into a gallop, but the last mile stretches my nerves taut and sharp.

"Home, sweet home," Sam says as we come up on the fence. I never thought those words about Glory, but I find myself agreeing with him.

"Who's that?" calls the guard.

"Garrett," Curtis calls back. "Open up, we got four coming in."

After a moment, the gate begins its horrible screeching and slowly opens for us. My heart beats wildly, still convinced something will go wrong.

"Come on, then," the guard says, and Curtis leads the way inside. I thought I recognized the guard's voice, and sure enough Amos Porter is waiting for us.

I let out a breath as the gate closes, the sound sharp and final.

"When'd you get a horse?" Amos asks.

"It was Dollarhide's," Curtis answers. "He won't be needing her anymore."

Amos grunts, taking the news in stride, then his face breaks into a smile. "Well, I'll be! Is that you, Willie?"

"Hey, Amos," I smile back at him.

"Thank god you're back. You know there's hunters after you?"

"I know."

Curtis halts the horse and I fling my leg over and slide down as best I can. My back and my rear ache from riding so long, and I wince when I hit the ground.

There's a stilted moment when we all realize we've actually made it back. I glance at Ben and Curtis; this may be the last walk I take with them. It makes me strangely wistful.

"And I see you came home, too, Doc Junior," Amos says to Sam. "Your pa's been hounding me night and day. Next time you feel like taking a trip, you might oughta tell him."

"Sorry, Amos," Sam says.

"Where's your friend, then?" Amos asks him. "Your brother, Willie, you hiding him?"

I brace myself. "He won't be coming back."

His smile fades slowly, the corners of his mouth dragging down. "I'm sorry for your loss, young'un."

"Thank you."

"Well, come on," Curtis says, always taking the lead. "Can't stop now."

We take our time walking the small distance down

the road. I breathe in the smell of Glory, the tang of wire from the fence and the yeasty scent of bread coming all the way from the Homestead. It stirs up memories, both good and painful. We walk toward the center of town, the street empty and the shops deserted, just like always. I find myself appreciating the quiet; I have to get my head in the right place before I walk into the saloon.

The silence is disrupted when we get closer to the Homestead; rowdy voices drift out, and someone is singing loudly and off-key. I take a deep breath and push the door open, ready to get this over with. One last task and then, like the song says, it's home, sweet home.

71.

I didn't expect anything to change, but it still feels odd that nothing is different in here; the tables, the spittoons, even Elsie behind the bar, everything is right where I left it. It's like Glory stopped in place when I went away, waiting patient and lifeless until I returned and it could start moving again.

"Willie?" Elsie's eyes widen when she sees me, and she runs out from behind the bar to take my face in her hands. "Sakes alive, you look like death warmed over. I expected you days ago, I was that worried. I told McAllister, I told him—"

"I'm fine, Elsie," I tell her as she examines my face. "The Garretts took good care of me."

"Thank you," she says, looking at Ben and Curtis.

"For bringing her home safe. She means a lot to me."

"I'd never want to disappoint you, Miss Elsie," Curtis says, taking his hat off.

"You," Elsie says, pointing her finger at Sam. "You best get home, and quick. Your pa is fit to be tied."

"I'm going soon, I promise," Sam says, holding his hands up in surrender.

"Mm-hmm," Elsie mutters, and takes me by the shoulder. "Let's get some food in you, you look thin as a barber's cat."

"Some other time, Elsie," I say. "I got things to do first."

I scan the room, and it doesn't take long to spot McAllister; he's sitting at the Judge's table. The sight of the two of them sets my teeth grinding, and I don't even attempt to hide my disgust.

"Ready?" Sam asks quietly, and I nod.

I march over, my blood rising up with each step I take. They see me coming and McAllister looks shocked to see me alive and walking; the Judge looks like he always does, bored and inhuman. There are two other hunters sitting with them, but I take no notice of them.

"Miss Wilcox," the Judge says, nodding to us as I

approach the table. "Garretts. And Samuel Kincaid, is it? I believe your pa is looking for you."

"So I hear," Sam says.

"Didn't expect to see you back," McAllister says, schooling the surprise off his face and crossing his arms.

"I got held up," I tell him. "But I'm here now, so you can go ahead and call off the bounty."

He sniffs. "Not unless you got something for me."

"Call off the bounty," I say, my voice too loud.

McAllister starts to smile, and I reach into my pocket and slam down Micah's pocket watch and the crumpled bills Pa gave me.

"My pa's dead," I say. "And that's all that's left of your money."

He picks up the bills, smoothing them out on the table, while the Judge slowly flips the pocket watch over to reveal Pa's initials.

"He's dead," I say again. "You want the rest of your money back, you can take it up with the devil himself."

The Judge looks past me to Curtis.

"You saw this?" he asks.

"Yessir," Curtis lies. "We did."

Ben clears his throat. "What the girl says is true."

McAllister balls the money into his fist and bangs it

on the table, swearing harshly.

"Enough," the Judge orders. "Call off the bounty, the man's dead. Make your peace with it, McAllister."

McAllister glares at me, his hand still clenching the money. "We're square," he spits out.

"We're not square," I tell him. "We'll never be square, and don't you forget it. If you ever step one foot on my land again, I'll kill you. I don't care what your friends do to me after, it's enough to me that you'll be dead."

"You don't scare me," McAllister says with a laugh.

"Don't matter. The brave die just as easily as the scared," I tell him. I pick up Micah's pocket watch from the table and tuck it away. "Either way, I'll bury you."

I turn my back on him and ignore the name he swears at me as I walk away. He can call me whatever he likes, but I meant what I said. He comes near me or mine again, I'll be more than happy to kill him.

"Miss Wilcox," the Judge calls after me. I steel myself and turn back to face him.

"Yessir?"

"My condolences on the loss of your father," he says, his pale eyes roving over my face.

"Thank you," I manage to say.

"You should get some rest. You don't look . . . well."
He smiles thinly at me.

I nod stiffly and turn away. It's enough to tell me
he thinks I'm lying. How much he suspects, I can only
guess, but my insides are crawling with doubt.

"That went as well as it could, I reckon," Curtis
offers as we march out of the Homestead.

I shade my face with my hand so I can look up at
him. "Thanks for saying what you said. Both of you."

Ben shrugs. "I'll take any chance to lie to the Judge."

I wince slightly, hoping the Garretts at least are
safe from his grasp. We head slowly back down the
road. The brothers are staying at the Homestead, so
they'll just have to turn right around, but I can't bring
myself to tell them they don't need to come with us.
We've been walking together so long, it just feels right.
I didn't even know them two weeks ago, and now it
pains me to think I'll wake up tomorrow and they
won't be there. I won't have Curtis to give me orders I
don't want to follow, and I won't have Ben to—well, I
won't have Ben.

The fork in the road comes sooner than I want. Ben
reaches it first, but he waits for the rest of us to catch
up, and we gather in a small circle.

"Well," Curtis says. "I gotta say, this was the worst job we've ever been on."

That surprises a laugh out of me, and he grins.

"I ain't sorry, though," he says. "Doc, it's been a real experience. I'm glad we had you along."

Curtis holds out his hand, and Sam shakes it. "Anytime you need patching up, you let me know," he says.

"Thanks for all your help," Ben adds, taking Sam's hand next.

"And Willie." Curtis turns to me, his kind eyes crinkling at the edges. "I don't know what to say."

I'm about to hold out my hand when he envelops me in a tight embrace. "It's been a real education, young'un," he says in my ear. "I'll miss you."

When he lets me go, my cheeks are hot and I'm sure I'm blushing. "Me—me, too," I say, stammering. "I can't ever—" I stop and get myself under control. "Thank you," I say firmly. "For everything you've done."

"You're welcome. Now, then," and Curtis claps Sam on the back and steers him away in the worst attempt at subtlety I've ever seen. I meet Ben's amber eyes and glance down, not ready to face what's there quite yet.

"I guess this is good-bye," he says.

I don't know what I would do if Ben tried to hug me, but thankfully he just holds out his hand.

"I reckon so," I say. His hand is warm and big, and I hold it just a moment too long before letting go.

"You know, we'll be at the Homestead for a while, till we hire on a new job." Ben looks at me, then ducks his head away. "Don't be a stranger."

I nod. I should say something else, but all the words I can think of sound so stupid in my head. I want to say something significant, something he'll remember. I want to tell him that I feel something, that I don't understand it but I think he feels it, too. And that I wish things were different, that I was a less complicated girl with a less complicated life. But I don't say any of that.

"Good-bye, Ben."

"Take care, Willie." And he half turns away, but hesitates. Then, in a rush, he leans forward and kisses my cheek. It happens so quick, I almost miss it, the slightest pressure of lips skimming my skin and the scratch of an unshaved chin. It feels like a blink and it tastes like a promise and when I catch my breath he's already walking away.

"Come on, Will," Sam says, tapping my shoulder. "Let's get you home."

"Yeah." I bite my lip and take a chance. "Hey, Ben," I yell at him, and wait for him to turn around.

"What?"

"You should grow the beard out again. I like it."

And he's too far away to see clearly, but I can picture his smile.

72.

Sam and I walk side by side along the path toward our houses. I'm anxious and full of my own thoughts; now that we're home, facing the twins is a daunting task. We pass the storefronts in silence, then the hollow remains of the church. I've walked this road so many times I would know every step with my eyes closed. Here's the ruined wall with the stain that looks like a sideways cat, there's the pile of glass from busted windows. And here's Sam's house, the porch empty and the windows dark.

"You think your pa's home?" I ask.

"Doesn't look like it," Sam says. He hops up the porch and opens the front door with a bang. "Pop, I'm home!" He waits a minute before turning back to me.

"Didn't think so. He'll have to worry a little longer. Come in for a minute."

"I better not," I say, backing away. "The twins have waited long enough."

"At least let me check your bandage."

"It ain't even itching anymore," I say, but he's already ushering me inside.

I've only been in the Kincaids' house once or twice, and each time I leave confused. It's like they don't know what furniture is used for; there are piles of books on the table and stacks of dirty plates on the chairs. I'm in no position to judge, but at least I know better than to hang laundry inside. Sam clears a chair for me, then opens dusty curtains to let some light in.

"Sam, why does your pa live here?" I ask, pushing aside a stuffed crow.

"What do you mean?" Sam sits next to me and motions for my arm.

"In Glory, in this house. There are better places a doctor could go."

Sam shrugs his shoulders and starts to unwrap my bandage. "We've always lived here. I don't think Pop notices what's around him most of the time. And Glory needs a doctor." He pauses working on my arm to look at me. "I guess I never thought much about leaving. This is our home."

I trace a line in the wood of the table. I've never felt much affection for Glory, not until I thought I wouldn't make it back.

"Do you still want to leave?" Sam asks.

"I don't know. I did. Now I can't think farther ahead than supper, and how I'm going to get by without Micah."

"Will, you're practically family, you know Pop and I will help you."

"Thanks, Sam," I tell him. I don't want help, though, not even from Sam. I don't want to owe anybody, not the Judge and not a friend. I want to be able to take care of me and mine, and I'm starting to think there might be a way for me to do that. "It just ain't the same."

Sam looks at me with sadness written wide across his face. "I know," he says simply.

I draw a shaky breath, not sure I'll ever be ready to talk about it. I lost a part of myself when Micah died, lost something more than an arm or a leg. I can feel it missing, a phantom pain in the empty space where he should be.

"I hardly ever went a day without talking to him,"

Sam continues. "He was my best friend. He was my only friend."

It occurs to me that Sam knew my brother better than I did. It hurts, in a soft and new way. But here is someone else who loved him, someone to share the load of grief; one death and a thousand tiny ripples.

"I liked coming to your house," Sam goes on. "It's always so loud and full, even when it's quiet it's a loud quiet. The twins running around, Micah and I trying to avoid them, you yelling at all of us; it's not like my house, all empty and lonesome."

"You're always welcome, Sam," I tell him. "I know it ain't the same; I'm not Micah, but you do have another friend. And it'd be nice, to have someone to talk to— someone who knew him."

"Listen, Will—" and Sam stops speaking, staring down at my arm.

"What?" I ask, uneasy. It hasn't been bothering me since we came through the gates, but Sam's face looks upset. "How bad is it?"

"It's—it's not," Sam says, and he gazes at me with wide eyes. "I think it's healing."

"What?" I yank my arm away from him and look at it closely. The skin around the bite marks is pink, but no streaks of red. I use one finger to press the wound gently, but I don't feel any puffiness and no blood seeps out.

"How did you do that?" I ask Sam.

"I didn't do anything," he says. "You said it was—" and he slaps his hands to his forehead. "I'm an idiot."

"That's one thing you're not, Sam."

"No, listen," he says, his eyes lighting up. "Inoculation."

"What?"

Sam stands up, too excited to sit still. "Cuts itch when they're healing, too. It makes perfect sense."

"Sam, would you kindly sit down and explain what you're talking about?" I try not to yell at him, but I think I'm being very patient under the circumstances.

Sam bounces back to his chair and perches on the edge of it. "Remember that smallpox scare years back?"

"Yes," I say slowly, not sure what he's getting at.

"Well, you remember how your ma brought you and Micah over to see Pop? She had him inoculate you, so y'all wouldn't catch the pox. He did it for lots of folks."

I meet Sam's bright eyes, hoping I understand. "I'm not gonna get sick again."

Sam smiles at me, a real, honest smile. "You're not

gonna get sick again, Will. You won't ever get the sickness again."

I blink a few times, my slow brain trying to catch up.

"Willie, don't you get it? The shakes can't hurt you. Even if you get bit again, your body already has . . ."

Sam's voice drones on, but I've stopped listening. I stare at the bite mark on my arm like it can tell me what to do. An idea is solidifying at the back of my mind, but mostly what I'm thinking is that I'm tired.

"Sam," I interrupt him. "I have to go home."

"Sure, Will," he says, his enthusiasm deflating a little. "I'm sorry, I know you want to see the twins. I'll come by tomorrow to check on you."

"Thanks, Sam." I get up to leave and Sam follows me to the door. I stand in the doorway for a moment, and turn back. "Hey, Sam? How much can you let go of—how much can you give up—and still be yourself?"

Sam cocks his head to the side, frowning. "I don't know."

"Yeah. Me neither." Impulsively, I reach out and wrap him in a tight hug. It takes Sam a moment to overcome his surprise, then his arms snake around my shoulders and he squeezes. I close my eyes, and it's almost like hugging my brother again.

When I finally pull away, Sam's eyes are slightly pink behind his glasses.

"You'll come and see me, won't you?" he asks.

"No," I tell him firmly. "You'll come and see me. Help keep the house loud."

Sam laughs a watery laugh and ducks his head down. I hate to leave him here, alone in his perpetually empty house, but the twins are waiting and my thoughts are coming fast and hard.

I give Sam a last, quick hug and leave him standing on the porch, watching my back as I walk away. He'll always be watching my back, that one.

"Willie," he calls after me. "Remember that they can't hurt you. You don't have to be afraid anymore."

I'm not.

73.

Almost home. Almost home. The words pulse through my mind, and I walk to their beat, tracing the familiar path to Bess's house. I think I figured something out. There has to be a reason all this has happened to me, there has to be some light at the end. So much has been taken from me: most of my family and pieces of myself. Surely there must be something given back in return.

I think about those names scratched into the wood at the station and how many of them must be dead now. What did they leave behind besides a name? Micah left so much: half-finished projects, ruined watches, and curiosity. He left a deep rip in my side, one that I see echoed in Sam; we're two broken pieces that can never be made whole. If I had died in the desert, what would

I have left behind? Some dirty clothes and a fistful of flour. Two children and a lizard, all with short memories. Have I done enough to be remembered, have I made enough, loved enough?

I hear the twins before I see them. They must've been at the window, and my heart tugs to think they've been watching for me for days. I drop to my knees as they come running and they slam into me, one after the other.

"You came back, you came back," Cath cries into my shoulder.

"I told you I would, tumbleweeds," I say.

"What took you so long?"

"How many shakes did you see?"

"Did you find Pa?"

"Where's Micah?"

Calvin asks the last one and I can't even begin to answer.

"Micah is . . . he's . . ." My first thought is to tell them a story, say he found a job in Best. But Micah hated lies.

"Give her some space, little ones," Bess calls from the porch, stamping her cane. The twins peel off me and I struggle to my feet. I'll never understand how she gets them to obey her; pure fear, perhaps.

Old Bess takes a long look at me, and I'm sure she sees my healing bruises, my cracked lips, and my red eyes. She gives me a small nod, her eyes crinkling up in her face.

"Looks like the desert chewed you up and spit you back out, my dear."

"Feels that way, too," I say. "I'm so sorry I'm late. Miss Bess, how can I even begin to thank you—"

She waves her cane at me to stop. "None of that. They were no trouble and I enjoy the company." She tilts her head, appraising me. "You take care of what you needed to?"

I nod sharply. "I did."

"Good."

"Willie," Cath says, pulling on my arm. "Where's Micah?" Her small face is drawn with concern. "He said he was going to help you. Did he help you?"

"Yes. He helped me," I say, and my throat closes up. I look at Bess pleadingly. I don't know how to do this. Her dark eyes meet mine, a depth of understanding there.

"Your brother is gone, child," Bess says gently. "He's with your ma, wherever she is. I'm sorry."

Cath starts to cry and even though she's too big, I scoop her up and hold her close. Calvin throws his arms around my waist and presses his face into my shirt.

"It was quick," I tell them, even though that doesn't make it better. "And he was so brave."

"I didn't want him to die," Cath cries into my neck.

"I know. But it ain't up to us." I look over to Bess, my eyes burning. "Thank you," I say. I could say a hundred thank yous and never come close to how grateful I am to her.

"Take them home," she says softly. "Grieve together, and come back when you've healed."

I carry Catherine in my arms and hold Calvin by the hand. Almost home. It pounds in my head. We started as six, and now only half remain. I make a silent promise to Ma: no one else.

I never thought much about the future. Never thought I had much of one. It seemed foolish to make plans, to tempt fate and dare life to come and ruin everything. In Glory, planning for tomorrow is the quickest way to make sure you don't get one. So I kept my head down, thinking it was enough to get through each day. To keep my family safe, to put a little food in my stomach and a few dollars in a tin. I thought that would count for something, that each little piece could add up to a life.

And it turns out none of it mattered. Fate came for us anyway. Life doesn't care how hard you're trying, doesn't care how much you've already lost, it will still break in and crush you and leave you bruised and bloody. And still expect you to keep going, because what else can you do?

I promise, Ma.

It's not enough, just getting by. I want us to remember what it's like to be happy. I want a real life for us, with a real future. And if fate isn't going to give it to me, then I'll damn well take it. I may not be smart like Sam, or clever like Micah; I'm not a leader like Curtis, or a great shot like Ben. But there is one thing I'm good at, and that's surviving.

I promise, Micah.

So I'll be a hunter. I'm not afraid anymore. The sickness can't touch me. The desert doesn't scare me. None of it is permanent and nothing stays the same. It doesn't matter if I'm a hunter, or a shake, or just Daisy Wilcox. Life can do its worst to bring me down. When the dust clears, I'll still be standing.

74.

One Month Later

There's a moment, in the early morning, when the rising sun hits the perimeter just right. It turns the ugly tangle of barbed wire a deep orange, makes the fence light up like it's glowing. My eyes linger on the blazing wires and I wonder if some things are more beautiful because they are deadly. A tug on my shirt drags me back to the house and the two small faces waiting in front of me.

"Do you remember the rules?" I ask, kneeling down so I'm level with the twins.

"Stay close to the house," Calvin says, his small brow wrinkling.

"Mind Miss Bess," Cath adds.

"And stay out of trouble," I finish.

I stand up, ruffling Cath's hair, and look to the cluttered porch in front of me.

"You sure about this, Miss Bess?" I ask. "I can ask Sam or Elsie—"

"You're wasting daylight," Bess calls from her rocking chair. "Go on and get. We'll be fine."

I nod and squeeze Calvin's shoulder one last time. "Look after one another," I tell them. "I'll be back in four days."

"What if you're not?" Calvin asks.

"I will be," I say. I trace my scar lightly with my fingers, feeling anxious and invincible. "I might be late, I might be injured, but I will always come back to y'all. I promise."

"Micah always said don't make promises you can't keep," Cath says, and my heart twists. "You can't swear that."

"Can't I?" I ask, kissing the top of her head. "Well, we'll see if life makes a liar out of me, won't we?"

I watch them walk toward the house, and a part of me goes with them.

"Love," I call out, and I wait until I hear their voices call back before I turn to leave.

Some days I'm not sure I made the right choice. Ma

wouldn't approve, I don't think. But then again, what do I know. Maybe she would. People change; I changed. And this was my choice, and if it's a mistake then it's my mistake to make.

The path forks and I go left, the sun climbing high above the fence. That's all choices are, really; a step in one direction instead of another. Every scuff my boot makes in the dirt feels like a beginning. It will never be easy, I know that; life will never let up, it will never give me room to breathe. But there are still things worth fighting for. There are still people worth protecting. And maybe this town is still worth saving.

The gate looms ahead, solid and still, but my eyes go to the figures in front of it.

"You're late," Ben says, his hat tucked low over his eyes.

"Quit scowling at me just 'cause you're tired," I tell him, and he grumbles under his breath.

"You ready for this, young'un?" Curtis asks, smiling at me.

"As ready as I'm gonna get, I reckon."

Curtis whistles to the guards on the gate and gives Daisy's saddlebags a once-over. She's loaded up with everything from flour to bullets, but the weight doesn't seem to be bothering her.

"Wasn't sure you was gonna show," Ben says quietly, coming to stand next to me.

"For my first supply run?" I nudge my shoulder against his, just hard enough to send a spark through my veins. "I wouldn't miss it."

I catch the barest ghost of a smile on his lips before it disappears.

"Open her up," Curtis calls, and my heart thunders at the squeal of the gates.

"You ready to go back out there?" Ben asks.

I take a deep breath that smells like dust and metal and fate.

"I'm ready."

He tilts his head up and his eyes are gold in the sunlight.

"Then after you."

I adjust my rifle and put my hand to my belt and wrap my fingers around the hot metal of my revolver. I know what this road leads to. The desert took almost everything from me, left me broken and heartsick and hard. I stare at the path I need to follow, and I dare it to cross me. Give me blood, give me pain; I've survived worse. It's what I'm good at, it's what I do. This is the life I've chosen for myself, and this is the path that I take. I pull out my gun and I walk it.

ACKNOWLEDGMENTS

First and foremost, I owe thanks to Heather Flaherty for starting me down this long, dusty road. Thanks for taking a chance on me and holding my hand through this entire process. Sorry for all the emails.

Martha Mihalick, every day I'm grateful that this book ended up in your care. Thank you for seeing the potential in my words and for digging out something better than I could ever have hoped for. Again, sorry for all the emails.

Katie Heit and Tim Smith, Paul Zakris and Sammy Yuen, all the folks in marketing, publicity, sales, and Epic Reads, thank you all for your hard work and enthusiastic support of this book. Y'all are the best and I am forever thankful to be a part of the Greenwillow team.

I'm lucky to have the Herd at my back, an amazingly talented group of writers and friends. Thank you for your constant inspiration, commiseration, and celebration. Y'all make the highs higher and the lows bearable.

Thanks to Graham Norris and Lee Arcuri for your insightful critiques and much needed encouragement. You may be fancy-pants writers but you're even better friends.

Thanks to Adrian, Katherine, Laura, and Leah, my earliest readers and loudest cheerleaders by a wide margin. Special shout-out to Gene Kincaid for keeping me alive all those summers in the real Silver, Texas. Thanks to all my friends (you know who you are) for standing by me through thick and thin. I love you all, you beautiful weirdos.

I have a big dumb family that I big dumb love. Thanks to Hillary, my first and most persistent fan. Peter, I swear Micah isn't based on you (mostly.) Emily, thanks for geeking out over YA with me. Willa, when you're old enough to read this, remember that I came up with the name first. Mom and Dad, thanks for never suggesting this might not be the best career choice.

Finally, thank you to Mike. It's not an exaggeration to say this book wouldn't exist without you. I don't hate you, too.

31901062816147